SON OF WOMAN IN MOMBASA

Charles Mangua

HEINEMANN KENYA LTD.
NAIROBI

Published by
Heinemann Kenya Limited,
Brick Court
Mpaka Road/Woodvale Grove
P.O. Box 45314, Nairobi.

First published 1986
Copyright © Charles Mangua 1986
Reprinted — 1988
Reprinted — 1990
Reprinted 1992

Typeset by
Josaphat O. Mithiga
P.O. Box 31355,
Nairobi, Kenya.

Printed and bound in Kenya by
General Printers Ltd., P.O. Box 18001, Nairobi

ONE

Sunday Afternoon

Well, well, well, so here we are at last. I have been waiting to meet you for the last couple of months to tell you about a few things that happened to Tonia and Kiunyu down there in Mombasa, but I never got round to meeting you till now. Just in case you are wondering, Kiunyu is me. Not that I am dying to tell you the story of my life -- oh, no. Why should I? I don't know you and I don't care a fig about you, anyway. The only reason I am opening up to you is that last week I met some wogs who thought I'd died during the Oceanic Hotel bomb blast a year or so ago — which is all slimy stuff and nonsense. I am not dead. I am very much alive because I am the Son of Woman and the Son of Woman doesn't die easy. He dies hard — so bless his African Soul; my soul, that is.

And now just in case we haven't met before, let me introduce myself to you, whoever you are. We might as well start by knowing one another right from the start, although the knowing is fairly one-sided. Maybe one day you'll tell me a few things about yourself but meantime here are my vital statistics:

Full name:	*Dodge Kiunyu — best known to my friends as Dod, and Son of Woman to you.*
Wife's name:	*Tonia — daughter of Miriam (both ex-prostitutes).*
Father's name:	*Kiunyu — never knew his first name. Imprisoned for life and only met him two minutes before his death.*
Mother's name:	*Theresa Ngendo — Miriam's companion — died when I was around eleven. God bless her soul.*
Place of birth:	*Eastleigh, Nairobi, Kenya.*

Date of birth:	*None of your business — but to tell you the truth, I do not know exactly. I believe that I am around thirty-something or thereabouts.*
Family status:	*Married — no children.*
Qualifications:	*Degree in Geography. Subject matter forgotten within six months of leaving College.*
Profession:	*None. Lately a black-marketeer and looking for a job as a member of parliament.*
Previous experience:	*With Ministry of Labour, Kenya Shell, Ministry of Lands and Settlement and lastly with the Ministry of Home Affairs as an insider of Kamiti Prison — blast them cops!*
Any other statistics:	*Find out for yourself. It is contained in the following pages. If, however, you are as dumb a statistician as I am and therefore still require further information, please write to Son of Woman, c/o Parliament Building, Nairobi where I expect to be in a few months — explaining why I should waste any more of my time telling you more stuff that is none of your business anyway.*

So there you are my friend. Now you know all about me, or probably think you do. Anyway, I don't give much of a damn either way. I am the Son of Woman that was, is, and shall be, ever one Kiunyu — world without end — and that doesn't mean I have grown very Christian either. I am the same old me only a little eaten up by the tooth of time and enfeebled by this lousy Mombasa climate but worst of all harassed by hungry cops who are no more than any beggar-man thief. I've learnt their ways and they have learnt my ways so I reckon that God willing, we shall all go to hell together, the cops and I. May be you shall find us there if you happen to come that way; that is if you will not already be there waiting for us. Anyway, welcome to my world.

Just in case you have forgotten, the last time we should have met was when I came out of jail and Tonia came out of jail and we put our little money together and decided to put our lousy past behind us and move away from Nairobi to Mombasa where we were not known as jailbirds and where we would start a new and fresh little life. We were going to try and make a good out of two bads and that's what we've been trying to do for almost three years now.

What we did was we got to Mombasa and honeymooned for a few months before marriage, after which Tonia landed herself a job with the *Maendeleo ya Wanawake* and which entitled her to this big bungalow we are living in along Cliff Avenue. I got myself a hotel job which I lost two months later because I didn't need it then, so I've been jobless since. I married Tonia after three months of honeymooning and it was all plain sailing till our little money packet started getting eroded, mainly as a result of my bad habits and my ignorance of statistics. The only sensible thing we did is that Tonia bought a car and that is the only fixed asset we have. Anyway we are still here in the same bungalow but I reckon unless I can make some fat kill somewhere, or get myself a job, we may go back to square one someday. Tonia is very mad at me and I reckon one of these fine days she may divorce me and join the church as she had earlier intended to do. She's been giving me real hell, if you want to know.

Right now we are at home and it is time for me to sneeze again. Haachioo! Bless my African soul. It is my seventh sneeze in a minute. I think I have a cold coming. Anyway, I am taking my time in the toilet because I don't want to face Tonia. We may quarrel again.

The toilet is the wrong place for a sneezing session. I am having a leak and this sneezing business is interfering so that I am wetting the whole place. I am also keeping an eye on this mosquito which is hovering over my head, yearning for my blood. It has already given me one bite and I don't fancy another.

I flush the toilet and then go after the mosquito. I am in a murderous mood. The damn mosquito seems to read my mind and it perches right on the ceiling, upside-down! I climb over the toilet bowl, support myself with one hand on the wall and try to squeeze it between the ceiling and my palm. I miss! It flies off in a huff, zigzagging all over my head and nearly getting into my mouth. I curse it as I try to smash it again and as a result, I lose my hold on the wall and I slip. My left foot goes 'plop!' right into the toilet bowl. Nearly broke my poor ankle, I did. I look at my wet shoe and curse. Fuck all mosquitoes!

I get out of the place and remove them shoes. I am mad. Tonia starts to ask me what the matter is and I tell her to shut her mouth. She is always asking me what the matter is even when there is nothing the matter with me at all. What I want is to shed that damn mosquito's blood. I want to let off steam.

I march downstairs into the kitchen, grab a broom and then steal back and into the toilet. I close the door after me and start searching for the mosquito. The creature is nowhere to be seen. I am searching all over the place — even behind the dusty toilet bowl when the door suddenly opens. Tonia puts her head in and looks at the broom in my hand with an open mouth.

"Are you sweeping up the place?"
"Leave me alone," I tell her.
"What is the matter with you? What do you think you are doing?"
"Look Tonia — just leave me alone, will you."
"But what are you looking for with a broom in your hand?"
"Now, now. Can't I do anything in this house without having you run after me asking loudly what the hell I am doing? I can't even kill a mosquito without reporting to you?"

She sets her teeth and hisses, "O.K. big man. I shouldn't ask, I know. You are the boss. You don't like to get bothered. It has become a song now. Go on singing, Mr. Big Stuff". She bangs the door shut so loudly that I have to hold my ears. I spit right into the bowl and flush the damn thing violently just to let off more steam. I nearly break the chain. I stand there stupidly watching the action of the water in the bowl. I've forgotten what I came in the goddam toilet for. Oh yeah, the bloody mosquito. Anyway damn the mosquito and damn Tonia. Right now, I'd like to get her angry. She spent the whole of last night divorcing me. I need to revenge.

You may not know, but Tonia and I are at war. We've been at it for the past several months and I reckon I am going to strangle her one of these fine days. I've already told her so and she told me in turn to go fry myself an egg. That's how happy we are. Very happy. So happy that the only serious conversation we hold in this house is about frying eggs or jumping from the Likoni ferry.

I get out of the toilet and bang the door with vengeance. Damn silly of course but when man and wife are at loggerheads even innocent doors have to suffer. Why shouldn't they? I throw the broom on the floor just to get Tonia angry and then get into the bathroom where I proceed to put on my crocodile skin sandals. Very pretty sandals. I bought them on the black market from an Arab hawker who's also promised me two six-hundred-shillings-french-suits for two hundred shillings a piece. I didn't ask the guy where he gets all this stuff. That's none of my business. After all, a good buy is a good buy no matter who you buy it from. Maybe you know.

I am wondering whether I should have a wash on account of my left foot which got into the toilet bowl, but then I decide that there is nothing terribly dirty in the toilet bowl except my piss and that I'd just flushed. Anyway, I can't be bothered about washing my feet because I am intending to take a walk and they'll get dirty anyway. What with the dust and the wind and what have you? Mombasa is lousy!

Tonia is watching me but right now. I don't want to talk to her. I am not in a talking mood. I want to get the hell out of here and saunter to the Railway Club where I am a member, and give a good bashing at them snooker balls over a pint of cold beer. I am all hot and I want to cool my nerves. What with mosquitos and a nagging wife, and toilets? A man needs a breather.

Tonia sits on the long sofa biting her fingernails and absent-mindedly staring at her bare feet. She never wears shoes or slippers in the house. She looks beautiful when she is biting her fingernails and ignoring me, only it is irritating. I stand there with my hands in the pockets of my khaki trousers and look at her with amusement in my eyes. She pretends not to notice me at all. I decide that she is too goddam obstinate for my liking. How the hell can she just sit there and ignore me?

"Since you are so busy I am going out for a while", I tell her.
"Are you coming back for dinner?" she asks calmly without looking at me.
"No."
"Where are you going?"
"Where men get drunk. Why? I never ask you where you go and where you don't go with your *Maendeleo ya Wanawake* job, days on end and world without end". She shrugs her shoulders and looks at me with a sneer.
"Did you take your key?"

"Why?"

"I may not be here when you come back."

"I was not expecting you to be here. You are never here except when you are too tired to be elsewhere with your gossiping women friends. See you", and I start making for the door.

"That is one of your lies," she snaps. "Do please grow up and take your dirty shoes and the broom to their right place. You should have enough sense to remove them from off the carpet without being told. I am not your slave you know."

"And that is your big luck. If you were my slave, first thing I'd do would be to amputate your leg so you wouldn't go gallivanting all over the place talking about family planning when you can't even have a family."

I shouldn't have said that. Tonia is very touchy about kids because she loves them and she can't have any. Her uterus was taken out several years ago. I see her body stiffen and become rigid. There is so much hatred in her look that if her eyes were guns, I'd be a dead man. She chews her lower lip slowly and thoughtfully and then walks up to stand at the window, giving me her back. Maybe I should apologize but I am not in a mood for apologies and I don't think that Tonia is in a mood to receive them either. We are all square. She rattled me the whole of last night so why shouldn't she get rattled in turn?

Instead of grabbing the moment and getting the hell out, I light a cigarette and sit down. Life is very tough for married folks these days. That is why they are divorcing like nobody's business. Right now it is the fashion. If you haven't divorced your wife or she hasn't divorced you, there is something wrong with either of you or both. It's a sign of affluence. Me, I am a poor chap. I can't afford it but I know that I am going to have to go through it, for better or worse, one of these days. I can ill afford it but it is preferable to the type of life I am leading. I am nothing but Tonia's little man. I put on one hell of a brave front but she knows me through and through. According to her, I am 'the little man who keeps her married.'

I knew even before we got married that Tonia could not have any children. She'd told me. It didn't matter at the time because I didn't care about children anyway, but the more I think about it now the more I understand that it was all one big mistake; I mean, marrying her. At the time I could not figure out how a woman incapable of bearing kids would behave after the first passionate romantic spell was over. Don't let anybody kid you. It is OK if a woman who can have kids doesn't want any, but when she knows for sure that she can't have any, not even an angel of a husband can stop her from getting moody when the feeling of being inadequate catches up with her.

To compensate for this, Tonia now loves all mothers and all their kids. I think she loves them out of spite. She wants to behave as if she owned the mothers and their kids and is a great adviser on family matters. Poor mothers must be advised how to look after their children! She knows more than all mothers put together and she is a great compaigner of the *Maendeleo ya Wanawake* movement.

She has done a lot for the movement, that I cannot deny. From what used to be simple women clubs for knitting and weaving and dress-making and cookery, it has now become a formidable family planning affair with a talk of civil rights and equal opportunities for women. Frankly, I think that all she is doing is conniving with these women on how to give men hell. Women are clamouring all over the place for equal rights — whatever that means — but I am not bothered with all that stuff, though I do very seriously object to the hell she's been giving me. Why should I be bothered about how many women have taken to the pill and other contraceptives and the overall campaign for birth control? Me, I have no family to control or plan. I am waiting for my seed.

Tonia has important work to do. Sometimes she goes out into the Province and stays a couple of days. During this time I have to cook for myself or eat in restaurants. Yet I am not supposed to open my mouth about it. She can't bear the thought of having a house servant because she is supposed to be setting a good example to her fellow women. Consequently I've had to do without a clean shirt sometimes unless, of course, I wash my own things. Damn her! Every time she's away out in the Province and I hire a houseboy, he is fired the moment she gets back. I am supposed to have no say in the matter. She gives the orders, I have to obey them.

She now turns towards me slowly and says emphatically "You are extremely mean. Do you expect me to keep my mouth shut when you act like a half-wit?"

"Exactly, I want you to keep your mouth shut for ever. I am tired of this life".

"I agree with you. It is no use."

"What is no use?"

"You and I. I've said so before and I know I am right".

"It's your old song. I imagined that you realized something new just now. I was wrong".

"Not now you goon. I realized it a long time ago. It was a mistake in the first instance. We shouldn't have been married at all. We are too different. Now that it happened, I can't forgive myself. I never realized that you were capable of descending so low. I am not sure now, that I can live with it all. I don't think I can stand you anymore."

"Who asked you to live with me in the first instance? Who forced you?" I retort angrily.

"You know the circumstances as well as I do. It was good when it happened. It's no longer fun. Why pretend?" She is shouting now.

"I certainly have no pretensions as far as our relations are concerned. We have failed miserably and I have often told you so myself. I don't care for marriage any more. I am convinced that marriage is one of the most obnoxious institutions invented by mankind and that it will lead to his doom. The only thing that is reasonable in marriage is the production of kids but that is not important either. Kids can be produced without having to go through all the marriage nonsense and besides, you can't have kids anyway".

"But I told you, Dod, that I could not have kids long before we got married".

"I know you did".

"Why then hammer the point with a mallet? Or is it merely a deliberate attempt on your part to hurt me? You know I love kids and I would very much like to have some, but it is physically impossible. Why do you have to be so cruel?"

"O.K. I am sorry. I don't want to hurt anybody and I don't want to get hurt either".

"Do I hurt you Dod?" she asks softly.

"Of course you know you do. I am not made of wood. Just because you were going to join the nunnery and I stopped you doesn't mean that you are holier than I am. Your 'holier than thou' airs are very annoying. You want to watch every movement I make as if I am sinning all over the place. I can't leave the house without your blessing, even if it is to go out and talk to friends. That is not fair. You have to trust me. I am the man. I am your husband and not your wife. I am boss. You have completely usurped my manly powers."

"That is utter nonsense. All you want to do is sneak out of the house and come back at two in the morning reeking of drink and smoke while I have to take my meals alone. And I shouldn't say anything about it!"

"Do I complain when you go out on duty in the Province and stay away for four days at a stretch?"

"But that is duty. I go to work and not to mess around. You should understand."

"I reckon I am too daft to understand such devotion to work. As far as I am concerned, you are first and foremost a housewife. That is what you are. You are the housewife. I am not. I am the man in the house. You are not. That's simple. Trouble with you is that you want to play your role and mine. I don't want to be controlled and dominated. I want to be a man."

"If anybody is stopping you, from being that, it is not me. I don't play your role and even if I tried, you wouldn't let me. The question is whether you really play your role. I have to work to run the house. I have to cook for you. I have to wash your clothes and tidy the house. You want to have the best of everything while you sit on your ass and I labour for you. Slave days are over. What do you contribute? What do I ever get from you except complaints and misery and dirty clothes and . . . and an empty stomach? I have to pay for the house and yet that is your role. It is through no fault of mine that you do not do so. Why are we broke? It's because you drank all our money."

She pauses to scratch her elbow and then continues, "I am your wife, Dod. What have you ever done for me as your wife? Have you ever bought me a dress or even a small present? Grow up man. Life is made up of many small things. All that you have ever done for me is fuck me. And even that is no longer fun. There's nothing left between us now; just wedding rings."

"And that is why I never wear it," I retort.

"So that you can go out and cheat young girls that you are not married".

"Yes," I mimic her voice. "So that I can cheat young girls that I am not married."

"Swine!"

"O.K. I don't want to quarrel. I'll come for dinner."

"At midnight?"

"Ah — there you go again. Please try and understand one thing. If I am late and you raise hell, it doesn't help any. All it does is ruin everybody's sleep. Nobody wants to go back where a sharp tongue is waiting to lash out at them".

"So?"

"The best thing then is to go home very late when the wife is sound asleep and sleep in the guest room. That way, at least there is no tongue lashing till the following morning, and all parties get their share of good sleep."

"You don't seem to understand me. I don't want you to be with me all the time and I don't want to quarrel with you every time you come in late. All I ask is that you devote some of your free time to me when I am at home. You may not have noticed, but you never try to please me any more."

"Neither do you for that matter. I come home late — no food. I ask why and I am told that I am familiar with the kitchen so why don't I do the cooking myself. If that is your way of loving me then I am very much loved indeed."

Despite the seriousness in my eyes and the serious tone of my words, she laughs outright. I find the laughter very unbecoming because I derive no fun from boiling eggs at midnight.

"And what is so amusing, my dear Tonia?"

"I am simply amused. At least I am gratified to know that you get so mad when there is no dinner. I can imagine you fuming in the kitchen and getting your fingers burnt and..."

"Don't gloat over your sins," I cut her short.

"I wish I could really commit a sin."

"You have a whole lifetime in front of you to commit all the sins you feel like committing, my dear Tonia."

"Go on talking, Dodge. You sound clever. Say some more clever things."

"This issue of you lashing at me when I am a few minutes late for dinner. Let me give you a hint. If I come home late, please don't start a quarrel. Have some food ready. Let me feel welcome. Let me feel at home as I eat and then we go happily to bed. You can bet your last cent that I'll remain awake for hours cursing myself for being such an inconsiderate beast — thinking about how unfair I am for keeping you awake, what a wonderful person you are, and how I must mend my ways. The whole thing is a process. That sort of thing happens two to three times and I would be full of remorse. I wouldn't want to go out again. I'd be terribly ashamed of conducting myself in such an irresponsible manner when you are patiently at home waiting for me. I would be there when you want me. My dear girl, the wildest man can be tamed by a clever woman. She can twist him around her little finger by just a little play on his vanity. Let him understand that he is boss even when he isn't. Let him understand that he is a man and that you are a woman. That way you'll get away with most things. Simple lesson baby. Take it to heart."

She looks at me contemptuously and stands up. There is a sneer on her face. She shrugs her shoulders resignedly and says in like manner, "Thank you but that is not the sort of lesson I have to learn from you. In my life I have met men, and better men at that, and I know exactly what they are. Up to now, I haven't met one that wasn't a swine. I don't need any advice from you on the treatment of swine!'

I decide to say nothing. I am too angry for words.

She looks at me for a long time and then advances towards me as if she wants to hit me. She stands just in front of my nose and fixes her eyes on my angry face. She then lifts her right arm and places it on my shoulder. There is dead silence. The muscles of her neck are moving like the underside of a frog. Her face is so set that it looks like it would harden into glue. She clears her throat and then slowly and deliberately repeats what she'd said earlier.

"It's no use." I nod my head in the affirmative. "I am happy you concur. I see no alternative but parting ways," she says, and again I nod my head.

"Fine," she hisses. "I am the one paying the rent so I expect you to leave this house the earliest possible." Again I nod my head.

"And when is that?" she asks tersely.

"Right now, if you so desire," I tell her. She is not in a joking mood, but neither am I. Truth of the matter though, is wouldn't want to move out right now. These things need a little planning if you see what I mean. It is not the sort of thing you want to go through on a Sunday afternoon when you should be resting your bones like God said. But so what? If it's got to be, let it be.

"That is alright with me, Dod. You can leave now or any other time you choose. I hope to God that I've tried my best. I can't go any further. I don't like the way you are always pulling me down. You don't want to work anymore; all you want to do is to drink. I even got you a job with the Social Welfare Department and you turned it down. You are reducing everything to nothing and you want to do nothing. Choose your moment. I need peace."

Again, I decide to say nothing. I get out of the place fast and walk briskly through the gate. I take a peep back and see Tonia standing at the window. She stares at me the way you'd stare at a disappearing apparition. I walk faster and disappear behind the Jacaranda trees and then reduce my pace. I wipe my face and let out a sigh. What a life?

What I'll do is, I'll quit Mombasa and go back to Nairobi. I think that's what I'll do. I don't want to live in the same city as Tonia. Mombasa is only good for tourists. I don't have to think about these things now. In fact I don't want to think about anything anymore. All I want is get to the goddam club and get myself wet on a few drinks. Tomorrow morning I shall come back, pick my things and hit the road. God! I feel cheap. I feel real cheap. I think that more than fifty percent of the blame for this whole sad affair is imputable to me. So what? I need a drink to think straight.

Sunday Evening

The Railway Club is one of those old colonial affairs with tennis courts, badminton courts, swings for kids, a football pitch and lots of green grass. An open terrace separates the badminton courts from the bar, behind which you have the snooker tables. The place is quite airy and comfortable.

I get into the club and there is a lot off Hi Dod, Hi Son of Woman, Hello Mr. Kiunyu, long-time-no-see-you... old horse greetings. I am shaking hands here and I am shaking hands there. There is the income tax chap who is saying, "Dodge, old dear, I'll have one on you," and there are these three buddies of mine from the Kenya Navy who are demonstrating their drinking prowess through the use of bad language, who are shouting, "How are you fucker? Have a fucking drink on me." The place is lively as hell.

Four women are playing darts and making a hell of noise over it. Their husbands are getting drunk or are in the inner room playing snooker. There are three white guys and their wives having a drink on the terrace. They seem to be remembering the good old days they used to have before the noise-making niggers became club members. I make a mental observation that we niggers are very accommodating because if we believed in tit for tat, we'd have kicked out these old colonials a long time ago.

Kungu, the income tax chap, keeps pestering me about the drink I am supposed to buy him and I tell him to go to hell. As a matter of fact, we are not great friends. He doesn't like me because I have no fixed source of income and I reckon that's the reason why he likes to bleed a drink out of me whenever he gets a chance. Anyway, I am always beating him at snooker and he doesn't like that either because he is supposed to be a great sportsman. That's how friendly we are.

There's also this chap called Wambua who is the Provincial Engineer for the Ministry of Works. He's a terribly conceited chap because his father is a member of Parliament and owns a maize mill either in Kitui or Kangundo or some other such place. The two of us can never see eye to eye. We are the sort of friends that club members should be. He has a high spirited fiancée who I had the good chance to lay in the car once on one of them days when we were juiced. She is quite a dish, that girl. Her name is Cecilia. I don't know whether Wambua has smelled a rat or not, but I don't like the way he looks sideways at me. I am in one of them high spirits, so after we shake hands I ask him where Cecilia is and he tells me that he is not her keeper. I swallow hard and turn to my navy friends.

There is Harrison Wainaina, Claude Kunyiha and James Kagunyo. They are all lieutenants and great buddies. Always moving together and chasing girls all over town. They are saying all sorts of naughty things and the women playing darts have to plug their ears.

Claude asks me what I'll have and I tell him that I'd like two fingers of scotch. He asks me what I'll have it with and I tell him that I'll have it with porridge if they don't have water. I get my whisky on the rocks and say "cheers warriors" and we clink glasses. I gulp the stuff down because I am really thirsty and Harry gets me another double which he holds at my nose and says, "Hey, son of a bitch, this is my blood. Let's drink until we go under the table. Today is my day off. Then we'll play a foursome at snooker when these married people go home for dinner."

"You are forgetting I am married, Harry!" I tell him.

"Fuck yourself man. I am married too. How is Tonia?"

"Fit as a fiddle," I lie.

"Lucky bastard. Everytime I want to come to town, Esther starts a war. She's an intolerable bitch. I am a tortured man. Mark you old man, my father had six and he managed them fine. Why can't we bums manage a simple *one*, even when she is pregnant? Let's have a drink."

"I advised you against marriage, Harry," says Jim, "and you thought I was nuts. Anyway that woman was *managing* you even before you got married, so why the fuss?"

"Shut up man," says Harry. "You spend all your blinking money paying for abortions and bribing go-betweens. You can't afford one round of booze even just for the record."

"OK, rich man. You think you are the only one who has money. The next three rounds are mine."

We are hitting the bottle hard. Claude starts talking about some girl he wants to see at the Mombasa Hospital while Jim is talking about the mayor's daughter. Jim is scared of the mayor. He is talking in whispers. Harry tells him that he'd better watch out because if the old fella got wind of the abortion that Jim had paid for two months earlier, then there would be no telling but that the old geezer could even get him excommunicated from the city.

"Stella is a terribly nice girl, Harry, and she loves me. I don't want you to speak ill of her old man. He is a great guy."

"And why don't you get married, fucker?"

"And be like you?"

"What do you mean?"

"Quarrelling and fighting and..."

"Look Jim," Harry says seriously, "just keep your bloody long nose out of my private family affairs, will you? It is extremely bad taste on your part."

"I see," Jim says sarcastically. "Listen old chap, no offence intended, but really why don't you make it a *private family affair*? Everytime you have a quarrel at home you run into the Officers Mess hollering all over the place, telling everybody what a quarrelsome bitch your wife is and all that. That's not fair on yourself. It's bad taste. You should keep your private affairs to yourself."

"Don't advise me on how to run my house," Harry snaps viciously.

"Why don't you guys change the subject?" I ask them. "In the first instance, I want to buy a kingsize around. Like Harry said, I really want to go under the table today. I want to wake up tomorrow dead, sick, fuddled and blank."

"What is happening to you, Dod? No family problems I hope? I swear I shall never get married. Lieutenant Jim Kagunyo shall die a bachelor at the age of seventy. I don't want to live longer than that. After you are seventy your bloody balls don't function no more anyway, and I just don't care for being alive toting a dead rod. No use to anybody."

"You are obsessed with sex my dear Jim. Have a drink," I tell him.

"It's not an obsession, Dod. It's a fact of life. Take away sex and then you've no life. Even blinking plants have their little bit of it. When there is no more sex left in my little man, let me pop off. The damn thing wasn't given to me just for pissing. It has a reproductive angle."

"Ha, and how about aborting the fruit of your labours?" Harry teases.

"Shut your hole, man. I don't stop anybody getting his bitch to abort, so why don't you try it one day?"

I reckon that Jim is being too hard on Harry. He is hitting below the belt but you never can tell with these navy guys. They never seem to get angry with each other, so I shout at the bartender at the top of my voice just for the heck of it and the guy looks at me open mouthed as if I'd hit him.

"Yes, Mr. Kiunyu," he inquires timidly.

"One double scotch and three beers. Make it snappy."

"Sure, sure, Mr. Kiunyu". He brings the drinks hurriedly and looks at me suspiciously.

"Do you want something else, Sir?"

"No thanks, but please don't call me "Sir" again. You folks got so used to calling the Britons "Sir" that you say "Sir" to your own brother. The whiteman is no longer "Sir" and neither are we. You understand?"

"Yes, Mr. Kiunyu."

"That's a good man," I tell him. "Have a drink on me."

"Oh, thank you very much, Sir... I mean Mr. Kiunyu. I am sorry. I..."

"Alright. No apologies for short memories. Have your drink."

He is very nice, this bartender. His name is Salim and he speaks four languages. When you buy him a drink, he doesn't take it but he keeps the money. If you give him a good tip, he may give you a triple whisky and charge for a double. He's a very honest chap, this Salim.

I count four ten cent pieces and jingle them in my hand.

"Excuse me folks," I say. "I'll be back in a minute. I want to get out and make a telephone call."

The public call box is outside. I get in there and ring the port. I want to speak to my friend, Ben, because I want to know the exact time of arrival of a Greek cargo ship that is supposed to be docking sometime this evening. Ben is working overtime. Gets a lot of dough, the blighter.

After a few impatient rings, somebody picks up the phone on the other side and a female voice says, "Hello!"

"Hello, and good evening. May I please speak to Mr. Mwaura. Benson Mwaura."

"Who is speaking please?"

"His brother. John Mwaura."

"I didn't know he had a brother. Hold the line please."

I chuckle to myself and after a few cracking noises in my ear Ben comes on the line.

"Hello, Mwaura here."

"Hi, Mr. Man. This is Dodge here. How is you?"

"Over-worked. Who told you I had a brother?"

"A little bird — but skip it. Tell me, Ben, when is the Athenia docking?"

"You sure are going to get into trouble over this black-marketeering business. Can't you get an honest job?"

"Listen, Ben. Just tell me when that cargo ship is getting to Mombasa."

"Hold on a minute and I'll check." He's gone for half a minute. I can hear the opening of a drawer and the riffling of papers. Presently he's back on the phone.

"Hi Dodge," he calls.

"Yeah!"

"The vessel in question will dock at twenty one hours, zero minutes."

"Thank you Ben."

"Where are you?"

"At the Railway Club."

"A lousy place."

"It would appear so to a guy who is also making his secretary do some overtime."

"Blast your dirty mind. Be seeing you."

"Will you be in the office by eight thirty this evening?"

"Yeah"

"I'll see you there."

"Ah — ah. I'll be too busy and I don't want my office to be mixed up with your black-maketeering business."

"You shouldn't say such things on the phone."

"O.K. buddy, *au revoir*," and he hangs up. I put down the receiver and go out of the booth. I reckon that too many people are getting wise to this little profitable business I am on. I reckon I'll have to give it up. I have to give it up before the cops nail me on the cross. Damn the cops.

I get back to my scotch and give it a sip. It don't taste so good. I am no longer thirsty. Instead I am starting to get high and I don't like this place no more. The place is too goddam full. The women wouldn't even let you have a game of darts. They are monopolizing the damn game. Damn them.

I decide to get the hell out. I decide that the Bristol Bar might be more interesting. They even have snooker tables there. I drain my drink and Jim asks me to have another.

"No thanks," I say.

"Come, come Dod. You aren't chickening out."

"This place is stiffling."

"You'd have to invent a better lie. You sure are having some problems. Is it your Indian girl? I have doctor friends."

"And so have I, Jim. You are off on the wrong track. I merely want to take a stroll and breathe fresh air into my lungs."

Jim is drunk. He grabs me and imprisons my left arm while he orders another whisky. He says,

"You might as well stagger while you stroll. Don't act like a holy sneak. I told you I've got dough and it doesn't even belong to me. It belongs to a boat which is sold and therefore no longer mine. Let us drink to the extermination of the boers."

Salim is smiling as he places the drink in front of me and I notice that he's given me three tots. I smile back. He's a real sneaky bastard.

"This is murder," I tell Jim.

"Change to beer."

"Too filling."

"You on diet?"

"I've no weight to lose."

"Then stick to beer. That way you can feel it coming and go slow, but this whisky stuff just gets you all of a sudden and before you know where you are, you've blacked-out with your mouth open and saliva drivelling down your chin. I know a guy who pissed inside his pants at a party. He just sat there dead drunk and pissed. People were so mad that some chaps used his open mouth as an ashtray."

"What are you trying to do, Jim — scare me?"

"Ah — ah," he shakes his head. "I know your capacity."

I've just cleared this last drink and I am saying to myself that I'll have to sneak away without letting anybody know, when Cecilia walks in. She's looking wonderful in a white blouse, brown skirt and suede sandals. She comes right over to me and says, "Hi Dod" and I say "Hi". She gives me a very hot smile. Then she shakes hands with the lieutenants and excuses herself. As she goes to join Wambua she gives my hand a little squeeze. That feels good. I don't want to sneak away no more. I order myself another drink because my friends haven't gone halfway through their pints. I am just starting to sip this drink when Cecilia comes back.

"Where is Tonia?" she asks me.

"At home, I suppose."

"She didn't want to come out?"

"She was expecting some *Maendeleo ya Wanawake* friends." A bloody lie.

"You buying me a drink?"

"Would your friend approve?"

"I am single and free."

"Better try and get him to understand that, my dear. What will you have?"

"Same as you." I order a double scotch for her and we clink glasses. She then turns and clinks glasses with Harry, Jim and Claude. Jim is looking at her as if he'd like to eat her there and then. I wink at him and he smiles. He is a terribly sexy bastard.

We are standing there chatting about nothing. Harry is telling funny jokes and Cecilia is laughing her head off. Wambua keeps throwing a disapproving eye in our direction and I am wondering why he doesn't have enough guts to come and join us. I ask Cecilia to bring him over and she tells me that the guy ain't got it in the kidney. I ask her what the hell that means and she tells me that I don't have it in the kidney either. We are all baffled about this kidney business and we pester her about it, but she merely laughs and tells us that it's a lousy joke. Claude is not satisfied.

"But what does it really mean -- not having it in the kidney? You mean sexual power or pissing power or. . ."

"Don't be vulgar," Cecilia interrupts. "If you don't have it in the kidney you don't have it in the head. That's all it means." We are laughing when Wambua comes over and grabs Cecilia's free hand.

"Come!" he says.

"Let go of my hand," she snaps back at him.

"I want to talk to you."

"That doesn't mean that you've got to grab my hand."

"I want to talk to you," he repeats.

"When?" she asks sarcastically.

"Now."

"You'll have to wait like you made me wait last night."

"Wait for what?" He's embarrassed.

"Wait my time."

"But you are doing nothing right now."

"I am talking to these gentlemen."

"But they can wait."

"So can you. Don't be rude." She's very angry. I am angry too. I'd like to sock this punk in the mouth.

"Is something the matter with you, Cecilia?" He asks incredulously.

"Come, come. You can do better than that surely. What do you mean, anyway?" she asks.

"I invited you here and you cannot..."

"Please, please! Don't bother me. I can do what I please. You are not the only Club member around." She turns away and faces Jim. He in turn laughs and claps his hands and says, "Hear! Hear! Let's drink to that." Wambua focuses his angry eyes on him and clenches his fists. He opens his mouth and virtually spits the words at Jim.

"Why don't you speak when you are spoken to?"

Jim ignores him completely and continues to laugh as if the poor chap had said nothing. He turns to Harry and says, "Hey man, let us celebrate," and Harry says " Sure man, let us drink to our kidneys", and we all laugh like mad. Wambua is not in the know so he just stands there with an open mouth like a surprised porpoise hating everybody and probably even himself.

We get drinks and Harry raises his froth laden glass solemly, makes the sign of the cross, clears his throat and says in a solemn priestly voice, "Drunkards of the world, unite! You have nothing to lose but your kidneys." We burst out again and Wambua spits out,

"Shit!"

Jim puts down his glass suddenly and glares at him.

"Look my friend, why can't you leave us alone?"

"Who asked you to speak?" Wambua asks him.

Wambua is getting on my nerves. I know that chap is after me. He wants me to say something so he can pick it up from there, but I am not giving him a chance. I simply act unconcerned.

"Let's be very frank with one another," Jim says seriously. "I have no quarrel with you, Mr. Wambua, but if you insist on ruining my drink, I shall most certainly clout you. Get that straight in your head."

"And who are you to talk like a tiger? Clout me indeed!"

"I pray you, go away!" Jim is shouting. His eyes are red with anger. I must say he is doing his best to keep himself under control. The rest of us are mute. The ladies playing darts have stopped. Claude goes between Jim and Wambua. He says,

"Please, gentlemen, this is unnecessary. Let's enjoy our drinks."

"And who spoke to you — you little nigger?" Wambua snaps. That was a grave mistake. Claude is a small chap. He is short and has a terrible complex about his height. Immediately the words are out of Wambua's mouth, Claude gives him a right-handed dig in the stomach that sounds like a football kick and as he caves in, Claude gives him a knee lift that almost bursts his nose. It's all too sudden. Wambua reels, grabs a stool and swings it like a discus thrower. Claude ducks and the stool lands on Cecilia, knocking her completely over. She lets out a howl that you could have been heard in China. Wambua is momentarily off balance. Claude gives him an undercut on the chin that throws him right into my hands. I am not feeling very friendly towards him so I fling him off me, pushing with all my might. He careers backwards, trips over Cecilia who is being helped by Jim onto her feet, and crashes onto a small side table thereby upsetting the dart-playing women's coca-colas.

For a moment I think that the guy is spent. He isn't. He springs onto his feet like a tiger, grabs the little table in his hands and before I've the time to gasp, there is this big explosion on my face and I hit the floor with the back of my head. I am dizzy like hell. All I see are fighting shapes but I am even too weak to stand. I can vaguely see Wambua's boot as it comes towards my ribs but I can't evade it. I take it with a groan.

When I come to, I notice that Harry's face is a mess. He is bleeding profusely through the nose. Claude is on the floor and Jim bursts in through the door holding his head. I don't see Cecilia or Wambua but there is a crowd of punks all around us making a hell of a racket. Whenever there is a little fight you can't keep crowds off. The whites are murmuring in a group.

"You OK, Dodge?" Jim asks.

"I don't feel so good. What happened?"

"The blighter messed us up and took off."

"He's gone?"

"With the bitch. Dragged her all along."

"What were you doing?"

"The punk'd bashed me on the head with a bottle. The bottle didn't break though, otherwise my brain would be on the floor. I was dizzy and fucked."

The women are starting to withdraw on account of the bad language. We help Claude onto his feet and we get the hell out. Harry's hanky is so bloody that I have to lend him mine. Claude is still out. He can't drive his car. The idea is to rush him to hospital just in case he's cracked a bone and besides, Harry may need something for his nose.

By the time we get to the hospital Claude has come to. He's swearing that he doesn't want to see any doctor or nurse, so we ask him how he is feeling in general. He says he feels lousy and that there are bees in his head, but that is no excuse for seeing no blinking doctors. "Besides," says Claude "we've a bull-shitting naval doctor who sits on his ass the whole day trimming his nails. I want to go home. I am ashamed of myself. How can four guys be fucked by one blighter?"

I ask Jim to drop me at home because I don't feel like going to meet this Greek ship while there's a big lump on the left top corner of my face just below the hair line. I don't feel no good at all.

Within half no time, the car comes to a sudden stop in front of my house and the three guys are off again. I'd told them to drop me at the gate because I want to sneak in without being seen. I get in through the garage door making sure that I make no noise and wonder how I can sneak into the spare bedroom without being noticed. I want to rest, that I surely do. Can't stand Tonia jabbering at me and asking why I came back after I said I'd sleep out. Anyway, I am in no mood for them goddam questions or arguments. My head is aching and I need perfect peace.

There's nobody in the sitting room. I thank my stars for that. I take off my sandals and tip-toe to the guest room and I am just about to turn the knob when it occurs to me that I should piss first. My blinking bladder if full. I stand for a while and reflect. I decide that I can't go into the goddam toilet without making a racket. I stand there undecided and then remember that there is a wash basin in the spare bedroom. I'd piss in it.

I turn the knob stealthly and push in the door slowly just in case it has developed the creaking sickness and shut it carefully behind me. It's half dark in here on account that the sun is just about disappeared behind the ocean and there are these deep green window curtains that Tonia got as a home-made present from one of her *Maendeleo ya Wanawake* friends.

I've just unzipped my pants and I am happily letting out the first relieving gush from my over pressurized bladder when I notice a dangling figure where the mosquito net should be hanging. I am momentarily frozen. I feel like screaming something, but no words come. Only an open stupid mouth and staring, unbelieving eyes hypnotized by the hanging body. I am dead fixed. Then it comes back to me. My life comes back. I make a leap onto the bed and hold her legs up, hopefully to ease the pressure on her neck just in case there's some life still left in her. I am all frantic. I can't reach her neck to undo the knot. I've to get a knife or a razor, or something for chrissake. The only thing is to cut the goddam rope and I can't get anything to cut it with as long as I keep holding her up. I am mad. I've lost my wits. I can't let go and go chasing into the kitchen for a knife. Every split second is precious. I let go slowly and make a mad jump grabbing the rope just above her head and we both crash on the bed as the hook on which the rope was attached tears off the ceiling with a snarl.

I undo the knot frantically tearing flesh off my fingers and then stare at her in the half darkness. She's all limp and lifeless. I feel her heart but I can't feel a thing. My own heart is beating like a hundred drums. I let go and move to the door, switch on the lights, leave the door open, rush out madly, get a bucket from the kitchen, and proceed to fill it up with water. My mind is completely blank except for one thing. Water. I am not even considering whether she's dead or alive. My mind cannot accommodate such things.

I dash back into the bedroom, bucket full of water in my hands and splash it all over her at one go. I dash out again, get another bucketful and again splash it on her. I repeat the operation four times. Finally, I throw the bucket away and feel her heart again. No use. I can't tell whether it's my heart or her heart that is beating. Must get a doctor. I try the telephone. Line engaged. Damn the telephone company. Damn everybody. Jesus! Am I drunk or crazy, or both?

I grab her and fling her onto my shoulder. I never realized that she was so heavy. I dash out through the garage door but then the goddam car is locked. Where the hell are the keys? They must be somewhere in the house. Probably in her handbag. I dash back into the house, my dripping human cargo still on my shoulder. I am all wet. Jesus! I can't find the goddam key. Oh, blast! I must think. Must compose my whirlpool mind. Why did God give me such an empty dashing head? Why? Dash Him, too!

I finally find the key on the dressing table in the bedroom and I am out again. I get the car open, lay Tonia on the rear seat, hop into the driver's seat, reverse the car out of the garage and drive like hell, ignoring all traffic rules and with the hooter blasting away like a siren all the way. Nearly got rammed into by a blinking bus. The guard at the hospital gate gives me one look as I pass through, then immediately starts telephoning. Maybe he thinks I am nuts.

I park the car just outside the out-patients reception and virtually have to pull Tonia out of the car. I get a better hold of her and march up three steps, and find myself face to face with a nurse. She looks at the lifeless form in my hands and then at me and shrugs her shoulders. I just feel like strangling her.

"Get a doctor." I tell her tersely.

"What is the matter with her?" she asks.

"Get a doctor!" I snap. She's sort of frightened by my hagard look and my curt way of address.

"Wait a minute," she says timidly and starts to walk away.

"I can't wait. At least show me a place where I can rest her. The operation theatre or some place." She beckons me and I follow. Four doors away and around the corner she opens a door alright, but there is no doctor inside. I look around and then notice the usual examination bed with a mackintosh cover behind a movable light green screen. I don't wait for instructions. I move over and lay Tonia on the table. I flex my tired hands and then face the nurse. I am dripping wet.

"Where's the doctor?"

"You just wait a minute. He's out but he is on call. I'll get him on the phone. What's the matter with her?"

"Can't you see for yourself for Chrissake? Can't you see she's dead? Get the doctor and stop gawking." I am shouting.

"Did you say that she's dead?"

"Oh, for crying out aloud! Do I have to keep repeating myself? I said she's dead."

"Then what do you want a doctor so urgently for? She should be taken to the mortuary instead."

"Listen, nurse! You call the doctor right now or I'll strangle you. You understand?" My hands are shaking. I make a movement towards her baring my teeth and clenching my fists and she just about collapses with fright. She starts pleading. "No. Please no. I'll get the doctor.

Please." It's hardly a whisper. She's as terrified as a rat that had been thrown into a snake's cage. Gosh. I must be looking awful.

She moves to the doctor's table, lifts the phone and tries to speak into it. Words choke in her mouth. She's trembling and looking at me as if I am the only thing between her and death, and even then, I must be death's private executioner.

"Make it snappy girl," I say encouragingly. "I wouldn't hurt you. Never harmed a thing in my life." After what looks like a whole ten years of holding the phone to her ear, somebody comes on the line on the other side and she says:

"Please get me through to the medical officer on duty . . . The new one . . . Yes . . . Dr. Kihagi . . . Yes . . . Out-patients . . . emergency . . . thank you, I am holding." After another ten years she starts speaking again. "This is out-patients. We have an emergency . . . Yes . . . no Doctor . . . It's a dead woman and a crazy man . . . I haven't checked Doctor . . . No, not . . . drowning . . . I beg your pardon . . . the police? . . . No . . . I can't . . . I can't explain . . . The man is . . . No . . . Please come at once." She puts down the receiver and stares at me. I stare back and ask, "Is he coming?"

"Yes," she says timidly.

"You think I am crazy, eh?" She doesn't answer me. Instead she moves to the screen and shuts herself in there with Tonia. In a moment she comes out with an embarrassed smile and asks me.

"Why did you say she was dead?"

"Isn't she?"

"No, she isn't."

"I beg your pardon?" But again she doesn't answer me. She goes back behind the screen and I follow. She turns Tonia's face down on the little bed, holds her by the bowels and starts lifting her up and down. After half a minute of this she lets go and turns to face me.

"Did you give her artificial artificial respiration?" she asks.

"What is that?"

"Artificial respiration," she repeats. "Did you give her any after you fished her out of the water?" I notice that she's looking at me sort of funnily, averting her eyes. What's the matter with her?

"She wasn't in water. She was hanging."

"Oh," she says in a giggly timid voice that I consider completely out of place. Then I follow her eyes and notice them rest for a furtive moment at a point just below my tummy. I look towards my navel and — oh God! My pants are still unzipped and the circumcised head of my little man is sticking out like a dog's tongue. Of course I didn't remember to zip up. Take my advice. Never piss in a wash basin.

Instinctively, I turn round and I am stuffing my man back and trying to zip up frantically when the door opens suddenly and a young fellow wearing a doctor's uniform bursts in. He is directly in front of me. At seeing my frantic zipping act his mouth pops open with horror. Trouble is that the goddam zip is all wet. I turn sideways and give it a final pull as a result of which the piece I am holding comes off in my hand and that's just about the end of my zip. Blast the manufacturers!

I look at the doctor sympathetically, shrugging my shoulders. He looks at me and then at the nurse, walks past me and asks the nurse in a whisper, "Is this the mad fellow you talked about?" The nurse nods her head in the affirmative. "OK", he says, "call the police".

"Look doctor, I am not crazy. My name is Dodge. Dodge Kiunyu and the lady lying there is my wife. She was hanging when . . ."

"Shut up and get out," he snaps me. I obey him, but then he comes out of the green room two minutes later and now wants to know how it all happened. I tell him everything the way I saw it but in the end he merely shakes his head. He then goes back, holds a short conference with the nurse and then faces me.

"You are crazy", he tells me. "To begin with, that woman there is nobody's wife. I know her. She's called Tonia. Before I was transferred from Nanyuki to Nakuru and then to this place, that woman there was whoring away with all the soldiers in Nanyuki and I treated her for V.D. several times. So if you tried to strangle her because she wouldn't screw you unless you paid her in advance, then you'd better organise your head because the police are going to be here any minute.

I am so mad at the doctor that I could hit him. Oh God! How can he say such things? I can hardly open my mouth.

"Look," I blurt out finally, "you say such a vile thing to me again and I'll knock out your teeth outright." I am shaking my clenched fist at him. I reckon he thinks I am real nuts because the next thing he says is, "I see. And why were you sticking your penis out at the nurse? If you had no thoughts of rape, then you have to be mad. Why should a sane person stick his penis out at a woman?"

"Doctor I wasn't sticking anything out deliberately. It was just unzipped accidentally. When you came in I was simply trying to. . ."
"Spare your breath for the police," he cuts me short. I am mad. The blighter won't listen to me.

"But I am trying to tell you that. . ."

"You are telling me nothing. You are crazy!" he shouts.

"You are crazy too, doctor. I am trying to explain. . ."

"I have listened to you long enough. Now get out of my hospital before I throw you out."

"This is not your hospital!" I shout back. "This is a Government hospital and you are just an employee, so don't think you can push me around. This is a free country."

"If you don't get out on your own, I'll throw you out myself — and now."

"Why?"

Instead of answering me, he comes at me and gives me a bulldozer push that lands me in the verandah where I bang my head against the opposite wall. I am just about to make a mad dive at him when I see the police. There's one inspector followed by two constables and I decide that this will be the end of my fight with the doctor.

I am not given a chance to say anything. The doctor does all the talking after which I am hustled into a police vehicle and driven to the police station. Blast them cops and doctors.

Sunday Night

Cops are a bloody nuisance. If I become a judge one day I'll put the whole of the copper tribe in prison. They have been harassing me for ages, and they are still harassing me. They keep taking turns so no sooner do I finish with one cop than he goes out and another one comes in and starts the whole thing all over again. I am so fed up that if their words were sweet meats, I'd have already puked ten times. At last it is the Inspector and I am praying God that he will be the last. He grins at me, sits down and relaxes as if he is quite happy to spend the whole night having a chat with me. Blast him!

"Your full name please?"

"Dodge Kiunyu."

"Age?"

"Thirty two."

"Place of birth?"

"Eastleigh, Nairobi."

"Occupation?"

"None."

"How do you earn your living?"

"I don't."

"How do you live then?"

"On my savings and my wife's income."

"How did you get your savings?"

"I used to work before."

"And when did you quit working?"

"About a year ago or thereabout."

"You haven't worked since?"

"No."

"You must have had fat savings to last you that long without gainful employment."

"Don't you think you are digressing, Sir?" I ask him.

"We are just trying to get the preliminaries straight. Where do you live?"

"Cliff Avenue."

"Where on Cliff Avenue."

"The house overlooks the Golf Course directly in line with the New Florida Night Club. It's Plot no. 17 on Cliff Avenue."

"Fine. Now give us some details about your wife — name, age, place of birth, occupation and so on."

"But I have been giving those details ever since I got here!"

"Just give the same details again," the officer says.

"OK," I say. "Her name is Tonia Miriam. She is as old as I am — approximately that is!"

"For how long have you been married?"

"Around one and a half years."

"Any children?"

"None."

"You are much too careful, don't you think?"

"I don't have to think. I know."

"Now Mr. Kiunyu, we shall discuss your wife's and your own family background later on, but for the moment just tell us what happened this evening."

"It's as I told your friends earlier. I went out for a drink and when I got home my wife was . . . well, she was hanging on a rope in the guest room."

"Do you have family problems?"

"Nothing special."

"Did you quarrel with your wife over something lately?"

"Nothing that would prompt her to hang herself."

"But did you have a quarrel?"

"I would like to meet a married couple that does not quarrel. Simply put it that we have our own family misunderstandings like everybody else."

"How did you get that bump on your head?"

"Some chap hit me at the Railway Club."

"You are sure that your wife did not give it to you? You can swear that you have not been involved in any physical fight with your wife?"

"That is absurd. I tell you that some chap hit me at the Railway Club. That can be verified and I have not had a fight with my wife. I am not a wife fighter."

"And why did this chap hit you?"

"There was a fight and the chap got crazy so he was hitting everybody. You probably know him. His name is Wambua. He is the Provincial Engineer. Go and ask him."

He simply twists his mouth and continues.

"And now to come back to your wife, how did you happen to discover her? How did you happen to go into the guest room? Does she normally sleep there?"

"I was trying to sneak into the guest room unnoticed. I thought that she was in our bedroom and I didn't want to talk to her just then."

"Why?"

"She doesn't approve of my drinking habits and I was drunk. I was merely trying to avoid a confrontation."

"So you let yourself into the guest room and found her hanging?"

"Yes."

"If your wife disapproves of your drinking habits, how come that she gives you money to go out and get drunk?"

"She doesn't give me money every time."

"So you have been drinking your old savings for a year?"

"That could be a fantastic way of putting it."

"How would you put it?"

"Listen Officer. Did you call me here to get an insight into my life history?"

"We are asking the questions, Mr. Kiunyu. As you put it yourself, I think it's fantastic the way you've been able to economize your savings so that you can afford a drink when you want one."

"What is wrong with economizing?"

"I am merely wondering whether you have not been stealing your wife's money and I am also wondering whether that would not be sufficient cause for occasional fights. Tell me truthfully; has your wife ever accused you of stealing her money?"

"I think that this interrogation is taking a ridiculous turn. Why should I want to steal my wife's money? I never heard such nonsense in my life."

"O.K., O.K. You don't have to lose your head yet. We shall come to that later. I am merely trying to figure out your family problems why you have constant quarrels."

"I didn't say that we have constant quarrels."

"Of course you didn't, but it is apparent from the way you guard your responses in that respect."

"I don't understand you."

"You can tell as much by simply refusing to tell."

"That's even worse for my stupid brain."

"But you do have constant family quarrels, don't you?"

"Certainly not," I snap.

"But your wife disapproves of your drinking habits, doesn't she?"

"So what? It's within her rights. Doesn't your wife disapprove?"

"So if you drink every day, then your wife complains every day and that is why you would prefer to sneak into the guest room and forgo your dinner just to avoid a confrontation. Doesn't that tell a tale?"

"What tale?" I was getting very angry with this chap. I didn't like his insinuations one bit. I didn't like the way he was prying into my private life but I was intrigued by his approach. I was wondering what he had at the back of his mind. He continued.

"Are you familiar with your wife's financial situation?"

"What do you mean?"

"What I mean is, do you know what your wife does with her money or how much she has in the bank?"

"Why should I want to know. It's her money."

"Do you ever discuss your financial situation?"

"No."

"Does your wife have an insurance policy?"

"I don't know."

"How do you run your house?"

"My wife runs the house."

"Don't you even discuss how your house should be run?"

"What is there to discuss?"

"So you do not discuss?"

"I don't think that there is anything to discuss — not unless something went wrong. I mean, we can't discuss what time is lunchtime or what food is nutritious, what soap we should use for washing clothes and when to polish the floor. All these things go without saying. Of course we don't just sit and stare at each other like goons. We talk about all sorts of things like everybody does. But when a man talks with his wife it can be both discussion or no discussion. Discussion implies that there is a subject to be discussed. You can talk to your wife for ten years without discussing any particular subject."

"Are you happily married, Mr. Kiunyu?"

"What business of yours is that?"

"This is an attempted suicide case. Your family life just became our business. I repeat my question. Are you happily married?"

"And I give you the same answer. It's none of your business."

"Fine. You've already answered the question. Now we are starting to understand each other. So I'll ask you another question. In your own opinion, Mr. Kiunyu, is your wife mentally stable? Have you ever had doubts about her sanity?"

"None whatsoever."

"Has she ever consulted a psychiatrist?"

"To the best of my knowledge, no."

"Have you ever threatened to divorce her?"

"You are getting personal again."

"When did you last threaten to divorce her?"

"I haven't said that I did."

"But you have at one time threatened to divorce her?"

"You are repeating the same absurd question."

"Which you have repeatedly refused to answer, isn't that right?"

"Divorce is a common word."

"And you've been using it repeatedly at home I suppose. Tell me, this afternoon before you went to the Railway Club between you and your wife was there any talk of divorce?"

"Are you insinuating that she'd hang herself if there was such a talk?"

"That's what I am driving at."

"You are driving at the ridiculous."

"O.K. Let's grant that it is ridiculous, but I still want to know if you had a quarrel this afternoon during which you discussed divorce."

Finally I have to tell him about the disagreement we had this afternoon which I think was a mistake because he then proceeds to sweat me out about all sorts of things. I have to tell him about Tonia's past life of prostitution and my own previous life. At the end of it all he made me feel like a psychopath who had unwillingly driven his deranged wife into committing suicide. Finally he calls somebody on the phone and asks him to bring out a camera and then he says to me, "I . . . we are going over to your place to have a look around."

He agreed that we could pass by the hospital so that I could collect my car and also find out how Tonia was fairing. On leaving the hospital, the inspector sat in my car while the photographer followed behind in a police patrol car. I was feeling awful. He was whistling all the way. He had his right hand dangling out of the window of the car and he kept drumming on the outside of the door in rhythm to his whistling as if he was at perfect peace with himself.

We got to the house, parked the cars and entered. There was water on the floor all the way up to the guest bedroom. We got into the guestroom and the Inspector started pestering me with questions again. He wanted to know where I stood when I noticed the body, how the body was hanging, which side it was facing, why I had to spill so much water all over the place and how, in my opinion, Tonia could have tied the rope on the hook attached to the ceiling since there was no chair in the room. I told him that his guess to all that was as good as mine.

The assistant took measurements of the distance between the window-ledge and the spot where the rope was hooked, and then measured the distance between the bed and the ceiling and also the distance between the bed and the window. The cameraman was taking photographs from various angles, sometimes focussing his camera on the wet bed and the rope and sometimes focussing it on the ceiling from different angles and positions. His bulbs were blinding me.

The officer was standing at the door, staring at the whole scene and contemplating. After a long while he asked his assistant, "What is your opinion, John?"

"If what Mr. Kiunyu says is true, that he did not remove any furniture from this room this evening, then I find it very difficult to understand how the lady hanged herself. She had to fix the rope on to the hook on the ceiling but that is understandable. She could have removed whatever she placed on the bed in order to reach the hook after she'd attached the rope."

"That makes sense", the officer said.

"Having attached the rope, then she had to climb on something while putting the rope round her neck. Something that she'd have to kick away so that she could dangle. Whatever it was, it should have been in this room when Mr. Kiunyu came in. She couldn't possibly throw it out of the room when she was already dangling down."

"That is what I've been thinking all along," the Inspector said. "Think again Mr. Kiunyu. Are you sure that there was nothing?"

"I don't remember noticing anything. Besides, whatever it was, it should still be here."

"What about the bucket. Are you sure it wasn't in this room?"

"I am not sure anymore. I wasn't in any state to notice details, but I do remember getting the bucket from the kitchen downstairs. This bucket always sits in the kitchen and to the best of my knowledge that's where I got it from." The officer scratched his head, made two steps and stood in the middle of the room.

"It's got to be the window. She must have stood on the window ledge, tied the rope around her neck and then let go so that she could swing."

"That is very unlikely, Sir. From the measurements I have taken, that theory would be impossible. She would have to lean at an angle of forty-five degrees while she was putting the rope round her neck which is impossible but even then, she would hardly have any clearance from the top of the bed. She would virtually be standing on it instead of swinging. Mr. Kiunyu says that her feet were at least a foot from the top of the bed."

"What is your idea then?"

"Well . . . the only logical conclusion is that the lady did not hang herself. She was hanged."

"And how do you explain that?"

"Either Mr. Kiunyu is lying that he found the lady hanging, or if he is speaking the truth, then somebody else hanged her. It is unreasonable to imagine that somebody from the outside would come in here, walk into this room, remove the mosquito net and then call out to Mrs. Kiunyu to come in, and put her neck into a noose while he supported her. He would only be able to do that if he'd hit her and made her unconscious first, but still he couldn't hang her limp body without using some sort of a pulley system. We know that no pulley system was used because the rope is still attached to the hook and besides the rope is not long enough for a pulley. On the same grounds Mr. Kiunyu himself could not have done it because, otherwise how does one explain why he later wanted to save her if he was the original hangman?"

"All that you are telling me," the Inspector said, "is that you can't explain how it happened." The assistant nodded his head.

"I think your measurements are wrong John. I still maintain that she climbed on the window, tied the rope round her neck and let herself go. We'll do an experiment. We'll re-attach the hook at the same spot on the ceiling, get a piece of stick that's just about her height and hang it one foot from the top of the bed and then try to figure out whether that stick could hang itself from the window if it was a human being."

"Excuse me, Inspector," I horned in. "Don't you think that you are carrying this investigation of yours to a ridiculous extent? Are we not wasting time trying to figure out possibilities and probabilities, and I don't know what, when as early as tomorrow morning my wife will be able to tell you how she did it? From the theories you are advancing one would imagine that my wife was already dead. This is not a murder case. Nobody is dead."

"I am interested in these possibilities, Mr. Kiunyu. This could just as well have been a murder case. Suppose you'd come in five minutes later? I don't have to tell you, but we shall be prosecuting your wife for attempted suicide if your story is true. How do you like that?"

"Of course I don't like it. The ridiculousness of your argument is that I did not come in five minutes later, and my wife is very much alive. I feel confident that she will tell you the whole truth."

"We are going on with the experiment, anyway."

"I don't like the way you are soiling my bed."

"You shouldn't have poured so much water on it," he retorted.

They carried out the experiment and came to the conclusion that it was possible for Tonia to have used the window ledge when trying the rope around her neck. The chances were fifty-fifty. I maintained that the whole investigation was wrong and wasteful since Tonia would furnish answers to all their questions in the morning. The Inspector nodded his head. I then asked him whether he'd mind transporting himself and his assistant out of my house 'cause I was sleepy and he nodded his head again. At least we were now getting somewhere.

They looked around the house for a suicide note but there was none. Tonia decided to leave no messages behind. To say the truth, I would have liked her to leave a message. Up to now, I can't figure out why she wanted to take her life. As things are, I'll probably never know. The Inspector and his assistant got out and as I closed the door, he turned and said

"Goodnight, Mr. Kiunyu. Don't leave town till I say you can. There's more to this than meets the eye." I banged the door wihtout bothering to say goodnight. I was tired. Very tired.

TWO

Monday Morning

"Oh shut up, you old stubborn fat-headed clock," I curse as I stretch my hand to stop my old table clock from ringing. It always rings too loud and I had no business setting it for 7.30 a.m. except that I was afraid I might oversleep on account of these sleeping pills that I swallowed last night after the cops left. It is 7.30 a.m. now, but it looks like 8.30 a.m. 'cause I slept with the curtains open and the sun's rays shine directly through my window.

I light myself a cigarette, which is a thing I always do before getting out of bed and which irritates Tonia to such a point that she refuses to make breakfast for me at times, and then I scram out of bed. I look at myself in the mirror and scowl. I don't look so good. As a matter of fact I look positively bad. My eyes are red and sunken on account of last night's booze and my face is a greasy dead pan with a trickle of dried saliva at both corners of the mouth. I blow smoke at the mirror and then proceed to the toilet to rid myself of stuff that has been accumulating in my sleep.

What I have to do is, I have to wash up quickly, make some breakfast for Tonia and be at the hospital at eight o'clock. That leaves me a busy half hour between the toilet, the kitchen and the hospital. What I don't know is what I should make for breakfast. My usual breakfast is a cup of tea but Tonia likes to eat things. She insists on toast and butter and marmalade and fruit and bacon and eggs and sausage and porridge. . . . crazy! She eats like a blasted white. That, of course, has led to occasional arguments which she has always won on the grounds that it's mostly her money that buys the food. Anyway I have to make some breakfast and be at the hospital at eight. Luckily, I have no hangover. Thank God.

I get to the hospital at 8.10 a.m. on the dot. A short ten minutes late. I have a flask of hot sugared tea and a covered bowl in which I have mixed sausages, eggs and four slices of bread. There was no decent way of carrying these things short of bringing a tray along, so I hoped Tonia wouldn't mind. Normally she would of course object very strongly but these are special circumstances. I make straight for the special room where they put her last night. That is right at the other end of the ward so I have to pass these many beds where women with all sorts of illnesses are lying or sitting and I don't feel so good 'cause it's not a pleasant sight. Few of them are wearing bras.

"Hey, where are you going?" a nurse aks me. It's not the same nurse I saw last night. This is a different one and she don't look so bad. As a matter of fact she looks good. I give her my morning smile and a little suggestion of a wink and say, "I am going to see my wife. She's at that small room at the other end of the ward"? I point with my finger and she says, "You mean Mrs. Kiunyu?"

"Yes. That's the lady — my wife."

"You are Mr. Kiunyu then?"

"I sure look like him, don't I?"

"But you are. . ."

"Sure, I am him. Bones, nose and eyes."

"Your wife is with the sister in charge. She's in her room now."

"Does that mean that I can't see her?"

"I don't think that the Sister is examining her. I think they are merely chatting. I'll go and see."

"And who is this sister?"

"Oh, she's new. Her husband is a doctor here."

"O.K. Go and check." I follow behind her and as we get near the door to the room, I hear hearty laughter coming from within. The nurse stops.

"I think it will be O.K. for you to see her. I need not check," and she turns to go.

"Hey, tell me. How is she?"

"Of course she is fine. You can hear for yourself."

"And how about a date one day, you and I?"

"Goodbye, Mr. Kiunyu. I am glad to have met you." And she walks away. I look at her buttocks for a moment and then turn and proceed to the door inside which there is still much laughter. I knock, turn the knob and peep in. Tonia is lying on the bed holding hands with a uniformed lady who is sitting on the bed beside her. They both turn their eyes towards me and I notice immediately that they resent my horning in on their privacy without warning and that they'd rather be left alone. There's momentary embarrassment all around so what I do

37

is, I shut the door behind me, smile broadly and say, "Good morning, and may I come in?"

"You are already in. What do you want?" the sister asks.

"Eh ... I ..."

"It's OK, Julian. This is Dodge — my husband."

"Oh, I am sorry. Do excuse me, Mr. Kiunyu. I thought that perhaps ..."

"No need for an excuse. You are perfectly in order. I am glad to meet you sister ..."

"Kihagi, but you can call me Julian."

"What?" Truth of the matter is I didn't like Dr. Kihagi when I met him yesterday so I am wondering whether the nurse is his sister or his wife or is she another Kihagi all together? Perhaps I did not hear properly. The momentary surprise on my face is directly transmitted to her and she asks in surprise:

"What's so shocking about it?"

"Oh — nothing. It's my stupid head. I imagined that you said that your first name was Julius and that brought Caesar to my mind and..."

"You are bizarre, aren't you? Or are you merely making a stupid joke? How can you imagine that a lady was called Julius?"

"My apologies sister."

"I said you could call me Julian."

"My apologies Julian. Eh ... are you a sister to Dr. Kihagi?"

"I am Mrs. Kihagi. Have you met him?"

"Yes I met him last night. He was the doctor on duty. He's the one who attended to Tonia when I brought her in. Eh ..." I turn to Tonia.

"I brought some breakfast, love. Sausage and eggs. Better eat it while it's hot. How are you feeling?" I put the breakfast things on the side table by the bed.

"I feel fine thank you ... and I have already had breakfast."

"Eh?" I was surprised by her dry, icy tone.

"I've had my breakfast already and don't act so dumb. Sit down." I feel terribly uncomfortable. I feel unwanted. In a way, I am dumb. First I meet Tonia laughing with a nice beautiful woman who turns out to be the wife of the fellow who practically kicked me out of the hospital last night and then Tonia talks to me in this very unfriendly cold voice. The thing is that I'd like to talk to her in the absence of this other woman but I don't know how to go about it. It looks like they'd like me to disappear so that they can continue with whatever they were doing. I decide one thing. I decide that I don't particularly like Julian Kihagi and that it's high time I acted like a tough loving husband. I say to Tonia, "Have the police been here yet? I want to talk to you before they do."

"And why would the police want to talk to me?"

"That's what I want to talk to you about."

"What do you have in mind?"

"It's the whole thing. You know how it happened. They'll be here any minute."

"I am sorry, I don't understand. I'd also like you to know that Julian and I are good old friends. We knew each other in Nanyuki. We are old friends. I am very glad that we've met again and very disappointed that we lost track of each other through the years otherwise we wouldn't have lived in the same city since they came down two weeks ago completely oblivious of each other's presence. I am glad I came to the hospital although we'd have met accidentally in due course, anyway. The point I am trying to make is that Julian and I have no secrets."

"Oh, it's OK, Tonia. I'll go out and do the rounds. I'll be back as soon as I can," says Julian.

"No, no. Stay. My husband is leaving soon." Then she turns to me. "It's O.K., Dod. Feel confortable. Why do you think that the police want to talk to me?"

I feel like strangling her. Looks like all she wants is to let me down. She wants her friend to understand that I don't figure in her life at all; that I don't mean a damn thing to her.

Julian fidgets with her fingers and then says, "But my dear Tonia — you know what it's all about. The story that Mr Kiunyu told last night."

"That's the whole trouble. I don't understand. All I know is what you told me he said, but of course it's all nonsense."

"The police want to know why you tried to . . . to . . . well, you know what you tried to do last night." I say.

"What do you mean?"

"That's what I want to know before the police get here. What prompted you to . . . to . . . well, you know what you tried to do last night," I say.

"And what did I do if I may ask?"

"You know damn well what you did. If I hadn't come in on time it would be a different story altogether." I was getting angry. What was she trying to pretend about, anyway? She hanged herself and I didn't have to remind her.

"What are you talking about?" she snaps.

"So I take it that you do not know why you are in a hospital ward?" I retort.

"Honestly, I don't know. All I remember is starting to faint. I know I hit the floor and that is all I remember. I was in the sitting room standing at the window when I started to feel dizzy and was trying to make it to the bedroom when I passed out. I know I didn't get to the bedroom."

"Who are you trying to kid?" I ask her with a sneer. "In any case what's the point? I found you hanging by the neck in the spare bedroom and that is quite different from swooning onto the floor, if I may say so. The police want to prosecute you on a charge of attempted suicide."

"You are crazy," she snaps. "How could I hang myself in a state of unconsciousness? You are merely making the story up so that you can get some grounds for divorce. You don't have to descend to that level of cheap lies to accomplish your designs. I am terribly ashamed of you. God! I hate you. How can you tell such lies and then show your face in public? You should hide your face, Mr. Kiunyu."

"There's no point in arguing." I tell her. "I don't really think that you are in your right state of mind yet. The doctor's report will clarify matters. I . . . well . . . I don't know what to say. Do you think they'll let you out this morning? I mean . . .eh. . . are you well enough to go home?"

"That's hardly your business now, is it? You go about telling abominable lies about my trying to hang myself just so that you can get me into some sort of trouble and now you have the cheek to pretend that you care whether I am well or not. My very dear husband, allow me to congratulate you on your great kindness. You have ruined me you bastard — can't you see?"

"I am very sorry Tonia but I don't seem to understand anything anymore. I found you hanging and rescued you before it was too late and then brought you here to the hospital in a state of unconsciousness. As I say, the doctor's report will show the facts."

"Have you finished?" She asks me tersely. There's so much hate in her eyes that I feel it was all wrong to reapeat the story again. I can't understand her attitude. I want all the best in the world for her and I am planning to bribe the police officer so that the whole thing is dropped and forgotten for ever but instead she acts as if I am trying to drive her into the grave. It's all very unfair to me. One doesn't expect this sort of return for trying to be kind and useful. I have no words. I merely stare at her and all I see is hatred. Julian just stands there like an elephant, shifting her eyes from Tonia to me and biting her lower lip in contemplation. It's like a scene in the movie.

"If you have finished your piece, you may go now. . . . . . and don't forget your breakfast. We shall not be needing it." She dismissed my presence completely and turned to Julian.

"Hey, Julian, you didn't tell me what happened to Tay after her quarrel with the captain. Did she fight the other girl like she always said she would?"

"Really, Tonia, I don't think that this is the right time to talk about it. I can't begin to understand why. . ."

"Oh come, come Julian. Dodge is on his way to. . ."

"OK! OK! Tonia I'll be on my way although I wouldn't have expected you to mind my presence 'cause there are supposed to be no secrets between a man and his wife. Please do me one favour, Mrs. Kihagi. Please try to make my wife understand the situation. That would be more important than discussing old Nanyuki friends. As a nurse and a friend, I would expect it to be your duty."

"I understand you, Mr. Kiunyu, and thank you very much. I am glad to have met you and I am sure that we shall meet again under different circumstances. Tonia will be getting out of here as soon as the doctor has seen her probably in one hour's time. You may wish to bring the car along at. . ." There's a loud knock at the door and Julian finishes her speech in mid-sentence. She moves to the door and yanks it open. She lets out a gasp.

Framed at the door is the police Inspector. He smiles at Julian, looks into the room and says, "Oh, I am sorry to disturb you, Sister. I was coming to see Mrs. Kiunyu but since you are examining her, I think I'll come after you are finished."

"I am not being examined if that's what you want to know Inspector," interrupts Tonia who now sits on the bed casting deadly eyes at me.

"Eh, may I come in then? I just want to talk to you for a minute. Eh, do you mind if I speak to you alone? I'd prefer to speak to you alone."

"Look Inspector, I have no secrets from the world so what is this nonsense of wanting to speak to me alone? Dodge here is my husband though he should be gone by now I dare say, and Julian is a good old friend. I have no secrets Inspector."

"It's not really the secrets Mrs. Kiunyu, it's the nature of the business. The matter is somewhat delicate and. . ."

"Look here, Inspector," she interrupts. "I don't think that I have any delicate business to discuss with you and your one minute is just about gone, so if you have something to discuss, go right ahead without hawing and hedging."

"I don't want there to be some misunderstanding, Mrs. Kiunyu. You see, I am a police officer and I represent the law. I have the right to demand to see you alone if the nature of the business, to the best of my knowledge, so deems it necessary. And the business at hand is such that I am forced to..."

"You are still hawing and hedging, Inspector," Tonia snaps. "Your minute is gone anyway so would you mind awfully, Inspector . . . Would you mind really to close the door after you as you leave. We don't have the whole day."

"I think I'll go," says Julian.

"No, no. Wait and hear what he has to say. After all, I am a patient."

"Very well," the Inspector says. "I gather that you are being dismissed this morning, Mrs. Kiunyu. Would you please report at the police station as soon as you are released?"

"Certainly not. What should I report at the police station for?"

"For questioning."

"About what?"

"About attempted suicide."

"Are you in your right mind? You talk like my husband and he is certainly sick. Why should I want to commit suicide?"

"That's exactly what I want to know."

"Then you better talk to my husband. He's the only one who seems to know something about it, at least that's what he says. I can assure you, Inspector, that I know absolutely nothing about this nonsense!"

"You mean you didn't hang yourself?"

"That's absolutely ridiculous. It is the most preposterous lie and the very mention of it brings tears into my eyes. I could never have imagined that even a madman would invent such a monstrous lie about his wife. It will take me time to recover from the shock." She paused as if to let her outburst sink. Finally she added, "I know nothing about this malicious story. My husband is the only one who seems to know. Talk to him."

"I don't know what you are trying to make me believe, Mrs. Kiunyu. The fact is that you were brought here last night in a state of unconsciousness and your husband plausibly explained what had happened. I had the chance to examine the room in which you hanged yourself. I am quite satisfied that Mr. Kiunyu is right, unless you can give me a different explanation."

"To the best of my knowledge, if I may borrow your phrase, Inspector, I lost consciousness when I fainted and hit the floor somewhere between the sitting room and my bedroom and from that oblivious sleep, I woke up sometimes last night in this room. I didn't know where I was till the nurse told me that I was in hospital. From what I gather, I had an attack of epileptic fits though it is something I never suffered from before. It will take months to cure as Dr. Kihagi will explain to you if you care to ask him, but of course I don't have to be confined in a hospital. And now Inspector, since I couldn't possibly know what was happening when I was in a state of unconsciousness, I reiterate what I told you earlier. Ask my husband how he found me when he came to the house, how he brought me here and ask Dr. Kihagi about my physical condition at the time and thereafter. I think, Inspector, that I have told you all that you want to know from me and if you don't mind awfully, eh — I want my rest now."

"Just one minute," the Inspector says. Then he turns to Julian. "Is that what the medical report says? Does it say she had a fit?"

"Yes."

"Your husband was in charge of the examination, wasn't he? I mean last night."

"Yes he was. He was on call and is coming on duty at 10.00 a.m."

"I would like to ring him from your office if you don't mind."

"I wouldn't mind, but I am sure he will. He didn't have sufficient sleep last night. It's going to nine now. He'll be here in an hour. The medical report is however ready and you can have it. He asked me to give you a copy of the report when you called. If I understood correctly, your instructions were that you should be furnished with a complete report in the morning and my husband didn't want to be woken up. If you'll please follow me to the office, Inspector."

"I can't seem to understand this whole business," the Inspector says thoughtfully. Then he moves over to Tonia, goes on the knee and examines her neck.

"And how do you explain these marks on the neck?" The Inspector asks accusingly.

"The medical report explains all that," Julian tells him.

"Damn it all. And what have you got to say Mr. Kiunyu? What was all this stuff about your wife hanging herself? You didn't cook that up did you?"

All this time I've been standing here wondering whether I am really nuts or not. I know I am not nuts so the other party has to be nuts whichever way you look at it. That Tonia was hanging and that I rescued her is true. I could walk through fire or go to bed with my grandmother, if I had one, just to prove that. It is true. She was hanging and she is lying. How she could have had the doctor to collaborate her story by giving a false report, I cannot understand. Not unless after she met Julian she spilled the beans and persuaded her to make her husband tear up the original report and substitute it with a false one. That is the only way it makes sense. If the doctor's report talks of epileptic fits then it must be false. Trouble is, can I contradict a doctor's word? Can I prove that he is lying? Would it serve any purpose to have another doctor examine her? Why should I want another doctor to examine her? In other words, have I any alternative but collaborate with Tonia and the Doctor? I'll be damned if I know.

To begin with, the lie is a good one. At least Tonia will not be prosecuted for attempted suicide and that will save us a lot of unnecessary trouble and bribe money. In a sense, the blasted doctor has come to our aid. He's helping us get out of a jam now, although he wouldn't listen to me last night when I was begging him to listen to me. His wife must have given him a very good reason. So we are clear on the main issue but I am separately in a jam. If it can be shown that I fabricated the story, then the cops will not leave me alone and no amount of bribing will stop them. If Tonia wants to insist that I fabricated the story in order to obtain sound grounds for divorce she easily could. Judging from her attitude right now, I don't think she'd mind if I spent a couple of days in jail. I think she'd love it, blast her!

I don't know how to play this thing any more. Certainly a husband cannot keep on insisting that his wife tried to commit a serious crime while all other evidence shows that she didn't. There is no way of insisting on the accuracy of my story without betraying my trust as a husband and without making myself a ridiculous fool in the eyes of the public. Tonia has got me where she wants. Clever bitch. She could even accuse me of malicious damage to her name, et cetera. Can a wife claim damages from her husband for defamation of character? I don't know. Anyway, I've to play it along her way. I've no other.

When I don't answer, the Inspector repeats the question: "The story about you finding your wife hanging, did you just fabricate it? Why?"

"I think you better have a look at the doctor's report. It's bound to clear all outstanding misunderstanding."

"But if your wife had a fit how could she hang herself?"

"I remember telling you last night not to waste a lot of time carrying out all sorts of ridiculous experiments' cause my wife would tell you exactly how everything happend. You didn't want to listen to me."

"All right. There is a lot in this than meets the eye. Somebody is lying and the lie is so big that it constitutes a crime. Think twice, Mr. Kiunyu. Think carefully. Did you or did you not tell the doctor on duty and myself that you found your wife hanging by the neck in one of the rooms in your house?"

"I don't have to think twice or carefully about that one, Inspector."

"That is not answering me."

"Then don't ask me to think."

"Did you or did you not say that your wife was hanging by the neck last night when you returned to the house. I want an answer. Yes or no."

"I am not a doctor. If you want to know whether she was hanging or not all you have to do is look at the medical report. I don't see what you are waiting for. Sister Kihagi is waiting to escort you to the place where a copy of the report is waiting for you."

"All right. Please yourself. You'll remember that you made a full statement at the police station and that you were not under duress when you signed it. I'll teach you that you can't play with the law." With that he stares right into my eyes and then walks out followed by Julian. I turn to Tonia.

"You fool. Why didn't you warn me? Why didn't you tell me that the doctor had fabricated the thing so it wouldn't appear like suicide. You really made me look like a bloody fool. What's the catch?"

"I am sorry, Dod, but I don't know what you are talking about. Unless you think that you are more competent at diagnosis than a qualified doctor, I suffered from a fit as the report says."

"But my dear Tonia, you know as well as I do that you don't suffer from epileptic fits. It's caused by secretions from tape worms and you couldn't possibly have tape worms. That much I know."

"You are not qualified to discuss causes and effects in such medical matters. Your speciality is currency black-marketeering. Stick to your trade and don't advance theories in matters that you know nothing about. I shall say this and I shall repeat it again. You have told a very damaging lie about me for reasons known only to yourself. You couldn't have chosen a better way of discrediting and indeed ruining me completely. It is beyond forgiveness and I shall persue you till my name is exonerated and you have paid for it. I have nothing more to say to you except this — that while pursuing this matter to its ultimate conclusion, I shall, in my heart, forget that you are my husband and shall let the law take its course same way as it has always done in its combat of crime. In other words, Dod, you are nothing but another hateful criminal in my eyes. Please go away now but leave the car outside. I shall be needing it pretty soon."

"Well, I'll be damned! I am either crazy or you are." I hand her the car keys and make for the door. I am in one of them murderous moods.

I feel like hitting the wall.

"Hey, take these breakfast things with you, will you. I've told you ten times that I don't need breakfast." I look back at her and feel a great urge to slap her. Who the goddam hell does she think she is anyway? Oh, shit!

"Look Tonia," I tell her trying to control my voice. "You have the car and you'll be home in about an hour. Why do you want me to walk all the way home carrying that stuff?"

"You'd no business bringing it in the first instance. You should have had enough sense to know that they provide breakfast here."

"O.K. Shall I tell you what you'd better do right now? Just fuck yourself!"

I am walking out when Julian is walking in and as we cross ways, we don't even look at one another or say good-bye. I just go straight through the ward and when this nurse I'd talked to earlier on tells me that she hopes I had a fruitful visit, I tell her to go fuck herself. She drops her tray and I storm out feeling a bit better. But just abit. Jesus! How did I ever marry such a callous bitch.

The police Inspector is sitting in a police car outside reading the medical report. I hesitate but finally decide to ask him what the report was. He raises his eyes to my face and then continues to stare at the paper. After a moment he looks at me again and shakes his head.

"We have a case of a person suffering from epilepsy brought to the hospital and treated for epilepsy which is a perfectly normal thing to happen. The patient got to the hospital in a state of unconsciousness, wich is also a normal thing with the first attack if that attack happens to be full-fledged and this one was. Recovery of consciousness four hours after the onslaught of the attack. Again perfectly normal. Scratches on the neck of the patient made by the nails of the patient herself at the start of the fits when some forceful feeling of suffocation or strangulation may exist. Some flesh found underneath the patient's nails traceable to the patient's neck. Again perfectly normal under the circumstances. A little bump at the back of the patient's head resulting from a backward fall and hitting something solid on the floor. That is what this report says, Mr. Kiunyu. I believe it."

"Last night you believed me," I retort.

"No I didn't. We couldn't figure out how the lady hanged herself. Our experiment showed that she couldn't possibly have hanged herself. And now that I remember it, you were very anxious that we don't carry out the experiment. Why are you trying to put your own wife into trouble?"

"I don't know anything anymore, Inspector."

"You are a very strange man, Mr. Kiunyu. An ordinary husband would be lying like crazy to get his wife out of a jam. But you are doing the opposite up to the point of making a signed statement. Man, I think you've stretched your neck too far."

"So what are you going to do with me now?"

"One thing is clear. We can't charge your wife now. Not with this sort of medical report. I'll give it to our police Doctor and seek his opinion but something has to be done about you. You just can't send the police on a wild-goose chase on taxpayers' money and expect the taxpayers to keep quiet about it. In short, you have committed a crime against the state."

"Would your police doctor re-examine my wife if he was not satisfied with this report?"

"Doctors have confidence in each other. It's a question of ethics. He would have to smell a very big rat even before contemplating the step. Are you in anyway insinuating that this report is incorrect?"

"Yes."

"How would you know?"

"Rope marks on the neck. The doctor should have noticed those. I can't say anything about epilepsy. May be it is true. But the rope marks, where did they go? Why did the doctor call you in the first instance if it was a normal case of epilepsy?"

"He called me on the strength of your story and also because you were behaving crazy. He called me immediately, you remember? He didn't make a statement about the physical condition of the patient then. He told me in your presence that he'd only be able to make a statement after he'd examined the patient. Believing your story of course, he wasted a lot of time looking for the wrong symptoms. That was really callous on your part, Mr. Kiunyu. You should be charged."

"That's OK, Inspector. I shall plead guilty right from the start. Do you think you can give me a ride? I have to leave the car for my wife."

"No Thank you. The next time I give you a ride will be to the police cells. Don't get out of town yet."

"No. I wouldn't, but sincerely, I think you should just drop this matter. It was just a storm in a tea cup. Just drop it and forget it. I wish you'd give me that statement back. I would love you for ever. Seriously. Why don't you tear it and forget it? We shall all feel very thankful to you and it shall be the end of the whole bloody matter."

"Not much chance. Remember what I told you about taxpayers."

"You can always do somebody a favour, you know. You can decide out of your own generous heart to lend a helping hand."

"I didn't start it."

"Oh fuck it man. Drop it. What would it mean to..."

"Mind your language mister," he cuts me short.

"I am sorry... but drop it."

"Do you know that you need a doctor? If I were you, I'd see a doctor even before I see a lawyer. You'll need both. And now I must be off. Needless to say I'll have to obtain a written statement from your wife. Anyway, I know where to find her. I shall also get one from the doctor and we shall see where that leaves you. Man, you shouldn't play with the law."

"You and your inhuman law! Won't even give me a lift. I am a taxpayer for chrissake."

"You are forgetting that you have no source of income, Mr. Kiunyu. Frankly, you are a police case. You should be investigated."

"You are frightening me now instead of giving me a lift to the roundabout at the crossing of Kilindini and Salim road where I can catch a taxi. Do please drop me there."

"OK, for this time. As I said, the next time will be to the cell and I mean every word of it. You are going to end up in cell very soon. Hop in," he says. And I do.

He drops me at the Manor Hotel and I decide to walk all the way to Barclays Bank, Kilindini Road and get myself some dough. I reckon that seven hundred shillings should keep me going until Friday. It's more than I'd normally take out for five days but I want to get myself drunk and I may have to do a little bribing.

What I do is get out of the Bank and move across the road to this place they call Sunshine which is open day and night. I take two quick beers and then take a bus to the port.

I've decided to go over to this Greek ship — the *Athenia* and say hellow to Yanis. He is a very nice bloke, Yanis. You wouldn't think he was the captain of the ship 'cause he doesn't look like one at all. He just looks like an affable simple gentle small man of fifty that should be tending sheep on the mountain sides of Greece instead of commanding a huge cargo ship. We made friends first time we met and have remained so. I've in the past got quite a bit of good business from him and I bet he'll be disappointed when he knows that I intend to quit. I used to give him a little discount which I took into account when dealing with the Indians and which went to him as pure profit but that's all over now. I am going straight. I'll just drop in and say hello and maybe have a drink or two.

The *Athenia* is moored right out because all the off-loading berths are taken. There's always quite a bit of congestion here at the Port. Quite often ships have to hang around for days before they get to discharge their cargo. I get myself one of these boats they call K-boats and have the chap take me over to the Athenia. He's one hell of a rough boatman and I am afraid that he is going to crash against the side of the ship but he doesn't. He eases the boat nicely to the ship's ladder and I let out a sigh of relief. He asks me whether he should wait for me and I say no. I climb up the ladder and ease myself on deck.

Yanis is not on the ship. I am told that he's gone to town. I ask for the Chief Engineer who is a chap I also know, but whose name I can never pronounce, and I am told that he's gone to town too. I don't feel so good especially because the K-boat chap has gone back. I ask this chap whether he can signal a K-boat for me and he says he will. Then he asks whether I'd like a drink in the meantime and I say it's too early, which is a bloody lie. We get talking but the chap's English is so bad that most of the things he says are just Greek to me. I keep smiling because all he is doing is crack these Greek jokes which I don't understand. I reckon I am supposed to laugh. Then all of a sudden he says, "Hey, you know where buy pill for contraband V.D.? Doctor of pharmacy in town?"

"Sorry I don't get you," I tell him.

He explains to me that there is this very nice girl that has V.D. and that he would like to buy her some medicine. His English is so Greek that I really have to cock my ears to understand what the heck he is talking about.

"Why don't you give money to the girl so that she can go and see a doctor?"

"Because if I give money she drink money and get no cure for V.D. I don't trust her. Me, I buy good medicine for her and I make her eat it."

"Why don't you get some from your stock on the ship?"

"Oh, no! Ship medicine is not for African prostitute. For prostitute I pay. Ship doctor is for shipmen not for prostitute. So you know good chemist shop or no?" I tell him that I do and then ask him to get a K-boat and he signals one.

The K-boat arrives and we hop in. It is the same mad K-boat driver. He says I should have asked him to wait for me in the first instance as two trips were more expensive than one and I agree with him. Anyway, all I want is to get to shore and when we do, I let the Greek sailor pay. We then get a taxi and I explain to the driver that he has to drop me at the anchor and continue with my friend to Patel Chemists further down Kilindini Road.

I drop at the Anchor but again I am out of luck. The anchor is a favourite spot for the Greeks but there's not a single one today. The place is just about empty but Milka is there. She is the owner of the joint. She makes good money selling booze and a little of herself.

"Hi Dodge," she greets me with a sweet prostitute smile and I say "Hi Milka. Where is everybody? It's eleven o'clock and at the end of the month. You are not doing so well, are you?"

"It would appear so. On the other hand I prefer a few decent heavy drinking customers than a whole load of noisy ruffians. What will you have?"

"I'll take a beer, although I'd prefer to have it in another place where there's more noise. I want people around me."

"What about me? Don't you think I am people?"

"No."

"If you buy me a drink, I'll make a lot of noise."

"Have one."

"You know what, Dodge, you are a nice bastard and I am going to give it to you one day... for free."

51

"Thanks, I shall remind you."

I gulp the bottle and quit. I am feeling very lonely. I decide that I should go somewhere noisy and get myself drunk and then go home. I walk down Kilindini all the way to the Sunshine Day and night club and enter. Yanis and the Chief Engineer are sitting there at the counter having whisky. They are wearing uniform. They notice me and beckon.

"Hello, Dodge," Yanis says. "How are you?" We shake hands. "Thought I'd meet you last night. You are always on time. Have a drink." I shake hands with Asparagus — that is what I always call the Chief Engineer on account I can't pronounce his name — and then take a stool. Yanis orders a double whisky for me and says that he is on the way to the bank and that it's just as well I dropped in. I could save him the trouble. I don't say anything 'cause I don't want to ruin the drink by telling him that I ain't playing ball no more so we go on laughing and Asparagus orders a round. Yanis tells me that he wouldn't be coming this way no more 'cause he is being transferred to a South American route, and I say I am sorry to hear it.

There are quite a few folks in the place and the Juke box is playing *Hot Pants*. There are these two girls jerking away with the music and when the record is over they come over to where we are sitting. One starts talking to Asparagus and the other one who is wearing a blond wig leans on Yanis's shoulder and says:

"Hi, skipper. Want to buy me a vitamin?"

"Skip off, will you. And don't you dare put your greasy black hands on me again." He says it in a manner that gets her recoiling so she just stands there somewhat dumbfounded.

"You are not playing ball this morning skipper?" she continues, obviously embarrassed. He whirls round and faces her. He looks at her with such contempt that I feel embarrased myself. After all, prostitutes are prostitutes and all they want is a sucker with some dough to spare. Why get nasty?

"I said skip off bitch!" he yells at her. "Just get your silly stinking black cunt out of here, will you? Jesus! I can't have a quiet little drink without having some black bitch shoving her sweating syphilitic cunt into my face. All they wonna do is fuck, fuck, and fuck, they'll fuck a dog for half a fish. What a world! Grrrrrr. Better explain to your sister, my dear Dodge, that we are not in a black cunting mood," and he pushes her off with the palm of his hand.

The girl looks at him and then walks away swaggering contemptuously, pulling her friend along. They sit at a table completely oblivious of our presence. I look at them and get this strange feeling that they are my sisters. They could be my sisters after all. I mean, if I had a sister and she became a prostitute she'd just behave like these girls and Yanis would treat her the same way. Any white man would treat her the same way. Would he treat a Greek prostitute that way? Would he treat any white prostitute that way? All of a sudden I feel that all those nasty words meant for the prostitute were actually meant for me. He was insulting me. He was insulting my manhood. Would he stand around and let me treat a Greek prostitute in Athens like that?

I feel hate welling up in me. These white bastards will always remain white bastards and they have absolutely no respect for us niggers. It's in their blood. Bastards all. I work myself into such a mood that I want to hit something. I feel like smashing Yanis on the face, only he's fifty and I have no doubt that Asparagus would flatten me out 'cause he's one hell of a giant. What I do is I leave my stool and walk over to the girls. I want to buy them a drink. I feel rather sorry for them. They are my black sisters.

"Can I buy you a drink please," I ask them.

"Who are you pimping for?" the blond-wigged girl asks me. I don't even get angry. I just forgive her like Jesus forgave his murderers. I look at her and smile. After all she's just a prostitute.

"No. I don't pimp," I say casually. "Those are my friends. Mere drinking friends. A bit of business too. Are you going to have a drink."

"Is one of them your boyfriend?" she asks. This time I get angry. Jesus! She is intimating that I am a homosexual or something. How unkind. Maybe Yanis was right. That is the only way to treat prostitutes. Rough.

"Listen sister I am not that type. Do I look like one?"

"I am not that type either so how would I know?" I don't say a thing. I just walk back and resume my stool. I am very angry. Them prostitutes come begging for a drink from a white bastard who insults them and when I become brotherly, 'cause they are black like me, they insult me in return. I feel insulted from all sides. Today is not my day. It's not my day at all.

I order one round and Yanis asks me to save my little money for my unborn kids and then he asks me whether I am interested in one of them black cunts' cause if I am, he'll pay for me. I tell him that it is too early in the day but I don't tell him that I'd like to smash his nose though that's what I feel like doing. I let him pay for the drinks and then ask him how much dough he wants to change. He says that because of the congestion at the Port they may be held up for around a week and that he's got to change a few dollars' cause he's got to pay for provisions and pay some few sailors advance salary which is unfortunate because they'll waste the lot on black cunts. He asks me how much I'll give him for a dollar and I tell him the usual seven shillings and thirty cents and he starts complaining that I am getting lots of profits because I am selling the dollar for nine shillings. After a lot of bargaining we settle on seven shillings fifty cents a dollar. Officially he'd only get seven shillings. I make it clear that it's only for today and only because he is changing two thousand dollars at a go. He has it all with him. He wants to know when we can complete the deal. I decide that just for the heck of it, I am going to rob. I am gonna rob this nigger-hating captain.

"I don't have that much money on me. I'll have to get it before the banks close. If you'll just hold on a minute. I'll make a telephone call." I ask the waiter to pass me the phone and he asks me whether I want to telephone within Mombasa or outside. I tell him that I want a Mombasa number and he asks me for fifty cents in advance. He insists on getting the number for me so I let him dial. When the phone rings on the other side he hands me the receiver.

"Hello. Is that you, Khimji?"

"Yes. This is Khimji. Who is speaking?"

"This is Dodge. Listen Khimji, I want some fifteen thousand Kenyattas cash within twenty minutes for you know what. I've two thousand greens right here and the owner has to be cashiered off otherwise the birds will fly to another tree. Can you make it?"

"Wait a minute, Dodge. You mean you are asking fifteen for two thousand greens?"

"No. That's just the owner's return. Between me and you it's nine a green but I thought you may not need so much greens in your food and all I wanted is the fifteen so that I can dismiss the chap. Later we can fix it the way we want between you and me, depending on how . . ."

"I want it all Dodge. I want many times that. Where is this chap?"

"Right here with me."

"Where?"

"Come, come. That is not important."

"But where are you?"

"Look here, Khimji. If you want to deal directly with the chap you'll have to dig him up yourself. What are you trying to do, cut me out?"

"You sure do get a lot for nothing. You charge fifteen and you sell eighteen and that's a clean three for damn shit nothing. You are robbing me. Look, we are old firneds. OK? Eight-fifty. That's all I can pay. After all you have nothing with which to dismiss the chap and you need my help. Eight fifty a green and not a penny more. You agree or get another buyer."

"OK, Khimji. I agree. I will be right over with the greens in ten minutes. How long would it take you to have the Kenyattas ready?'

"It's all ready. I was just going to the bank to deposit."

"OK, I am on my way. Keep counting."

I've been talking right here next to Yanis so that he can hear what's going on. That should make things easier. I turn to him and tell him that it's all organised and that I wouldn't take ten minutes. He starts arguing again about my raising his discount and I ask him not to try any bleeding business. We move over to a corner and he gives me the dough. Forty crisp fifty dollar bills.

"You can have a tall round of whisky on me," I tell him. "I'll be loaded on return and I'll pay a round for those prostitues."

I get the hell out and make straight for Khimji's wholesale shop. I am there in five minutes. He is at the back of the shop in his office and has a bottle of whisky on the table. Just in case you don't know, I have decided to rob him too. After all he's a goddam mean thief himself.

"Come on in Dodge. This Johnny Walker black label is waiting for you. Where are the greens?"

"Right there with the goddam chap. He didn't give it to me, the bastard. He listened on the phone and wanted to do the deal straight with you so I told him he could go to hell. Then he shows the money — crisp fifties and says he ain't parting with it before he can smell the local cash right there in front of his nose and asks me to get it first. Can't blame him though. After all he is a stranger to these parts and maybe he has no right to trust anybody. I agreed with him."

"I thought he was a friend."

"I've had business with him several times before. You never know with these whites. I suppose he just wants to get nasty for a while. He's scared 'cause he's a little drunk."

"If he wouldn't trust you, why should I trust you?

"My God, Khimji, I'll cut your throat."

"I am merely joking. I had counted seventeen thousand which should have closed the whole deal at eight fifty a green but since we are dismissing the chap for fifteen only, you'd better take fifteen, dismiss the customer and then come for your cut. And Mr. Whisky, don't start drinking with that money in your pocket. Immediately the transaction is over, come right back."

I collect the fifteen thousand shillings and head straight for Madhivani's Self-service Super Market. Madhivani is one hell of a rich bastard but like all Indians, he's mean. Wouldn't even spend a hundred shillings a weekend. I once owed him a hundred shillings and he hounded me to death, he did. It's now a quarter to twelve and there are lots of people in the shop. Madhivani is sitting in his glass walled office when I knock and enter.

"Hello Dodge," he greets me and I say, "Hello mean Indian," and he laughs. I don't waste any time on preliminaries. I just go right ahead and ask him.

"Would you be interested in some greens?"

"What do you mean?"

"Dollars old chap. Green dollars." His mouth begins to water and his eyes shine a brilliant greedy brown.

"Do you have some."

"Yeah."

"How much?"

"Ten shillings a dollar."

"That's robbery."

"That's the price; take it or leave it."

"Look, Dodge, that's not the way to treat a friend. The price has always been nine."

"Things have changed. There's a great shortage of the foreign stuff. I sold a few yesterday for eleven."

You can't beat an Indian when it comes to bargaining. He will always win. Damn persistent, that's what they are. As bad as the Jews. Madhivani has managed to beat down the price to nine, and like Khimji he has this bottle of whisky which he says is all mine to the last drop. He hasn't got enough money ready so I have to wait till he gets some from the supermarket cashiers and that is done in a matter of ten minutes. He opens his safe and comes out with a wad which he combines with what he has collected from the cashiers and starts counting.

"There you are. Eighteen thousand bob," he says. I hand him the dollars and he starts counting again. Finally he nods his head

"When you get some more, bring them along." And I say I will.

I get up, collect the bottle of whisky and beg my leave. I head straight for Marshall's garage and pay twenty five thousand shillings cash for a green Peugeot 404 saloon and one thousand eight hundred shillings for insurance and road licence and ask them to have the car ready for collection by five o'clock. I scram out.

I am feeling like a bloody thief, but a satisfied one. This is of course the end of this crooked business as far as I am concerned, and I feel that I ended it rather well. This money I robbed from Yanis and Khimji is the payment for all the risks I have taken and it isn't really all that much when you consider that I could have been jailed and Yanis and Khimji can bear the loss comfortably. They dare not report to anybody of course. That would be tantamount to giving themselves away. All they can do is hunt me down but that wouldn't help either. I'd simply tell them to go to hell. I have a good mind to telephone them and tell them that I just robbed their money, but then that would spoil the fun.

I don't feel sorry for Khimji at all. He stinks with money and what I've taken is a mere drop in his money bucket and besides, he cheats on income tax. Yanis may find it harder to support the loss because he is merely an employed captain but I suppose they have insurance for this sort of thing if he cooks up a nice story. The whole idea of robbing him wouldn't have occured to me if he had not been so downright insulting to that black prostitute, and in a way to me and all my black brothers. I robbed him to punish him — no, I don't mean that. What I mean is, if he despised the blacks so, why shouldn't he despise them some more? Why, shouldn't I give him cause? What difference does it make anyway if he thought just a little bit worse of us than he already does? Anyway, to hell with him. At least I hope he'll stop peddling currency on the black market. I taught him a lesson. Nobody can teach Khimji a lesson though. Indians are persistent.

I take a taxi and go home. It's lunch time. I am not really going home for lunch. What I want is to leave this bottle of whisky and some of this money I am carrying in my back pocket locked up somewhere so that I can come back to town. I have altogether some six thousand eight hundred and eighty shillings and I can't go carrying it about with me.

Tonia's car is parked in the garage so I reckon she's left the hospital. I pay the taxi driver and get into the house. I've to figure out where to hide the money so that she can't find it because I have no intention of banking it. Not just yet. Then I have to telephone these navy chaps and find out how their bumps are healing after last night's fight in the club.

I walk upstairs and find Tonia sitting on a sofa reading the *Daily Nation*. She looks up at me as I enter and then continues reading. I am wondering why I came at all. I go past the sitting room and get into the toilet. I piss very loudly and then get out of the place. I get back into the lounge and sit down. There is this ice between us that is so thick that I don't know how to break it.

After five long minutes of sitting there and not speaking to each other I decide I can't bear it so I go to the bedroom and stretch myself on top of the bed for a while. It looks like there is going to be no lunch here so I might as well have a little nap before I go back to town for lunch. Or why don't I break the goddam ice? Why don't I be nice and invite her for lunch out and make amends? That's what I'd like to do but I am scared of one thing. I am scared of getting snubbed. I hate to be let down when I am full of good intentions. But what am I scared of anyway? I am the man in this house. I am boss, at least till we get through with the divorce if we ever get through with it, that is.

The truth of the matter is I don't want a divorce anymore. I think that Tonia needs somebody to look after her. I wouldn't want her to hang herself again. Trouble is she wouldn't bend. She's aloof all the time. All of a sudden I get angry. Who the hell does she think she is anyway? Just a lonely woman that needs a husband as much as any other lonely woman does, so why make our home a little hell?

I get out of bed and move to the lounge. She's still reading the paper and does not as much as look up when I come back.

"What's the news today?" I ask in the way of opening up a conversation. "I didn't have the chance to read the paper." She glances quickly through the back page of the paper and then throws it at me. I am terribly disappointed. It's extacly what I imagined she'd do. That's not the best way of opening up a conversation in a situation like this.

"Hey, you haven't prepared any lunch by any chance, have you?" I ask her. That should get her mad but it doesn't. She doesn't answer. I am wondering whether she's gone crazy or not. May be she's gone real nuts. She's got to be crazy to hang herself and then deny it, unless she was sleep walking. I hope she hasn't developed into a sleep walker. That would be damn scaring. She could cut my throat in her sleep.

What I do is I do something very stupid. I don't know why but I just suddenly throw the newspaper right onto her face. She lets out a loud "Aaaoh!" and then glares at me.

"What did you do that for?" she demands furiously.

"To get you talking," I reply casually.

"You are a primitive cold-blooded beast. How can you be such a beast. How can you be such a beast? You are not supposed to be here you know".

"I asked you about lunch and you didn't answer."

"Oh stop it, stop it," she begs me frantically. "Are you so foolishly conceited that you'd expect me to come from the hospital and prepare lunch. Oh God! How did I ever come to meet you!" She is almost pulling her hair with excitement or madness, and I decide that I am not going to get myself rattled. I don't know whether she's crazy or angry.

"Look. I didn't expect you to have prepared lunch. What I wanted was that we go out and eat somewhere in town".

"What heavenly kindness. I don't need your lunch, Mr. Dodge Kiunyu, Esquire". She sneeres at me. "I don't want anything from you. Not even your presence."

"Honest. I am not kidding. Let's go out and grab something to eat before it's time for you to go to the office."

"I am off-duty for a week and I need my rest. This morning at the hospital I told you very plainly that you should stick to your decision and since nothing has happened in between to necessitate a change in that decision, I demand that you leave."

"Something has happened in between. I've changed my mind. I can't leave you now. I am staying."

"No you are not. I don't want you. I don't even want to see you. Stop forcing yourself on me."

"I'll stay all the same," I tell her casually.

"By force?" she asks ferociously.

"Well, not by force of course. I'll just stay. I don't want to leave you alone. Not for the time being, anyway."

"And why, if I may ask?"

"Well, I don't want you getting upset and starting to do the sort of things that you did yesterday evening."

"When are you going to stop harping on that stupid idea. I did nothing last night to warrant your protection. I've tried to explain but you are so thick and vain you want to stick to your lies just because you told them once. That's one of the reasons why I can't live with you anymore. You are mad."

"Are you trying to make me believe that you hanged yourself in your sleep?"

"Oh shut up for crying out aloud. Who put this silly idea in your head, that I tried to hang myself? What are you trying to do to me?"

"Look me straight in the eyes Tonia."

"What?"

"Look me straight in the eyes and swear on your honour that you didn't hang yourself last night."

"What preposterous nonsense," she cries desperately. "What has got into your head? How could I do a thing like that? Oh, please God, help him. Help him to believe me." All the time she's been looking at me so steadfastly that I have had to blink. There's utter sincerity in those staring eyes. She focusses them on mine till tears well out and start rolling down her cheeks. All the time she doesn't blink an eyelid.

I am beat. I feel exhausted. If I should believe her it is now and yet I know that she can't be telling the truth. Tears are still rolling down her cheeks and we are still staring at one another. I am suffocating. My blood pressure has gone up so much that I can hear my brain. My brain is overflooded with hot blood and there is general redness all around the room. Am I crazy by any chance? Suppose Tonia did not hang herself and that the whole episode is a mere coinage of my crazy mind, what then? Is it possible that I am wrong? That sincerity in her eyes, is it faked? Why is she crying?

I close my eyes and hold my head in my hands for long seconds. I am trying to get into focus. I want to slow down the speed at which my brain is turning. I sit down on the sofa without opening my eyes and still with my head between my hands, rest my elbows on my knees. My mind is a whole mess of a confused wet blank, full of itself and full of nothing. It's just a full empty mind. I am thus sitting when she comes and kneels in front of me. She also rests her elbows on my knees so that our hands come togeher. I open my eyes and look at her. Her imploring pleading eyes are still red with tears.

"It's true, Dod. You must believe me. I don't have the least idea about this thing. What has come over you? Why, why do you still insist? What have I done to you? Oh! God, I pray you. Have mercy. Deliver us from evil."

You would believe her if you were me. Just the sincerity in those eyes and you'd know that her conscience was clear. I am having a great fight with myself. My heart is fighting my head. My heart believes her. It is practically forcing my head into tears. It's all useless. I am physically subdued. I stare at her steadily.

"I don't know what to believe. Not any more," I tell her. "I want to believe you. But tell me. If I believe you, will you believe me?"

"But how can I believe you, Dod? You know it's not true."

"But it is true, my dear Tonia. I swear in the name of my dead mother, God bless her soul, that what I've said so far is true. Let her come out of the grave and call me a liar. Let her come and confront me and I'll not budge. It's true. You were hanging when I came in. I've never had hallucinations in my life and I don't think I am mad. I beg you to believe me."

"How come then that I know nothing of it?"

"That's what is bothering me. How can you hang yourself without knowing. It is impossible. You must know unless you'd just become a sleep walker. It's all very confusing."

"But the Doctor's report does not collaborate your story."

"That's another thing that is bothering me. To the best of my knowledge it is faked. I told the Doctor the circumstances that occasioned your situation and he damn well believed because every evidence pointed that way. How he came to this other stuff of epilepsy, I just cannot figure out. He's got to be telling lies for chrissake. When did you become epileptic anyway? It's all crap."

"I don't know, Dod, and I feel terribly bad about it. As for the medical report, I have nothing to add. I have not seen it but Julian told me what it says. Your insinuation that there is some cheating involved is absurd, or are you implying that I probably made the report myself?"

"No. It is however likely that you could have influenced Julian and that she influenced her husband. It's possible."

"Oh, wouldn't you believe me! That report was ready in its present form when Julian came in this morning. So she couldn't have influenced her husband. You've got to be wrong."

"Did you talk to Doctor Kihagi last night?"

"Yes, but only briefly. He came into my room soon after I regained consciousness."

"And what did he say? What did you tell him?"

"Oh! come, come. We just talked like a doctor talks to a patient. He knew me in Nanyuki. He asked me how I was feeling and I told him I was feeling awful, then he asked me what happened and I told him I fainted, et cetera."

"You told him that? I mean, you told him that you'd fainted?"

"But of course. What else did you want me to tell him?"

"What else did you tell him?" I am getting excited.

"You are being ridiculous. He just questioned me and I answered him. That's all. Then we talked of old times in Nanyuki."

"Did he tell you about my story? Did he tell you that I'd said you hanged yourself?"

"Not in so many words but I remember him asking me why I was unhappy and why I was tired of living, but of course I told him that I didn't understand."

"He didn't talk about hanging?"

"I've already told you he didn't. The only thing he talked about was people wanting to take their lives and frankly he was talking out of context and I told him so. What are you trying to get at?"

"I don't know but I am starting to see a little light."

"I don't understand you."

"I am not very sure myself that I understand. There's just a chance that we are both right. Maybe the report doesn't say everything. But tell me, did you actually faint?"

"But of course, Dod. That is the last thing I remember. I just saw darkness and when I saw light I was in hospital."

"Well, it is still incredible. How the hell did you do it? Even supposing that the medical report was correct, how does one explain the events from the minute you fainted to the minute I rescued you?"

"You didn't rescue me! I am starting to get angry again. You want me to believe you but I wouldn't. As you keep saying yourself, the circumstances cannot be explained your way."

"Unless it is all one big lie." I tell her. She gets up abruptly and shrugs her shoulders.

"It's no use trying to talk to you. You are still persisting with your lie," she yells angrily. I get up too and we stare at each other. We are back to square one.

I have a great urge to light a cigarette and blow smoke onto her face but I don't. What I do is I decide to get the hell out of there and I am making long strides to the door when the phone rings. I stop and look back and notice that Tonia is making no attempt to get up from where she is sitting. I walk back past her and pick the phone.

"Hello, Kiunyu's residence here," I say.

"Hey, Dodge, is that you. This is Khimji. What the hell are you doing with my money?" I can hear that he is excited and out of breath. Poor bastard. He's in for a black surprise.

"I am sorry, but Mr. Kiunyu is not here," I tell him. "I am his brother," and I hang up before he can open his mouth again.

As I walk past Tonia, I say "Ciao" and then make for the kitchen where I stuff most of the dough in my hind pocket into an empty Indian curry can which I, in turn, place between the fridge and the wall and then scram out of the place. As I walk towards the town, I am again overcome by this old feeling of cheapness. God, I feel cheap. As cheap as an empty bottle of beer.

Monday Night

I've spent the whole goddam afternoon and evening in hiding. I don't mean hiding like a thief, oh no. I am talking of the other type of hiding. The type of hiding you do when you are not a thief. What I did was to collect my new car at seventeen hours and drive off to some joint in Mariakani where they sell palm wine. A wonderful place. It's like being in the country. The place does not even smell like Mombasa and the people don't smell like Mombasa either. They smell like the trees around them or like palm wine. Anyway I love palm wine, especially when it is served by innocent topless sixteen year old maidens who are completely unaware of the effect of their little eye-ball tits on the dirty minds of the palm wine drinkers. Anyway, that's how I've been hiding and I am praying, God that I don't smash the new car on the way home 'cause I don't feel very steady. That would be pathetic.

It's two thirty in the morning when I get home. I park the car alongside Tonia's, get out, fish the house key out of my pocket and open the door slowly. All of a sudden I feel scared. It just occurs to me that I might find Tonia hanging. I don't put on the light. I just grope my way upstairs in the dark just for the heck of it but when I get into the lounge I put on the light and listen. Then I here it. I hear Tonia talking to somebody in our bedroom. I am frozen. How on earth could she be having an innocent guest at two thirty in the morning in our bedroom. My mind works very quickly. There is this Masai Club that sits on the bookshelf as a decoration and I proceed to arm myself with it and then tip-toe towards the bedroom. I fling the door open and flick on the light. There's nobody in the bedroom except Tonia who is comfortably in bed and who is blinking her eyes on account of the light. I close the door and make a dash for the bed and look under. There's nobody there. Tonia is perplexed.

"Who were you talking to a minute ago?" I ask her. "No stories, I heard you".

"I was talking to the police"

"What?"

"I was on the phone. The Inspector asked me to ring him soon as you were back."

"What Inspector?"

"Same one who came to the hospital this morning."

"And what does he want?"

"He was here not a long time ago together with your sailor friends."

"What? Please explain." I am all excited.

"I told you not to drag me down with you but it seems like you'll never lift your head till you've hit the rock bottom. I am tired of this harassment and its all your fault. I want peace. I have told you before. You have sailors and the police after you which I suppose is your privilege, but I don't want any of it around me. God, I can't even have decent sleep even in my own house. What sort of man are you?"

"Please Tonia, tell me what happened". I am not even angry with her. Oh no. I just want to know what happened.

Tonia told me what happened. It was all about my friend, Yanis the Greek. He'd spent the whole afternoon trying to locate anybody who might know where I lived and it wasn't until late in the night that he managed to do so. Luckily I wasn't there and he found Tonia in bed. He practically had to break the doors down and quite unknowingly of course, Tonia helped me. She woke up in a temper and after he breathlessly explained what the trouble was, she asked him to get out but he wouldn't budge. He said he'd sit there and wait for me even if it meant waiting for ten years. He was breathing fire and fury. He was raving mad. He imagined that Tonia was an accessory to the act. He was implicating her. He thought that she was in league with me. That is the one mistake he should never have made, only he didn't know. He didn't know what sort of woman Tonia was.

What happened was, Tonia went to the bedroom and called the police. The idea was to put us both, Yanis and I, in the hands of the police and eventually in jail. We had had slight reconciliation this morning before I left but that wouldn't stop her from putting me in jail. This is how principled she has become. She is clean. She must not be mixed with dirt. Anyway, Yanis was sitting right there in our sitting-room when the police arrived. She had not told him that she'd called the police so it was one hell of a surprise for him. He nearly fainted.

It was the same officer who was handling the attempted suicide case. He had elected to come to the house personally just to see what more farce we were creating this time. Actually he thought we were fighting. He would have grabbed any opportunity to get me on a definite charge 'cause he wasn't feeling so happy about the run-around that we'd given him earlier in the day. He also was surprised to see a haggard white man smoking profusely in our sitting room. Tonia described the incident to me very vividly.

"Good evening, Mrs Kiunyu. Eh — you just telephoned about . . ."

"Sit down, Inspector," she interrupted. "This gentleman sitting here came bull-dozing into my house with a wild story that I do not understand and I thought that he may want to repeat it to the police. Do sit down please."

"He is a friend of the family I suppose and it. . ."

"No Inspector," she interrupted again. "I don't know him from Adam and he hasn't even had the courtesy to introduce himself. All I know is that he claims to be a captain of some ship and that he wouldn't leave this house till he sees my husband even if that meant waiting ten years. Talk to him. He's been insulting me and accusing me of . . ."

"Let me explain, Inspector," Yanis cut her short. "It's all one great mistake. The dear lady misunderstood me. My apologies please, Mrs. Kiunyu. You see, Mr. Kiunyu is a great friend of mine. We've been drinking together. He invited me for a night cap and we left the bar together, only he had some four people to drop at the New Florida night club first and then come for me. So I went back to the bar to wait for him. I was there when a taxi driver came and told me that Mr. Kiunyu asked him to drop me here 'cause he'd finally decided to invite everybody to his house. As you can see Sir, Mr. Kiunyu isn't here yet. I don't know what he could possibly be doing after sending that taxi to bring me here, so I imagine that he'll be here any minute. That's why I said I'd wait for him. Now that it would appear that I have caused Mrs. Kiunyu some inconvenience, I must apologise sincerely. Forgive me dear lady. It is all a misunderstanding that is not of my own making. If you will please accept my apology, I shall very humbly beg my leave. It is very unfortunate that the police have been inconvenienced. I hope you will accept my apologies, Sir."

"I don't seem to understand that set-up," the Inspector confessed. "Not when the lady accuses you of having been abusive and obstinate. Mrs. Kiunyu, do you want to make a complaint against this man? We already have the record of your call in our books."

"The man is lying. Immediately he came into the house and I told him that my husband was not in, he made a search of the house. He even had the audacity to go into my bedroom. He was cursing my husband all the time and claiming that he robbed him of some dollars. He went as far as accusing me of being an accomplice in the theft. He even looked into my handbag and threatened to pull the house apart if he did not get his money back. I couldn't understand his words clearly, but he claimed very emphatically that he gave some dollars to my husband to go and change in the black market and that my husband disappeared with the money. That is what he has been harping on since he entered this house."

The Inspector's mouth opened involuntarily.

"And what have you got to say to that?" he snapped, pointing his finger at Yanis.

"It's a fantastic story, Sir. I certainly never said such a thing. I can't believe my ears. I may be a little drunk but not to the extent of uttering falsehoods of that magnitude. I think the lady misunderstood me all together. If I did crack such a joke, and I didn't, it would be merely to stop the lady chasing me out while I am waiting for Dodge. But I am certain that I did not even crack the joke. If the lady is joking then I must apologise, but I find the joke just a little bit on the heavier side. It's absurd. Again I think I will beg my leave. Dodge must have got held up somewhere in another bar or something. Or may be they are all at the New Florida and the taxi driver misunderstood his instructions. I really must be going."

"You are a liar," Tonia shouted at him. "You are lying to save your own skin. You indulge in illegal money transactions and you are now afraid that the law will get you. I can assure you, Inspector, that I've told you the truth. My husband cheated him over an illegal money deal. That's what he's been yelling about all the time before you came. In any case, I am lodging a complaint against this man. He has insulted me, searched my house by force and disturbed my sleep without cause. I am making a complaint."

The inspector turned to Yanis. "You understand the gravity of the circumstances. I am sorry we'll have to get more insight into this matter. To begin with, let's start from the beginning. Who are you and what do you do?"

Yanis went ahead to tell the Inspector that he was a Captain of the *Athenia* and that he's docked in Mombasa several times and that he knows me very well and that we've drunk together many times only he didn't have a chance of coming to my house before et cetera. He however denied that there had been any money transaction between us. He was so impressive with his story that he Inspector started doubting what Tonia had told him. Evenually, the Inspector ruled out that since a complaint had been lodged, Yanis had to go to the police station and make a statement. He left after warning Tonia that he was getting alarmed at the incredibilities that seemed to hang like a beard on the Kiunyu household and asked her to ring him the minute I got back home.

After I got the whole picture well imprinted on my mind I decide to support the Yanis version. It was a good story. Very convincing. I don't have time to tell Tonia how I'll play it before the Inspector arrives. I open the door for him and we walk upstairs into the lounge. He does not waste any time. He just says a curt good morning and then proceeds to ask me what I was doing since sunset.

"Why do you want to know?" I ask him.

"Because your wife lodged a complaint. A Greek captain who had illegal money transactions earlier on in the day came here demanding your blood because you cheated him of his money. That is the story from Mrs. Kiunyu. Do you by any chance engage in black-maket currency transactions?" he asks.

"Ask me another, Inspector. I am sure you already know the answer to that one "

"That is not telling me."

"What do you want me to tell you? That I am engaged in some unlawful activities? Well, use your head."

"Fine. Your friend Yanis accuses you of having robbed his money while affecting such an illegal transaction. What do you have to say to that?"

"That he is a greater liar than Ananias, or that you misunderstood a joke. If he did make such an accusation then I shall have no alternative but to prove him wrong in a court of law and proceed thereafter to sue him for defamation of character. It's absolutely absurd. As a matter of fact, I think you are lying Inspector. Yanis could never have made such an accusation. It is not possible. We were having a happy time together all over the place, like good friends should. Your insinuation is absolutely absurd."

"Where were you having your drink?"

"All over the place: We were at Sunshine, the Anchor, et cetera."

"Who was paying for the drinks?"

"Why? That's a silly question. I was paying and he was paying. What did you expect?"

"How did you happen to lose track of each other?"

"That is the unfortunate part. I had to drive some people to the New Florida and then go back for Yanis so that we could both come here and have a drink. On reaching the New Florida I decided that the place was interesting and sent a taxi driver to collect Yanis and bring him along to the club. The taxi driver made a mistake of driving Yanis to my house." I was cooking up all this story from what Tonia had told me. I just explained it the same way Yanis had explained and I was hoping that there wouldn't be a catch somewhere. The Inspector was looking at me with a frown. I stared back at him confidently.

"What are you trying to make me believe?" he asked me.

"Oh, nothing. You come to me with a wild story and then I explain to you what happened which you do not want to believe after which you ask me what I am trying to make you believe. I should be posing that question. What is wrong with having a drink with a Greek Captain?"

"Your wife's story conforms with what Yanis told me later. You have to be lying, Mr. Kiunyu. You have got yourself involved in a very serious crime and I advise you to come out clean otherwise you are going to be locked up for six months even before your case is heard. I am offering you a chance to help yourself."

"I don't know what you are talking about. To the best of my knowledge, I've committed no crime and I am in turn advising you to invoke any goddam law you think I have broken and I shall answer you in court."

"I can prove that you are lying."

"Go ahead. You have to prove it in court. You don't have to do it here. You are an officer of the law. You have the law at your disposal. Use it."

"Would you fight against your own wife in a court of law?"

"What in the name of Jesus do you mean by that? Why do I have to fight against my wife. She hasn't lodged a complaint against me, has she?"

"I told you that her story ties in with Yanis confession."

"Confession! What sort of confession are you talking about?"

"Your friend Yanis made a full written confession of his illegal dealings with you."

"That is absolutely crazy. If Yanis was involved in any illegal activities, I have no knowledge of it and I am certainly not a party to it. Dear officer, you are really getting into my nerves." It's true. He is really getting into my nerves. The truth of the matter is, I am worried like hell. I have no knowledge of the sort of statement that Yanis made at the police station only I feel convinced that he would never confess. The Inspector is bluffing. If he isn't, I am licked. It would mean several years in jail for me. I am praying to Almighty God that the man is bluffing.

"In that case," he tells me calmly, "would you like to come to the police station and make a written statement?"

"Sure", I say confidently. I am beginning to sweat. I realize that I am hooked if Yanis spilt the beans. I would never be party to such a confession. It is a useless confession. It wouldn't reduce your time in jail. It would merely reduce the work of the prosecutor. I am not the prosecutor's brother so there is no reason why I should reduce his work. I shall claim my innocence right to the jail gates. I have nothing to lose.

"Mrs. Kiunyu, are you prepared to repeat the conversation you had with Mr. Yanis tonight before I arrived?" he asks Tonia.

"Yes"

"It's lies for chrissake!" I shout. "You can't repeat such stuff. You misunderstood the man."

"No, Dod. It's not lies," she tells me calmly. "I don't want to go through it again but it just happened as I explained to the Inspector. The man claimed that you cheated him out of his money."

"But he explained right here in front of the good inspector that you'd misunderstood him. I have gone further and now cleared the misunderstanding and you still don't want to believe. Where do you think this sort of thing will get you?"

"I am merely telling the truth," she snaps. "The man came in here crying murder and wanting his money back but when the inspector came he changed his story completely. He was lying and of course you are lying too. I don't care for you to accuse me of being a liar. You are only able to tell your story because I was foolish enough to tell you how the man changed his story. I don't even think that you set eyes on him again since the moment you robbed him. I have told you several times that I will not back up your lies."

I give up. I am in such a rage that no words can come out of my mouth. My mind is spinning. All I want is to grab her neck and strangle her. I feel terribly let down. The Inspector looks at us and laughs. I think it is a very stupid thing to do at that moment. He stands up and continues laughing so we just look at him like you'd look at a laughing clown in the house of parliament during a hot debate.

"You are the oddest couple I ever met in my life," he says finally. "It was just yesterday when you, Mr. Kiunyu, claimed that your wife hanged herself. She denied it bitterly and there is sufficient proof to indicate that you were either lying or she was lying... or both. In less than twenty four hours after the scene at the hospital where you managed to confuse me thoroughly, I find myself faced with the same situation. This time it is you, Mrs. Kiunyu, who is accusing your husband and he is denying bitterly. The roles have changed, but the situation is the same. What are you trying to do to each other? I am not married but I at least know that the sort of relationship that exists between you two is odd. Enough of this. I want a written statement from you, Mr. Kiunyu, so if you don't mind let's get moving."

We went to the police station and I repeated the same story Yanis had told. I did not believe that he'd confessed. It took a whole two hours and I was avoiding the detail that can be verified. After I was through, the Inspector said I was free to leave and that he'd be cheking on my story after which I'd be arrested. It was only when I was walking slowly out of the place when the police assistant who was taking notes caught up with me in the corridor and told me not to worry.

"The Inspector is bluffing," he told me. "Your story ties with that of the Greek". I dug my hand in the left hand pocket and separated one bill and then crumpled it in my hand so that when my hand came out, it was just a ball of paper in my hand. I then extended my hand to shake his in way of good-bye and left the folded bill in his hand. I don't know whether it was a hundred, twenty or ten shillings. I didn't look. He said good-bye and I said thank you. I went home whistling. At least Yanis had ousted himself off the scene although there was of course, the possibility that he might come after me with a gun or set thugs on me. I had to be on the look out. I could only feel safe after he'd sailed out into the open sea.

THREE

Tuesday Morning

Tonia is off-duty because Dr. Kihagi gave her five days to rest. She doesn't want to rise up early to prepare breakfast so I do. After breakfast I tell her that I have some surprise for her and would she please come down to the garage with me. Up to now, she doesn't know that I have acquired a green Peogeot 404 and that it is sitting there in the garage. She doesn't look impressed by my promise of a surprise. She just looks at me and reminds me that I'd promised to quit the house and that I hadn't and that the lies I told the Inspector are enough surprise for her. I am not rattled by this unfriendliness; on the contrary, I insist.

"It will be a green surprise and there are no lies about it. Please come".

"What surprise?"

"Come and see," I told her.

"Keep your surprises to yourself. When are you going to grow up? I have passed the age of running around looking for surprises."

"Oh, come, come. This is for real. Come and see."

"Bring it up." she said, shrugging her shoulders resignedly.

"I can't. Please come. You'll like it." I was smiling pleasantly.

"What is it?" she asked impatiently.

"OK, it's just a car." I told her, feeling deflated.

"Whose car?" She was getting curious.

"Our car."

"What do you mean? Our car?"

"Well, I just bought a car. Come downstairs and have a look. It is in the garage alongside the other car."

"That's interesting," she said, and we walked down to the garage. I was all excited and I suppose I was just rattling off as I opened the doors and showed her the inside of the car — the cream seats, the dash board et cetera. I hadn't noticed that she was not sharing the excitement till she asked:

"Is it on higher purchase?"

"No. It's all paid for."

"And where did you get the money?" I was expecting this but I had no ready answer. If I told her that I swindled two crooks and bought the car out of the proceeds she'd probably call the police and that would be the end of my car. It would be impounded and me with it.

"I've been paying for it since the last eight months. I paid in the final sum last week."

"You never told me about it."

"I was never sure that I was going to be able to raise the whole sum, so I didn't want to raise your hopes until I was certain."

"And you got certain after you robbed your Greek friend, isn't it?"

"Oh come, come. I am telling you that I finished paying for the car last week. Last week Friday to be more precise. I didn't meet my friend Yanis until yesterday and I certainly did not rob him. You've got to get that idea out of your mind."

"Where did you get the money to pay for the car? You haven't answered me."

"I told you I've been paying slowly by slowly. I get a little money now and then and I pay it to Marshalls."

"Little illegal money. That's what you are talking about, isn't it?"

"OK. You know all about it so why ask? All I had to do was act as agent between buyer and seller and I got my little commission. The fact that there is a law against that sort of agency does not mean that I robbed anybody in particular."

"Don't justify yourself. It is a crime."

"I know and I agree but who got hurt? Aren't the politicians robbing us blind under our very noses and nobody does anything about it 'cause those who should do something are the ones who are robbing? Who owns farms and hotels and shops and buses and lorries and what have you? Is it poor people like you or me? Even with my little crookedness, would I afford a Mercedes? Do you think that dishonesty and corruption is the prerogative of these rich and influential bastards alone? What are we? The little insignificant underlings that must live and die like beasts in a drought, while our fat brothers hold the key to rain and water for their forbidden pastures. Let us all have rain. We all need green grass."

"And green cars, I suppose."

"Listen Tonia, I am your husband. What do you have against me that can not be remedied. I am through with the business. Through. Really. I've decided to stop. Within a short while you'll see me in a regular job. No kidding. I am looking for a job. There's a limit to how far one can push one's luck in one direction and I have reached that limit. I am quitting. I quit yesterday. If you ever catch me blackmarketeering again, you have my permission to cut my throat."

"You are lying about the car. I know you cheated that Greek captain and like a fool went and put all the money in a car. You'll be caught. If you can't convince me you can't convince the police. You have a bad name and I hate myself for having ever acquired it. The police are after you. They were here last night and they will come again. Your friend made a confession. That is what the police inspector said. That confession incriminates you. I am therefore surprised that you can be so naive as to be smiling innocently and showing me the very evidence of your theft and expect that I'll smile with you. The fact that there are many criminals in this world does not mean that you have to be a criminal yourself. What you seem to forget is that criminals are punished when caught and you too will be caught. I am afraid but you are not going to park this car in this compound. This is a government house. What are you trying to do? Ruin my career? I simply can't allow you to park a car which is obviously stolen property, in my garage. I shall never be you accomplice."

"I give up. I don't think that you'll every understand me. The only person you can understand is God and I am far from being God. You are wrong about my freedom though. There's no threat to it. Yanis did not make any incriminating statement as our friend the inspector was trying to make us believe. He was merely trying to trap me into admission of a crime that I never committed. It was just a ruse. He was lying."

"Do you really want me to believe that you did not swindle that man? Swear on your sacred honour."

"Yes, I want you to believe it. I swear. I can promise you one thing. I would have nothing to hide from you if you would also swear on your honour that in the event that I should tell you something that. . ."

I did not finish. Khimji's car comes tearing through the gate and he pops out while the car is still moving. He is so furiously excited that he can't even talk. He comes straight and grabs me by the collar and before I have time to get my reflexes working, he is shaking me furiously and groaning from right deep in his throat in the most emphatic manner.

"I want it! I want it! You produce it! I found out! You give it! The truth! You bastard! I want it right now! Not tomorrow. Now!" He must have shaken me quite a bit before the momentary shock passed and I freed my neck from his grasp. I was angry and amused. I had never imagined that an Indian could ever lay his hands on my throat and I reckon that's what shocked me more than anything else. He must have been really pissed off or maybe he didn't know me well enough. On the spur of the minute, I decide to beat him up before he can open up his mouth again 'cause I don't want Tonia to know what it was all about. It would merely help to widen the credibility gap.

Pop! I smack him on the nose. Pop! Pop! And the shock is on his face. I suppose it was all too sudden. One second I was shocked and the next second he was shocked. He wasn't shocked for long though. I was punching his face when he landed a terrific kick on my groin and I had to double up with pain. What happened thereafter was just a general fight during which we practically hit each other alternatively only he was getting the better of me because he was more angry and put a lot of steam into his punches. Every time he rammed his fist into me I could feel devastating impact taking my breath away' cause he was shorter and concentrated on my stomach while I was smashing his hard head and thereby hurting my kuckles. Tonia was screaming. We were thus engaged when a police car with my old friend the inspector and his assistant whom I had given a little money earlier on in the day came and stopped right in front of us. The fight stopped and we just panted looking at the law, conscious of likely damaging consequences. Khimji was frightened too. I had ripped open his shirt and his nose was bleeding. He looked like a perfect ruffian. Of course I couldn't see myself so I don't know what I looked like.

There was sheer incredulity in the police officers' eyes. They didn't even hurry when getting out of their car. They just came out slowly and ready just in case we should start fighting again and stood right there in front of us. Tonia had stopped screaming.

"What is going on around here?" the Inspector asked in a dry husky voice that was full of authority. I was going to wait for Khimji to reply first just to see how much of the truth he would give, but it was Tonia who answered first.

"It's this Indian. He just came and without warning and without saying anything, he attacked my husband. He..."

"Keep out of this," I told her, "and get upstairs. This is a man's affair and I don't want you butting in. Get moving." I was surprised Tonia obeyed. She just turned and walked upstairs.

"And now Inspector," I said calmly. "You may pose your question again. I myself would like to hear the answer from Mr. Khimji here because he is the only one who knows what it's all about. I simply don't know what he came for and why he attacked me."

"You know why, you thief?" he shouted at me. "You are a filthy thief. I want my money back and I didn't start the fight. You hit me first."

"You better address yourself to the Inspector, Mr. Khimji. I don't have the foggiest idea about what you are saying but I must warn you about slandering my name. I could take legal steps."

"I don't care what you..."

"Shut up both of you!" the inspector snapped. "I was coming here on a different matter but now I find that the plot thickens. I want you to calm yourself and explain clearly what the cause of this demonstration of strength is. Eh, what is your name again?"

"Khimji."

"Mr. Khimji, would you please tell me what you gentlemen are fighting for."

"Sir, this man Kiunyu is not a gentleman at all. Not at all sir. He is very different. He is a thief. I defy him to deny it. Only yesterday he robbed me some fifteen thousand shillings. I want my money back. When I ask him, he told me he was his brother. Isn't that a lie, Sir? He is a liar too." The officer scratched his head. He wasn't understanding everything that Khimji was saying. He had got the gist of it though. Khimji was letting the cat off the bag and we'd both be in hot soup. We were both licked. I decided to keep quiet and let Khimji talk. There was no point in interfering.

"Are you trying to tell me that Mr. Kiunyu stole your money and that as a result you came here to fight him?" the inspector asked.

"No, Sir. He stole my money and I came to ask for it. I did not want to fight. I am not a fighting man. He hit me." The police assistant was taking notes. He'd placed his note book on the roof of the police car and was scribbling fast.

"Now let us get this straight," the inspector said. "You say that Mr. Kiunyu stole your money?"

"Yes, Sir."

"When?"

"Yesterday morning. He came into my office yesterday morning and I must have left the safe open. No. Come think of it, the money was right there on the table. I was counting it so that I could take it to the Bank."

"How much?"

"Fifteen thousand."

"How, in your opinion, did he steal it?"

"Well — eh — as I said, he came to my office to talk business. I had to refer to a file which was in a different room and when I came out neither Mr. Kiunyu nor the money was there. They'd both disappeared."

"What business did Mr. Kiunyu want to discuss with you?"

"He came to borrow money to buy a car. I refused to lend him the money although he is a friend. He was asking for too much."

"How much did he want?"

"He wanted fifteen thousand."

"And how was he going to pay you back?"

"That's why I didn't lend him the money. Mr. Kiunyu has no good source of income. Not any that I know of anyway. He just said that he'd pay it back in six months. I didn't believe him."

"For how long have you known Mr. Kiunyu?"

"Well over six months, Sir."

"Have you had the occasion to do business with him?"

"No, Sir. Mr. Kiunyu is not a businessman."

"How did you become friends?"

"We just met, we talked and became friends."

"You haven't had any money transactions with Mr. Kiunyu?"

"Certainly not."

"How come then that he came to borrow such a huge sum from you?"

"I don't know. I suppose it's merely because we are friends. If he wanted a small sum I am sure I would have given it to him. I have given him small loans before."

"Does Mr. Kiunyu sell foreign currency to you, Mr. Khimji?"

"I beg your pardon, Sir?"

"You heard me."

"Well ! Foreign currency! Sir, what would I want to buy foreign currency for? I believe it is illegal, isn't it?"

"You have not answered my question. Has Mr. Kiunyu ever proposed the sale of foreign currency to you?"

"Oh no, Sir. I don't indulge in such matters."

"Do you know whether Mr. Kiunyu does?"

"I don't know and I wouldn't want to know. I told you that I don't indulge in such matters. I am an honest businessman."

"So when Mr. Kiunyu came to your office yesterday you did not discuss foreign currency."

"Certainly not. I told you he wanted a loan."

"So you refused the loan and he stole the money?"

"Yes, Sir."

"How come that you had exactly fifteen thousand shillings on your table? Don't you think that it was too much of a coincidence that Mr. Kiunyu wanted fifteen thousand shillings and that you had the exact amount right in front of you when he entered your office. Is it not strange that you should then leave the said amount of money right there on the table and go into a different room while Mr. Kiunyu was there. Don't you think it is strange?"

"I agree, Sir. It is strange. A strange coincidence. But I didn't know he'd steal the money. I thought he was honest. To the best of my knowledge I don't know when he became a thief."

"What did you do when you discovered that Mr. Kiunyu and the money had disappeared?"

"I got very angry, Sir. He... well. I got very angry."

"Is that all you did?"

"Well I tried to locate him."

"How?"

"I thought... I... I thought he'd come back. I thought it was a joke. I thought he'd come back."

"So you didn't try to locate him."

"After he didn't come back, I tried to locate him.

"And did you locate him?"

"Finally, yes"

"At what time?"

"In the afternoon."

"At what time did he disappear with the money?"

"It was before lunch. Around midday I would say."

"And you located him at what time?"

"I told you it was in the afternoon. Around two o'clock."

"You were sure that he'd taken the money?"

"Yes, Sir. No doubt about that. He took it."

"Why didn't you report the matter to the police?"

"Well... I... wanted to be absolutely certain that Mr. Kiunyu was not playing a practical joke. I told you he is my friend. I wouldn't want to set the police on him if the whole thing was a joke. That wouldn't be fair on a friend."

"And when did you discover that it wasn't a joke?"

"When I talked with him on the phone and he told me that he was his brother."

"Say that again."

"Well I telephoned him at the house and when I asked: 'Is that you Dodge?' he said; 'No, I am his brother.' Then I asked him what he did with my money and he said that his brother was not at home and would I ring later. That's when I knew he'd decided to steal the money."

"That sounds like a joke to me, Mr. Khimji."

"But I knew it wasn't a joke."

"You then knew for sure that he'd stolen your money?"

"Exactly."

"Did you subsequently report the matter to the police?"

"No Sir. I... eh..."

"Why?"

"I decided that... I... well, I decided to talk to him first."

"But you'd just talked to him on the phone."

"I wanted to talk to him personally."

"Why?"

"To put some sense into his head. He's a friend. I wouldn't like him to go to jail. If he could refund the money I wouldn't lodge a complaint."

"But your are lodging a complaint now.'

"Yes, Sir. I am lodging a complaint because I am sure that Mr. Kiunyu no longer has the money. He used it to buy this new car you see here Inspector."

The inspector turned his head and studied the car. Then he turned his eyes and fixed them on me. He stared at me incredulously for a full half minute and then turned to Khimji. All this time the inspector's assistant was writing notes frantically.

"When did you find out that Kiunyu had used the money to buy a car?"

"This morning."

"How?"

"A friend of mine saw him driving this new car yesterday evening, so I checked from Marshalls."

"Was this friend of yours somebody in your employment?"

"Oh . . . yes. Yes. He works for me."

"You had your men out looking for Mr. Kiunyu, is that correct?"

"No, Sir. This was just a coincidence. This man just happened to see Mr. Kiunyu. Sheer coincidence."

"So when you found out from Marshalls that Mr. Kiunyu had bought himself a car you decided that you were certain that he'd stolen your money?"

"Yes, Sir."

"You were not certain before?"

"No, Sir."

"So you knew that he wasn't joking?"

"Exactly."

"And you knew that he'd used the money?"

"Yes."

"Therefore you also knew that he couldn't possibly refund the moeny since he'd used it to buy a car?"

"Yes. I knew."

"Why didn't you report the theft to the police then?"

"Well, you see, Sir. . . I wouldn't like to send a friend to jail."

"But you are now lodging an official complaint?"

"Yes sir."

"So you no longer care if he goes to jail?"

"Not anymore. I would like him to go to jail now."

"I see. That's interesting. Can you then tell me why you thought it necessary to come here and confront Mr. Kiunyu personally?"

"I told you, Sir. I was angry. No. I don't mean that. I mean. . . . . eh . . . I had to see if the situation could be saved before I reported the matter to the police."

"And what did you find out?"

"Mr. Kiunyu's fists. He didn't give me a chance."

"So you defended yourself?"

"I'll say I did."

"Very well, Mr. Khimji. You are going to lodge a complaint at the police station and you are also going to sign a statement on the lines you have indicated. It's a very interesting case." He turned to me and stared at me again. I was laughing inwardly because I knew that Khimji could never make a case that would stand on its feet unless he changed his story. It was of course too late to change since he was speaking to the police and they were taking notes. If he tried, he'd appear a bigger liar than he appeared then. It was sticking out a foot that the inspector did not believe him.

I had no doubt that the Inspector knew about the currency blackmarketeering angle. That was his main interest in the matter. After the Yanis episode of the previous night and the unconvincing story that Khimji told, it stood to reason that the police would put two and two together and get four. Trouble with Khimji is that he did not realize that he was putting us both in the noose. He wasn't clever enough to realize, like Yanis did, that it is safer to lose the money than to land himself a charge of contravention of exchange control regulations. Anyway, the Inspector turned to me and asked, "And what do you have to say, Mr. Kiunyu?"

"After all the precious time that Mr. Khimji has taken telling you all those lies, I reckon that it would be more prudent for me not to waste any more of your time. I would however like to make one thing clear. In telling his story, Mr. Khimji has implicated me and I want to take this opportunity to deny any complicity in the story that has been outlined to you. Further, I would like to add that I shall consult my lawyer to explore the possibilities of instituting legal action against Mr. Khimji when this unfortunate accusation that he has levelled against me is proved false in a court of law. I want to state here and now that I shall meet this filthy Indian in court."

"You haven't explained the circumstances, Mr. Kiunyu. Did you for instance call on Mr. Khimji yesterday with the intention of borrowing money from him?"

"Certainly not?"

"What? You didn't try to borrow money from him?"

"It's a lie. I did no such thing. How can I go to borrow fifteen thousand shillings from him? If I had no money and cause to want to borrow such a sum, I would simply go to my bank. As a customer I have a good record with my bank."

"I don't understand. Khimji is your friend, isn't he?"

"He is an acquaintance but certainly not a friend. For instance I don't know where he lives and I don't know how he found out where I live. Let's put it this way. I know him. I know him less than I know you, Inspector. That's how friendly we are." All of a sudden I decide that since Khimji had told unconvincing lies, my best bet was to tell a different set of lies that would be more convincing. Something that Khimji couldn't disapprove. If I didn't have a story, the inspector would start thinking that I was guilty. Khimji had opened the door. He had as much as said that he didn't mind my going to jail. There was no reason why I should spare him.

"There are things that can be verified, Mr. Kiunyu. When you tell lies to the police you risk a lot. When you make a statement to the police we check and counter check. I have been checking on the story you told me last night and I found a lot of lies. I want the truth. Do you understand?

"Yes," I told him.

"Fine. Did you go to Mr. Khimji's office yesterday morning?"

"Yes."

"Why did you lie before?"

"I object to that. I didn't lie. You simply asked me whether I went there to borrow money and I told you I didn't."

"Why did you go there?"

"He called me."

"He called you?"

"Yes."

"Why did he call you?"

"I didn't know until I got to his office. He simply asked me to go and see him if I had time to spare 'cause he had something urgent he wanted to talk to me about."

"And what was this thing."

"You got me there inspector. I couldn't believe it myself. He asked me to keep my dirty hands off his sister."

"What!" The inspector was excited. Khimji was completely aghast. He tried to say something and only managed to swallow. He nearly chocked.

"I couldn't understand it myself. I don't remember that I have laid dirty hands on his sister any time and his accusation almost struck me dumb." Khimji made to speak and the inspector asked him to shut up.

"This plot does thicken," the inspector said. "So you were accused of messing around with his sister, ha? What happened next?"

"I told him to go jump into the sea. I know his sister alright. She's a decent girl. She's over twenty one and free. If she wants to go horsing around she's free to horse around. She is no longer a kid. So why pick on me?"

"Inspector, that's a lie," Khimji managed to say.

"You mean she's not twenty one?"

"No. Not that. What I..."

"Will you shut up. You've given me your story. When you were talking Mr. Kiunyu did not say a word. If you open your mouth again, I shall clout you myself. Now, Mr. Kiunyu, what is the relationship between you and Mr. Khimji's sister?"

"That is none of your business, inspector."

The truth of the matter is I have laid Khimji's sister a couple of times, but of course he doesn't know. We have been very careful about the whole thing. She'd go to this hotel in Port Reitz right on the way to the Mombasa airport and book herself a room. From there she'd ring me up at some appointed place and tell me the room number. I'd simply go to the hotel and walk up without checking with the reception and of course the door to the room would be open. We could only do that during the day though. Most times we did it during the morning hours. Usually from ten to one o'clock then we'd part ways. It was fool-proof. Anyway, that is now all over. We are quits. It wasn't really my fault. The rubber I was wearing once burst and I paid for the abortion so I can't really be blamed. She's the one that said we should stop but I am not bitter. A girl has to protect herself.

"Why do you say that you were shocked when Khimji asked you to lay hands off his sister?"

"Don't you think that is outside the scope of your examination, inspector?"

"No?"

"In that case I'll tell you. I know the face of Khimji's sister. I have said hello to her once or twice in his presence. I don't think that I've even ever shaken her hand and I doubt that she knows my name because Khimji merely introduced me as a friend without mentioning my name. I have never met her except in the presence of Mr. Khimji and I have never even dreamed about her. What put the silly idea into his head I do not know."

"So you have had no overt relation with her?"

"No. I have had no relation with her; overt or otherwise."

"And yet Mr. Khimji called you to confront you on the matter?"

"He's crazy." I could see Khimji wanting to swallow his teeth. This is something he never expected. If he should mention it to his sister, I know she'll give him hell. I know her. She doesn't like Khimji. She says he is mean and possessive.

"Was there some money on the table when you got into Khimji's office?"

"No, certainly not. Let me just explain what happened. After he asked me to stop messing up with his sister, I told him to go to hell as I have just told you and he was very rude. He started threatening me. He said he could bribe the police to jail me on a fake charge or set some chaps on me. Still I said I didn't care. In the end I got pretty steamed up myself and I told him that he could go and fuck his sister for all I cared. Then he threatened me that he'd tip off the police that I engage in illegal currency exchange and I told him to go right ahead because the accusation was completely baseless. I reminded him that on two different occasions he has asked me to procure some foreign currency for him and that on both occasions I had told him that I wouldn't know how to do it because I don't indulge in such illegal activities. Finally he banged the table and asked to get out of his office. I spat on him and left."

"So how do you explain this fight you were having by the time I got there?"

"I can't explain it. Khimji just got out of his car, came towards me and grabbed me by the neck. As he shook me about, he kept saying that he'd found out the truth. He was saying all sorts of insulting things by the time I managed to free my neck from his grip and pop him one on the mouth. I couldn't figure out what he'd found out. If it's something about his sister and me, let him speak out right now in your presence. I give him the floor." The inspector looked at Khimji but Khimji had no words. He'd lost his voice.

"If you want to know how the fight started inspector, simply ask my wife. She'll confirm every word I've said."

"Let's hope she will," the inspector said. "Tell me one thing. Khimji says that you bought this car with his money. Would you like to tell me where you got the money to buy the car?"

"Look here inspector, I think that question is absurd and to prove it, I am going to give you a cheque for fifteen thousand shilings and ask you to buy me another Peugeot 404 with it. If you can do so without adding a lot of your own money, then I'll admit Khimji's charge. My God! Do you think that this car costs fifteen thousand shillings?"

"Did you pay cash or did you issue a cheque?"

"Really inspector, I am going to have to refuse to answer your questions. Why don't you go to Marshalls and ask them? I've told you that this man came here to pick up a quarrel with me because of his sister and I don't see how you can start connecting that with the purchase of a car. I bought the car with my own money and if I wanted to, I can buy myself another car right here and now. I have the money."

"How much did you pay for it?"

"Quite a fortune. If you want to know the price, you have my permission to use my phone. Ring the salesman and he'll give you a quotation. If you should then decide that you want to buy a similar car yourself and you are short of cash, you can always raise a loan from me provided that it is properly documented and secured against tangible assets, notwithstanding. . ."

"Stop being flippant, Mr. Kiunyu. You two gentlemen are coming along with me to the police station and you are going to sign statements. Needless to say, we shall have to charge you, Mr. Kiunyu. Mr. Khimji has accused you of theft and unless he withdraws, it will be the duty of the magistrate to decide on the matter. I also want you to know that I consider both of you great liars. Let's go."

We went to the police station and had to sign statements. We were shoved into different rooms so I don't know what sort of signed statement Khimji made. I only know that I was thereafter given court summons to appear in court on a charge of theft and that Khimji was the plaintiff. That's why I am going to court Thursday next week to hear my case mentioned. I haven't got a lawyer yet. I have to get one. Trouble with Mombasa is that most lawyers are Indians and I don't care to be defended by an Indian against an Indian. You never can tell what goes on when they sit on their mats and eat curry.

If I should get acquitted, I'll sue Khimji for slander. What I am afraid of is that this other currency business might come to light and that is a dam serious offence. To win his case, Khimji would have to bring it up and we shall both fry, so he wouldn't dare. He'll find it very tough. Suppose I should admit that he gave me fifteen thousand shillings to go and procure him some dollars in the black market and that instead of taking the money to the police I used it myself. What then? Can they convict me? Could I not argue that he gave me the money to break a law and that I refused to break the law? In that case my only offence would be the failure to report the matter to the police. Any reasonable judge would agree with me that using the bad money for myself instead of taking it to the police station, where I wouldn't get a reward, was very tempting. Maybe I shall do a little confessing.

Tuesday Evening

This is a lousy Tuesday. It is raining. It has been raining through the whole afternoon and quite a lot of people are trapped on the sidewalks and shop verandas waiting for the rain to stop so that they can walk home. There are pools of water all along the roads and the six o'clock traffic is splashing through, often wetting pedestrians on the sheltered sidewalks. It is a horrid evening. It's almost cold which is something we don't usually have down here in Mombasa. Anyway, I hope that the farmers are happy.

I park my new peugeot 404 outside the Manor Hotel and get out. I have no umbrella so what I do is, I dash very fast up the steps that lead from the street to the lobby. When I am safe from the wet menace, I take out my handkerchif and wipe my hair and face dry. I then proceed to the inner bar and install myself on a stool. There aren't many people around, at least none of my close friends, so I just sit on this stool and ask for a whisky. I want to warm my insides a little bit before I change to beer. The bartender places the whisky in front of me and I proceed to sip it slowly.

Just in case you do not know, the Manor Hotel is one of these old joints that can do with a little touch of paint here and there if only to hide a few leaks where rain has seeped through making funny maps on the roof. Some repairs are underway here and there and maybe the place will look OK, after they are through. The place has something colonial although I can't lay my finger on it. May be it is this picture they have on the wall with a typical bearded colonial in Khaki who is lazily stroking his bulldog on the head while puffing his ivory pipe. I don't know exactly what it is except that whenever I am in here, I expect to turn my head and see some colonials behind me. Only I don't see them. The place is popular with Africans, especially the rich married ones who need a quiet corner with their girlfriends. Strictly speaking, the place is not my cup of tea today. I am feeling like a rich nigger. The folks around here don't look friendly so I just sit at the counter and sip my whisky.

After two whiskies, I switch to beer and on my second beer I go to the loo. I contemplate the writing on the wall above the urinal and decide that crazy men don't only go to cheap places. Name any place and you bet some crazy man has been there.

I am walking back to my stool at the bar counter when I meet this blasted police inspector who's been giving me hell since Sunday. If there is one man I don't want to meet at all, it is this chap. I hate him though I don't even know his name. He never told me and I never asked. He is just a nuisance cop like any other nuisance cop and I am not very partial to cops. What the hell does he want to come here for? To ruin my drink? Blast him.

He is smiling. He is *smiling* at me! Blast him and may his teeth fall out. I am not in the mood for cop smiles. He's not wearing uniform though. I suppose he's just come to have his share of alcohol like everybody else. I don't smile back. I don't even venture a 'good evening' I just pass him and install myself on my stool.

I order myself another beer and before the barman gives it to me, this inspector chap comes over and says, "Hey, how about one for me?" I turn my head and look at him. My eyes are not friendly. I have no reason to be friendly to this guy at all, so I tell him:

"No objection, so long as you pay for it yourself." He asks the barman to give him a cold Pilsner and when he gets the the bill, he shoves it in front of me.

"That's very kind of you," I tell him. "But I really don't care for that type of kindness. Please," and I give him back the bill. He takes it back with good grace and then says, "Can I pay one for you?"

"No thanks." I tell him. "I've had enough."

"You look it," he retorts. I don't like him bothering me. I am in no mood for these things. I want some peace tonight. I lean very close to his ear and whisper.

"Please get off my back, will you?" And he laughs.

"I hope that my presence is not giving you goose flesh, Dodge. I am not on duty. I am off right now. So if you want to know, I am merely amusing myself."

"Fine. Amuse yourself to your fill. You are entitled to do so but please let me be. Talk to somebody else. By the way, I am Mr. Kiunyu to you."

"Touchy, aren't you, Dodge. I thought we were friends."

"Look mister, I don't even know your name."

"You never asked me. You are not curious."

"I don't intend to start getting curious now."

"Please yourself. Eh, just in case you weren't telling me another lie, my name is Masakalia. Charles Masakalia."

"Thanks."

"Oh, I didn't tell you what happened. I had a bad day. My wife burnt the clutch of my car some place on Malindi road. The car got stuck in the sand somewhere by the beach and she burnt the clutch out Very annoying of course. The poor car is still there stuck in the sand and you know how these things are. It will mean a whole thousand shillings to put it right."

"I dare say it will, only it happens to be your affair and I can't figure out why you deem it necessary to tell me. I have never been accused of being a mechanic. By the way did you get married today or yesterday? Anyway, forget it I am not touched."

"I know what would touch you," he whispers. "If I were to tear up the file containing all the stuff about the theft charge so that you wouldn't have to appear in court, you would be very touched."

It started to dawn on me. The chap was after a little present, as the police call it. He had merchandise to trade.

"I would be very touched", I tell him.

"And I would be touched if I could get my car in working condition. That's a whole thousand of course. These garages are very expensive and of course it is the wrong part of the month for me."

"And if the car gets repaired, the charge and the files also get repaired, is that it."

"That is just about it in a nutshell."

"What about this Indian extortionist? How shall he be silenced?"

"Just a little persuasion."

"He may refuse to get persuaded."

"Then he shall be told the truth. The truth is, of course, that you obtained some foreign currency from the Greek and that on the strength of it you got him to give you fifteen thousand shillings but you did not surrender the foreign currency to him. Thereafter you sold the foreign currency to a third party for about the same amount you got from Khimji and proceeded to Marshalls to buy yourself a car. I also happen to know that the third party was Madhivani and that you must be holding a lot of cash somewhere because you haven't paid anything into your bank account which I had the chance to scrutinize myself. All this much I know. What I don't have is the proof and I am not going to look for it because all four of you involved are great liars and the truth will never come out in court."

"You seem to know quite a lot Mr. . . . yes . . . Mr. Masakalia. All I can . . ."

"Call me Charles."

"Fine. I'll do better than that. I shall call you Charlie boy. As I was saying, you seem to know quite a lot only I can not admit that your story is true."

"You need not worry. You are just thieves stealing from each other. I am not going to waste any more public time with this thing.

I have to tell you one thing though. If I catch you again and I get the proof, I'll put you in. I'll make sure that you rot in remand for six months before your case is heard."

"OK, not so loud. I don't mind telling you just one bit of truth. I am through. No kidding. I made this last haul as a sort of good-bye to the trade. I am through and through."

"What about this story about Khimji's sister?"

"Oh that. He didn't actually accuse me because he doesn't have the foggiest idea what we've been up to but if he knew, he'd have accused me."

"Interesting. So you took his money and you took his sister."

"Brother, I am sure you know how hard it is to get anything from an Indian. I just had my little chance and I took it."

"OK. What about this one thousand bob?"

"When do you want it?"

"Right now."

"Well . . . I . . . of course don't have it on my person. I'll have to dash somewhere and borrow from a friend. It wouldn't take more than twenty minutes maximum. Just sit tight and wait for me." I get out and hop into my car. I am driving to my house. I am not very unhappy. Now, the whole thing is different. One thousand bob will do the job. It will save me a lot of nuisance. I suppose that the inspector is really entitled to it. He could cause a lot of trouble if he wanted to.

I get home and find a strange car parked in the drive just behind Tonia's car. I wonder who the hell this night caller might be. What I do is, I get into the house and make for the store. The store is behind the kitchen and there is a lot of junk on account that we have no houseboy. The sitting room is upstairs so if I am fast enough I can do what I want to do before Tonia has the time to come down. I flick the light on in the kitchen and proceed to the fridge. I pull it forward and the curry can drops on the floor. It makes a slight racket. I get it open with a spoon handle, count twelve notes of one hundred shillings each, close the can and place it back into its hiding place. I flick off the light and then gumshoe quietly out of the place. I then walk upstairs to see who our visitor is.

Tonia, Julian and Dr. Kihagi are comfortably seated in the lounge. For one brief moment I have a great urge to bolt out only I don't.

My mouth experiences an involuntary opening and shutting action but finally settles into an embarrassed smile as I walk in and say:

"Oh, hello, hello, hello." I can't figure out why I had to say hello three times but I said it all the same. Tonia gets into the motion of wanting to make introductions and I tell her that I know Dr. Kihagi. So what we do is, we shake hands. All the while I am asking myself why the hell I'd to come upstairs instead of simply getting back into my car and driving out. I really have nothing to say to these people but I have to pretend to be a good husband and all. What a bloody mess. Masakalia is waiting for his one thousand shillings and I didn't even pay my bill at the bar.

"I am very glad to meet you Doctor," I say, just for the sake of saying something. "It is unfortunate that we first met under rather trying circumstances. Who would have known at the time that our wives were friends?" He merely smiles and says: "Quite true," which is not saying much in way of conversation.

"And how is Julian?" I ask. "Hope you are no longer mad at me."

"Oh I am fine and I don't think I was mad at you at all. How about you? I understand that you haven't been getting on very well with the police." Now, that was annoying. I am forcing myself to be nice and all and she starts talking about my problems. What has it got to do with her for chrissake?

"Oh, nothing I can't put my foot on. As a matter of fact, it was just a little storm in a tea cup. I drank it all." Dr. Kihagi laughs and says that the police can always be expected to cause trouble for nothing and that the best thing would be to forget them.

Dr. Kihagi is helping himself to this bottle of whisky I got from Madhivani while Julian and Tonia are sipping orange squash. The one thing I can't do is sit down and have a drink with them because I should be right back at the Manor Hotel this minute. It is also apparent that they were engaged on some line of intimate conversation and that my horning in hasn't done nobody no good.

I apologise for not having been at home when the guests arrived and then proceed to explain that I have to be at this rendezvous where I am waiting for an up-country friend. I then explain that I just dropped in to find out whether he'd telephoned or found his way to the house and that since none of these two events had taken place, I have to be back at the Manor Hotel. I then ask the Kihagi's when they would be free next so that we can have a little come-together and Julian tells me that she'll communicate with Tonia. I then excuse myself graciously with a little bow while raising an imaginary hat off my head and walk out. What a relief!

I get back to the Manor Hotel and find my friend Masakalia talking to some people. There is this chap who is sitting on my original stool and I have no place to sit at the counter because all stools are taken. I indicate my half-empty glass of beer and tell this chap that he has taken my seat and would he mind giving it back. He asks me how much I paid for it which is as much as telling me to go fry myself an egg. Masakalia comes to my rescue and tells the chap to get off my stool and the chap grudgingly does so. I sit down.

Masakalia dismisses his friends and turns to me.

"Any luck?" he asks, and I nod my head. Then he says, "I want to piss. Would you like to come along?" I order two beers and leave them right in front of our stools so that anybody will know that the stools are occupied and then I head for the toilet. I give Masakalia his one thousand and then I too piss. That's done at least. I'll have no problem with the chap again so long as I can cough up a little sum. I only hope he won't get too greedy and want to bleed me again. I would certainly object.

We stay in the joint until it closes up towards midnight. I am thoroughly drunk. I've to go home and hit the sack. We get out of the place and Masakalia gets into his car. Needless to say, the car is perfectly all right. I understand. The blighter isn't even married but he has imagination. He had an imaginary wife burn out an imaginary clutch on some imaginary beach! I must say that takes a lot of imagination.

On my way home I am hoping that the Kihagi's will have left for bed. It would be awful if I were to find them still there. It.s time for all busy people to go to bed. Trouble is I have to go to the kitchen first and see if there's some food left. I've not had my dinner. It is one meal I skip often. What I wouldn't like, is to be eating my dinner when these people are sitting up there. I am sure they'll have gone. Let's hope so.

I get home and to my surprise, Tonia's car is not there. Where the hell can she be at this hour of the night. I imagine that she might have loaned her car to somebody and that she was upstairs asleep but I am wrong. The bed has not been slept on even for a siesta. I curse and walk back to the lounge. I look around like an idiot who doesn't know what he is looking for and then descend downstairs to the kitchen and get myself a beer from the fridge and open it. I am no longer hungry. I walk up again and stretch on the sofa. I decide that I am going to stay awake till she shows up and that before she goes to the bathroom, I am going to smell her all round. If by any chance I should sniff anything that smells like fucking business, then I shall strangle her with my bare hands tonight. I feel so bad that even this lousy beer I am drinking from the bottle tastes horrid. God. I reckon that this fellow who said that jealousy was a green-eyed monster did not know what the hell he was talking about. Forget the bugger anyway. Jesus, I am drunk.

Tuesday Night

"Wake up!"

"Um ——oh—a--oh"

"Wake up Dodge. Why on earth are you sleeping on the couch? Couldn't you find your way to bed?" Tonia shakes me up vigorously and I open my eyes half a slit. I rub them with the back of my hand, belch and let out a lion's yawn. I then open my hurting eyes all the way and focus on the surroundings. I am right here on the sofa where I sat hours ago when I parted company with Masakalia.

"Why didn't you go to bed?" she asks.

"Don't know. Old sleep caught up with me right here on the couch."
"Where are you coming from?" I ask her still rubbing my eyes.

"I went to see a damn good movie".

"Damn good, eh? Then it must have been damn good. I don't hear you say damn something or anything unless it was damn it. It is not your language. Jeez -- must get to bed. What time is it?"

"Three o'clock."

"Three o'clock, Good God! You are coming at three o'clock in the morning? Where on earth did you go after the movie."

"Would it interest you, Dod?"

"I am asking you where you've been. We are not talking about my interests." I feel like an empty balloon with somebody trying to pump air into it very unsucessfully 'cause it's got a big hole. Gosh. Movies end between eleven thirty and mid-night, so what has she been up to?

"Do you really want to know, Dod? I'll tell you. A very interesting evening."

"No. Come to think of it, I don't. I don't want to know anything. You have your life to live after all." She laughs.

"You get easily on and off my dear old man. OK, I'll tell you where I've been. After the movie we . . ."

"I don't want to know. Really. I just don't want to know." Trouble is I just got this feeling that she might have been out screwing somebody and that she is going to tell me all about it just to spite me. There's mischief dancing in her eyes and I can see right through that she wants to shock me somewhat. She wants to see my heart wring with a little pain while she just stands there like an independent rock defying me to do my worst. Otherwise why did she wake me up? The Tonia I know would leave me sleeping right there on the couch and sneak quietly into bed so that she can hate me more in the morning. Tonia doesn't wake me up anytime and I am not jealous anymore. What I have is a flipping hangover. Jesus, I am drunk.

"Ha-ha-haaah!" she laughs aloud. "Fancy my old man getting angry 'cause I am late. Very surprising."

"I am not angry," I retort. "You didn't have to wake me up you know. What did you wake me up for anyway?"

"OK, Dod. Sleep well. Good-night." And she walks haughtily to the bedroom. I just sit there wide awake and try to hold my head together. I am an ass. I really am. Tell me sweet Jesus. Tell me. Am I by any chance starting to get jealous in my old age? Am I? Why should it bother me if she screwed a little out of wedlock when I do it myself and I haven't given her any for months. Hasn't she the right to do that? Well, I'll be damned.

What I do is I get up and go to bed too. I find Tonia undressing and I don't even sniff around her as I'd thought I would. I sort of feel sorry for that womanly body of hers that has not had sex for months. We haven't had it for a long time but if I tried she'd refuse in a very dignified manner. That's why I've been having it elsewhere. Now suppose she were to do the same thing. Suppose she's been having it out with some chap. The very thought of it is so repugnant, so —

oh — no. Stupid thought. She puts on her bath robe and makes straight for the bathroom. Gosh, she's going to take a bath. Ha. I can hear the water running. She's running the bath. Why? Why take a bath at three in the morning? Is she trying to clean off some evidence? Is she? Oh God.

I get undressed and get into bed. I try to shut my mind to all thoughts. I don't want to think. I shut my eyes and hate myself. I hate myself because I hate jealousy. The sound of the running bath is distasteful to my ears. I think I hate Tonia. That's the way I feel right now and that's why I am trying to get her out of my mind. I know it's absolutely selfish but if I knew that she was screwing somebody somewhere, I think I'd murder her. I would. What a thought? Oh—heck! Get out of my mind woman. Get out. Please, please, please. What are you doing in the goddam bathroom anyway? Washing off somebody else's sperms? Is that what you are doing by any chance? Gosh! Is that what you are doing? Sweet heavenly goodness — that's what she's doing. Damn! That's what I think right now. Suppose she confessed — what then? Murder? Gosh, I am drunk.

I get out of bed and dash to the bathroom. I push the door open and stare at her. She's lying there contentedly below the soapy film caressing her body with a sponge. She looks up suddenly, stares at me for a while in surprise and then ignores me with an embarassed smile. She closes her eyes and goes on sponging herself. I just stand there and stare at the bath. I have no words. I just feel foolish.

"Care to scrub my back instead of standing there gawking?" she asks without opening her eyes. She looks playful. I don't say a thing. I just swallow, shrug my shoulders and then bang the door shut. I get back into the bedroom, hop into bed and hate myself more. I feel foolish. Oh, I hate myself. I think I hate the whole goddam world. The reason why I hate myself is that when I was looking at Tonia underwater, I got this great urge to jump into the bath and rape her while drowning her at the same time. I am a madman, I swear. I am mad.

I lie there on the bed and this madman idea gets into my head. Why in water? Rape her when she comes out. I just decide to rape Tonia when she comes out of the bathroom. I think she'd like to be raped. I don't mean we reconcile and get soft and kiss and feel each other. No I just want to jump her, rape fashion. I'd like her to scream so that I can stifle her and I'd like her to fight so that I can clobber her. I'd like her to be crying while I am at it. Now that's exactly what I am going to do; rape her. What an idea. I never thought of it in my life but I reckon it's damn exciting. Rape — ha, ha. I'll be damned if I don't rape Tonia tonight.

She comes from the bathroom gracefully, takes off her bathrobe and I peek between her legs through the light blue nylon nightie that she's got on and see that she has pants on. I start pretending to myself that I am some depraved American gangster hunted for murder and sexually starved 'cause I've been living in the bush away from the law, eating wild berries. I just feel like a gangster holding up some lady that strayed into my bush kingdom only I don't have this beard that gangsters wear. I fold my face and bare my teeth imitating this gangster that killed three girls in one movie.

"Hello lady," I say gruffly. Gosh I feel like a gangster.

"What?" she asks, looking at me in surprise.

"Would you like a berry? I got some wild berries."

"What are you talking about, Dod?" I laugh gangster-fashion "Ho! ho!" and then get out of bed. I am all nude and my little man is standing out eight inches. I am terribly excited. I advance towards her like a lion stalking game and then I pounce, both hands on her shoulders.

"Let's see the colour of your skin lady. Strip. You have one second failing which I'll strangle you."

"Have you gone crazy. What sort of madman game is this? Are you really in your right mind?"

I don't answer her. Gangsters don't answer. They act and act fast. I can see that she's frightened. Maybe she thinks I've gone really potty. What I do is I grab the nightie by the neck and tear it right down the front to the hem. She screams and jumps away from me as a result of which the torn nightie is left in my hands. I throw it away. She stands there five feet away staring at me wildly. I pretend to be devilish myself and stare at her with wild maniacal eyes like I was really going to eat her. I advance again, madman-fashion, and she starts moving back. I think I've managed to scare her. She starts to say something but it doesn't come out. Her lips just quiver. I have my fingers spread out like a witch's talons and my lips pulled back right to the gums to give the impression of a skull. I am a real Dracula. I advance slowly but deliberately and she keeps stepping back. She's completely frightened now. I reckon she thinks I've gone real nuts and that I mean to strangle her. I am acting my part perfectly.

"Dod, please. Dod, what are you trying to do?" She's pleading. "What have I done? What has . . ." She doesn't finish. I pounce on her again and she lets out a stifled scream. I grab her pants and tear them completely off her as she tries to run away from my grip. She is now against the wall stark naked and terrified as hell. I have never been so excited before. I have never been able to frighten Tonia. Not before now. I have never been a master of the situation. Now I am a lion and she's a mere gazelle. She's trapped. She looks at my stiff man and gasps. There's something choking her. She looks at my wild eyes then at my man again; at my eyes and finaly at my man as I advance towards her. She can only edge sideways 'cause there is the wall behind her. I am between her and the bed and I am also moving sideways in a parallel line so that we are facing each other all the time. She beats me to it though. She edges to the door and with her hands behind her, she manages to turn the handle and before I realize, she has it open and is out like a light.

I dash out after her in the corridor and see her disappearing into the lounge. We'd put the lights off so I can't see clearly but luckily I hear her feet shuffling downstairs. I get to the head of the stairs and snap on the lights. She's at the bottom and I see her dash left towards the kitchen and I make the steps in fours. I am only ten feet from her as she opens the kitchen door. I make a terrific dash but she bangs the door on my face. Nearly flattened my nose, she did. Then ensues what you'd call a show of strength. Here I am forcing the door from the outside and she is pushing it shut from the inside. We are almost equally matched but I am more determined. I can hear her small cries as she pushes with all her might against me but in the end I am gaining ground. The door is now a foot open. I summon all my strength and give a final push. I crash in with the door.

Tonia has let go at the right moment so that my own force sends me stumbling and crashing on the other side of the kitchen. It hit my head against the kitchen cupboard and upset cans. It is quite a racket at three thirty in the morning. I collect myself quickly but then stand right where I am. Tonia has snapped on the lights and is standing by the cooker, a kitchen knife in her hand. She's trembling with exhaustion.

"If you touch me, you devil, I'll stab you. Try, I tell you." She is panting. She is out of breath. She looks very nice in the nude with a kitchen knife in her hand. She looks determined. I am sure that she means business. All of a sudden I feel terribly ashamed. What a bloody silly thing to be doing at three thirty in the morning? Suppose we had house servants and they witnessed the show — what would they think? I think I am a real madman.

What I do is I laugh. I laugh because I feel very foolish and also because my man has gone down anyway so it's no use to anybody right now. You can't rape nobody with a drooping prick. All of a sudden I feel bad. I feel bad because I had no goddam right to start such a madman's game and Tonia does not deserve to be treated this way. Oh, do I feel ashamed, I feel bad. I feel terribly apologetic. . really tupid.

"O.K." I tell her. "Let's cut it out. I am sorry. I really am sorry." She just stares at me with fright and hate. "I am sorry!" I shout.

"Sorry for what?" she snaps back.

"Sorry for all this."

"Sorry for all this what? What is this? What are you trying to do?"

"Nothing. I don't want to do anything anymore."

"But what are you sorry for? What did you want to do with me?"

"OK, forget it. Just a crazy idea." I tell her.

"It was a crazy idea, eh? Are you sure you are normal? You want to kill me. Why? What have I done."

"I don't want to kill you. How could I do such a thing. C'mon, let's go to bed. I really am sorry".

"Go to bed? Go to bed with you? You are mad and before you are put into an asylum I am not sleeping with you under the same roof. I can't share a house with a maniac."

"Oh come, come, you know I am not mad. I tell you I was merely . . ."

"I know. Just a crazy idea," she cuts me short. "So strangling me is just a crazy idea. That's what you want to do. You want to get rid of me so that you can be free with your young women. Do I stop you cohabiting with them? Just because I went out and came back at three you think you have rights over my life? I have the right to amuse myself as I please." She went on rattling endlessly accusing me of things I never did and saying she had rights to do anything with any man if it so pleased her. In the end I was damn angry but I was still apologetic. I called the tune so I get the music. I don't like it at all but I have to take it. I thought I was at the top but now I am right at the bottom again. My usual place.

"I am your husband!" I shout at her to make her shut up.

"You are a madman!" she shouts back. We both look silly standing all naked away from each other like enemies at war right here in our kitchen.

"OK, I am going to bed," I tell her.

"No, you are not. You are getting out of my house. I can't share a house with a madman. If you don't get out immediately, I am going to call the police."

"And what are you going to tell them?"

"Get out of my house!" she yells. My God. We shall wake up the neighbours. All of a sudden I become mad again. I decide that I was better off as a depraved American gangster trying to rape a chaste maiden instead of being a poor husband taking orders from a domineering wife. What I do is I get hold of a cooking pot and hold it like a shield and advance like a matador pretending that she was a charging cow. I tease her a little with the cooking pot keeping my distance but she doesn't move. I go as far as touching the knife with the pot but she doesn't strike. I feel terribly disappointed. She just stands there staring at me and allowing me to tease her with the pot.

"Charge, you cow. Charge!" I tease her. She doesn't; instead she drops the knife. She just stands there looking at me shaking her head. Then she laughs. She laughs heartily pointing at the pot so I hang it back on the hook. She is till laughing.

"Madman," she says and walks out of the place laughing. I contemplate over the situation, put off the lights and then move out too. I've never felt so foolish. Am I getting mad by any chance? Jesus, I think I am real nuts. What's all this nude-walking about? I crawl upstairs determined not to say a word more. I even decide to go and sleep in the spare bedroom only it scares me since she hanged herself there.

So what I finally do is I go to bed. Tonia has already sneaked in between the sheets and is facing the wall. I sneak in quietly and face the door. Our buttocks are touching. Tonia has very soft buttocks. Warm and soft. I pretend to snore and she bursts out laughing. I think she's mad too. It's infectious you know, madness. I can never imagine myself capable of such nonsense and at this hour of the night. Straight forward childish craziness.

"Shut up", I grunt and she pushes me with her buttocks in way of answer but still continues laughing.

"Dodge Kiunyu Esquire, ha—ha! Do you really know you are mad?" she says between bursts of laughter. "Madman -- that's what you are. Stark raving mad."

"Oh, shut up. I want to sleep."

"Ha, so you want to sleep. Who's been stopping you. . . me?"

"Leave me alone," I protest. She turns towards me violently.

"Leave you alone, you bastard. Who has been hounding me since I got into the house. Who's been mad, me or you?" I refuse to answer. I just turn on my belly and bury my face into the pillow. I am terribly ashamed of my behaviour tonight. I really am. So unbelievingly stupid.

"So you are not talking to me," she hisses grabbing my hair and twisting my head so hard that I am forced from my belly to my back. She's hurting me and somehow I like it. I am paying for my sins. What I do is, I say nothing. I just close my eyes with pain. Tonia is now sitting up in bed. She is banging my head on the pillow furiously.

"So you are sleepy, eh? You are not talking anymore. Oh, you beast." She bangs my head on the pillow more violently and I can see that she is working herself up into a terrific rage. God. She slaps me. She is slapping me again. I have to stop this. Must protect my face. I am struggling to ward off the blows and she grabs at my hands furously, gets onto her knees and then sits astride my stomach, pinning my hands down at the back of my head. She is fuming into my face. I am not struggling now. Somehow I'd like her to hurt me if by so doing she'll forgive me.

"What is the meaning of all this tonight?" she asks breathlessly. "Have you gone nuts? You should see a doctor. I shall see to that."

"I am sorry," I say at last. "Please I am sorry. Let us forget it. Just a mad game. Forget it."

"Forget it, eh? What got into your head in the first instance? First you sleep on the couch. When I wake you up you become snorty for nothing. When I go to the bathroom you follow me there and when I come from the bathroom you tear my clothes and threaten to strangle me. What got into your head in the first place?"

"I don't know. Let us sleep. I am sorry."

"No. We are not going to sleep. You are going to tell me why." Gosh! What does she think, sitting on my stomach and breathing fire.

"Get off me," I tell her and at the same time raise myself to throw her off. She gets off balance and then moves her legs backwards so that she is practically lying on me whole length. She brings her face close to mine and the hardness on her face starts to thaw into some softness and motherliness. She is still holding me down by the hands so that the tips of her firm unsuckled tits are just about touching the tips of my manly tits. She wiggles her buttocks downwards so that our bodies become an entangled fit.

"Tell me, Dod," she says staring me right in the eyes. I have my mouth open but I haven't got the words. She wiggles some more astride my legs rubbing my dead little man with her shaved mount. I can't believe it. It's all madness.

"Tell me, Dod" she whispers. "Tell me." She's working herself up into a different kind of anger. She is rubbing against me furiously now. She lets go my hands so that her warm breasts spread neatly on my manly tits and then grabs my hair.

"Tell me Dod," she hisses from the inside her and when I say nothing she starts bouncing my head again with a different kind of frenzy. I think she's mad. She's rubbing herself against me so hard that it actually hurts. She's hurting my man. He has shrunk right into the balls. She is not looking at me anymore. She has her eyes closed, banging my head and rubbing herself against me completely oblivious of my presence. She is in her own world. I am starting to get annoyed with my man. At least he should come up a little in appreciation but he doesn't. Stupid bastard.

"Tell me, Dod," she utters with a groan. "Tell me, Dod."

I grab her hands and free my hair 'cause it's not honey being bounced even in ecstasy. She supports herself on the left elbow and moves her right hand down my body till she touches my man. He's dead beyond recovery. He's gone right back into the stomach. She's trying to pull him out of the hiding place but she's too excited to be gentle. She's hurting me. Jesus! This is madness with a difference. I can't stand it anymore. Her nails are sharp.

"Please, you are hurting me. Oh, please — not so rough," but she doesn't hear me. She's not listening to me. She can't hear me. She is deaf. She is in her own world. I let out a loud howl 'cause her nails get in the wrong place and she cries out.

"You beast. I'll hurt you. I'll rape you. Get your thing up, you beast. Get it up, you hear me — I say get it up!" God, the way she is manhandling me. This is a real war. Before I realise what is happening, she's got off me, turned round on her side and has my man right in her mouth. Sweet Jesus. I am crying.

Then all of a sudden she lets go, turns over quickly and sits right on me encasing my man with her woman. What warmth! Just like before, she grabs my hair and starts banging me again. What devilish business is this? She is muttering as she screws away. Along crazy screw. My life erupts out of me like a volcano and the lava fills the crater and spreads all along the slopes of the mount. A viscous river of hot lava supplemented by the natural waters of crater lakes filling the valleys and the crevices and overflowing the banks to flood the forests. What a volcanic eruption.

Tonia lies lifeless and mute all along my body. She's giving me little kisses. I feel so good that all of a sudden I start crying. I don't know where the tears come from but I start sobbing. What a silly thing. I just hold her there on top of me and cry. She is caressing me softly.

"What is the matter, Dod?" she whispers.

"I don't know."

"But why are you crying?"

"I tell you I don't know. I am just overwhelmed."

She gives me a little kiss and then dries my eyes with tissue paper.

"Dod."

"Yes"

"Please, Dod. I . . . I needed it badly. I can't have enough. You punished me for too long."

"I missed it too. I was pretending I didn't."

"I am yours, Dod."

"I am yours too." That's the way I feel right now.
"You will not abandon me again?"
"No."
"Why are you crying?"
"I think it's because I love you."
"You do?"
"I think I do. I don't understand myself. I don't know."
"You didn't want to hurt me tonight?"
"No. I wanted to rape you."
"Oh Dod, why didn't you ask me? Please have me again."
"Yes".
"You will not let me down again."
"I'll try not to."
"You'll try hard?"
"Yes. I'll try very hard."
"Is it true about the girls?"
"Of course not. I was trying to annoy you." That's of course a lie.
"You mean there were no women?"
"No. How could I. You are my life."
"Oh, Dod. I am so glad. Oh, God. You suffered like me?"
"I suffered more because I pretended more."
"Why then did you allow me to be nasty to you?"
"To amuse myself. I thought it pleased you to be nasty."
"Oh, Dod. That was beastly."

So what we did was we made love till dawn. I saw the grey rays of the morning sun before my eyes closed in sweet slumber. The only thought before the heavy hand of sleep put its pressure on me was that I was happy. I was happy we were reconciled in love again — or was it sex? Both I suppose. In any case I'd quit the dark alleys of making easy black money and was going to take up a regular respectable job so I might as well start respectability at home. Any respectable job goes with some sort of respectability at home. What did it matter anyway if I didn't take the old girfriends out. What did I get from them anyway? Just an occasional screw in a hotel room or in the car or in the golf course. Why spend money on them girls who don't even give it to you when you want but when they want or when they want to reduce the weight of your purse. I think I'll start consolidating myself. I have to try and make Tonia happy. Damn it, she's my wife and there is nothing wrong about adopting children. I think I'll adopt a child. A boy.

FOUR

Wednesday Morning

"I can't have slept for one hour when the goddam alarm clock explodes. Stupid clock. She should have remembered to put it off. Both our hands reach out for it simultaneously without opening our eyes as a result of which Tonia's hand hits mine and mine hits the clock. It drops on the carpet and continues ringing. It's on my side of the bed so I lean out pick it and stop it. As I put it back at the usual place I squeeze it with vengeance and hope that it will break. It doesn't.

It's Wednesday morning and Tonia is still off-duty. She however tells me that she'll go to the office at eleven to check on mail and we continue sleeping till the damn phone rings. It's another unwelcome explosion. Gosh, it's eleven o'clock. I pick up the phone and growl, "Hello". I don't care for phone calls on this particular morning. I am angry.

"Hello, is that you Dod?" the voice on the other side says. "Are you alone?" God, I nearly have a fit. Jesus, it's Khimji's sister. It's Sheila. I think quickly and pretend that I am talking to a man. I say, "Hey man, the answer is no. Maybe in an hour's time. Ring me after an hour. You understand?" I hear a whisper on the other side say "Yes, Dod. I am sorry." I hang up and cover myself again. I need more sleep.

"Who was it, Dod?" Tonia asks

"An invitation for a drink," I tell her.

"Who's inviting you?"

'Claude."

"You'll go?"

"Not just yet, but he owes me money. I've to collect it at least."

"Oh my God. It's eleven already. I'll just go in and see what is happening and I'll be right back. You'll be waiting. . . or are you going to meet Claude earlier than I get back?"

"I'll nip off and see Claude. Can't trust him not to drink his whole wad before I get there."

"At least you'll be home for lunch, I suppose. I want to make you lunch."

"And I'll eat it."

"Promise?"

"Promise."

She gets out of bed and goes to the bathroom. I cover myself and go back to sleep. I am feeling lazy. Very Lazy. I am also wondering what Sheila had to tell me. We are quits and she has no right telephoning except that she expected I'd be alone if I was at home 'cause she couldn't possibly know that Tonia was off-duty. I am wondering about it all when Tonia comes from the bathroom, dresses hastily and waltzes out of the room. I close my eyes and ask God to send me a small doze of sleep 'cause I want to sleep for another thirty minutes — or maybe I should go down to the kitchen and make myself some breakfast. Heck, I think I'll have a little shut-eye.

It's eleven thirty when the phone rings like an alarm clock. I nearly jump out of bed 'cause I've been having this dream where we are having a flying competition Tonia and I. We have wings and all and are flying above trees when this big vampire bat with a beak like the needle of a huge syringe starts flying alongside us, grabs me by my wings so that I can't flap them and then digs its syphoning-needle beak into my right buttock and proceeds to suck my blood. On seeing the bat, Tonia forgets that she is flying and thereby starts to fall. She's falling like a sack, twisting and turning all the way and the bat's needle beak is well planted into my buttock and I am screaming the hell out of my lungs when the damn phone rings. It rings just as Tonia is hitting the ground.

I grab the phone and say, "Hello, Kiunyu's residence."

"Hey, Dod. It's Sheila. Are you alone now?"

"Yeah, how are you, Sheila. It's been a long time."

"Yes it has. Was Mrs. Kiunyu in the house when I called first time? I felt sure she was, from the way you replied."

"Yeah. She was right there. She could have picked the phone."

"Listen. Can you come and meet me this afternoon at three? I want to talk to you."

"Meet you where and what do you want to talk to me about?"

"I can't explain everything now. I'll just give you the highlights."

"O.K. just brief indications. At least you have to tell me where to meet you."

"At the Rex Hotel." She whispers.

"But what is it all about?"

"About you."

"What about me?"

"What did you tell Khimji about us?"

"I didn't tell him anything. I denied everything."

"He said you told the police right in front of him. He knows everything. He told me so. He even knows about the abortion."

"He is bluffing. How could he know?"

"From the Doctor. You gave him a personal cheque. Khimji got to know by accident. The doctor did not know that Khimji was my brother."

"Oh come, come. The Doctor only knows that a chap called Kiunyu paid for his services on your behalf. What else could he know?"

"They were at a party last night in the house of one of his friends where the Doctor was also invited. The Doctor was talking of a bastard African boy called Kiunyu who got an Indian girl drunk and then got her pregnant. Khimji put two and two together and got four."

"I still don't get it. You gave the Doctor a false name and a false address. I know that I am the only Kiunyu around here but there are many Indian girls in Mombasa so it doesn't have to be you. It could be any Indian girl."

"I know. You are right, Dod, except that Khimji didn't ask me as such. He got me out of bed when I was very sleepy, tired and generally fuddled and proceeded to accuse me of sleeping with you. Said that he knew it directly from your lips and confirmed it with the Doctor who conducted the abortion. Oh, he insulted me terribly. I had nothing to say. He knew everything including the fact that we were doing it during morning hours in a hotel. I just went to bed and cried."

"Oh God! You should have blasted him. He knew nothing."

"I blasted him this morning but I didn't deny anything. I told him that I was free to do anything I pleased and had the right to conduct my life anyway it pleased me."

"God. How did he react to that?"

"He has already negotiated a husband for me — some son of a rich Kisumu businessman who is completing his graduate studies in Bombay this year, so you can reckon he was terribly upset. He slapped me."

"Do you want to marry the chap?"

"I don't know him. I don't even have his photograph. I sometimes hate being an Indian. I hate my people. I hate the whole community. I want to run away, Dod. I can't live under the same roof with my brother. He'll kill me with shame ten times a day."

"Oh, no. Don't be too hasty. He's your brother. He. . ."

"No, Dod. To me he is more repulsive than a gorgon. I don't want to see him. I can't . . . hey, Dod, there's somebody coming."

"What other thing did you want to talk to me about?"

"About you, Dod," she whispers. "Khimji means to do you harm. He was swearing about how he'll see you. . ." Silence. I hear a door open on her side of the phone and then Sheila's different voice comes on the phone. She's talking lightly in an excited voice. "Oh, no. I prefer the blue sari. Oh, yes. Not four. I said three. Ah yes, I know. That's Mrs. Shah's favourite. Sure. I wouldn't fail. What? OK, don't fail, bye—bye," and then she hangs up. I guess that somebody burst in when she was talking to me and she had to put on an act. I hang up and wonder what sort of harm Khimji is planning for me. I can't get the chap out of my mind. You don't know him. He's damn persistent. That's his number one fault. Anyway, what it boils down to is that I have to go to the Rex and meet Sheila so that I can get more insights into his plans. I don't like it. Right now I don't want to meet a woman. Not after my promise to Tonia and in anycase not at the Rex. The goddam hotel is right in town.

I get out of bed, run to the bathroom and come out in ten minutes. I dress in exactly five minutes, run down to the kitchen, open a can of pineaple juice, drink it in a mug, light a cigarette and get the hell out of the house.

With all this new love I am feeling for Tonia, I decide that the first thing I have to do is have a heart to heart talk with Dr. Kihagi about Tonia's condition. The fellow was in my house last night drinking my whisky so I don't see why I shouldn't exploit the situation by pretending that we are friends. I have to know the truth about the hanging business or epilepsy or both 'cause when a woman starts hanging herself the husband should have a jolly good indication as to why.

I drive to the hospital and Julian tells me that Dr. Kihagi is at home so after I get directions I drive there. I find him sitting on the verandah in pyjamas and decide that even busy doctors have plenty of time to take it easy sometime. He should be at the hospital.

I say "hi" and he says "hi" and asks me to sit down. He looks sorta surprised to see me around his joint in the morning. He asks whether I'll have tea and I say no.

"What can I do for you?" he asks. I tell him that I've been to the hospital looking for him and that Julian advised me that he was home and that I was personally OK, healthwise and so was Tonia and that my only little worry was about the hanging or epilepsy thing that happened to Tonia and would he, as a good doctor and friend, help by giving me broad indications about the root of the problem.

"There was a medical report", he tells me. "Didn't you have the chance to look at it?"

"I know what the report says but I have no reason to believe it."

"Then you are knocking at the wrong door my friend. I made that report you know."

"I know, but it was intended for the police and not for me."

"I am sorry I have nothing to add."

I decide to be nice and plead with him and after a good ten minutes, and after promising him two bottles of whisky which I can buy duty-free from my naval friends, he starts to open up. The language he is using is however much too technical for me to understand and I can see that he is laughing inside because he knows jolly well that I do not understand. What it all boils down to finally is that the Tonia I know did not hang herself. The Tonia who hanged herself was a different Tonia. It's all bullshit of course; absolute nonsense but its what he is trying to convince me about. When I tell him that he shouldn't give me any moon stuff in the morning of a bright day like today he gets angry and tells me that he has nothing more to add.

"How can you possibly understand such a situation?" he asks mockingly. "I am trying to explain to you a phenomena where the conscious brain is not in control of physical actions and where the unconscious is so deep that vital links are broken so that the subject cannot be accused of being consciously responsible for such actions. We are talking of a mental void where the links are broken but without causing a vaccum. A phenomena that could be triggered by circumstances that are higher in realm than the ordinary observable causes such as deep seated depressions or tensions, shocks, brain illness or damage or acute mental disturbance. I am sure you understand. Just imagine a fractional bifurcation of a momentary but deeply unconscious schizophrenic tendency, occasioned by remote auto-suggestion which is itself triggered by external phenomena from the higher realms in a situation where brain links are broken, and you will agree with me that Tonia cannot be accused of hanging herself. That is why that aspect did not feature in my report. It is not the same Tonia."

I give up. I feel convinced that he himself doesn't understand what he is talking about and that he is just as good as telling me to get the hell out of the place. What he is saying doesn't even make English sense. When I ask him whether Tonia is likely to hang herself again because of phenomena et cetera, he starts all over again! So what I do is, I get up and excuse myself.

"But do you understand?" he asks.

"Perfectly," I tell him.

"Now that you are here, there's something I wanted to talk to you about. We were discussing things with Tonia and Julian last night and there was a general concensus that you may want to adopt a child. That would make Tonia very happy. It would give her sound reason to want to live and I feel certain that if there was a child around the house she wouldn't have tried to take her life. It's the only fool-proof way of making sure that there is no repeat of . . . you know the phenomena I am talking about."

"This time, I understand you very well doctor. It's however a matter between me and Tonia and none of your phenomena business. If however I should need any advice on the matter I can assure you that you'll be the first person I'll consult."

"How about the whisky — would it be available tonight?"

"Most likely. I will buzz you later and let you know."

I note down his telephone number and disappear from the scene. What a blinking blighter. God is great. He can create any kind of creature that he feels like creating. Some people were created when he was really tired. What a boring fellow — Dr. Kihagi, I mean. He is a real phenomena. Trouble is I am not very much wiser than when I started, so if Dr. Kihagi thinks that I am going to buy him two bottles of whisky for telling me shit, then he must think that I am a real bum.

I hit Nyerere Avenue in half a minute, turn right and then drive to the Bristol Bar. It is the sort of joint you go to when you want a noisy drink. They have a snooker table in a separate room but it is usually monopolised by Indians. The main bar is fairly international with sailors from all corners of the world and prostitutes from as far away as Mogadishu and Kampala. It's a very nice place for a noisy drink. What I want is just two cold beers and then I have to dash to the supermarket for groceries.

What I do is, I don't ask for a drink straightaway. I move to the telephone coin-box and give Ben Mwaura a ring. Whenever you telephone in this joint you have to shout because of the noise, but folks are never interested in whatever you are saying. You are simply adding to noise. Ben picks up the phone almost immediately with a drowsy, "Hello... Mwaura here."

"Hi, Ben. This is Dodge. How are things?"

"Lousy," he answers.

"Because your secretary is not in; the phone came to you direct."

"Look man, I can run my office without your comments. As for my secretary, you can screw her right now if you go to the hospital where she is admitted following an unsuccesful abortion. I am sure you'd love it."

"I am sorry, Ben. I understand. Too bad for you. Hey, tell me. The *Athenia,* did it sail away on schedule?"

"No, Dodge. It's sailing off this afternoon. Why do you want to know? I thought you quit that business man. At least that's what you told me."

"Sure, Ben. I quit. I was merely asking for this sake of interest. I have some friends on board."

"Well, you have your chance. The ship is still here."

"Thanks, Ben. Thanks a lot. Meet you one of these days for a little booze. Ciao," and I hang up. I put in some more coins and ring up Claude. I merely want to tell him that I am supposed to be having a drink with him but I don't get him. I move over to the counter, take a stool and ask for a beer. I want to swallow two and then go home for lunch. I promised Tonia. There are all sorts of guys in the bar but they don't interest me. They are mostly sailors and I can never really get to like sailors. There is something of the prostitute in all of them.

I drink the beer quickly because I am in a bad mood and also because I am hungry. I know that Tonia is going to make a special lunch after which I know she'll insist on a small siesta. She is not a beach goer. Weekends are always a bother for her unless she's having a meeting or a tea with the *Maendeleo ya Wanawake* women. She didn't mention anything of the kind so I reckon that this is one of her weekends at home. What I can't figure out is how I'll excuse myself to go and meet Sheila. I have to tell a convincing lie 'cause she's a very good detector of lies. The sad thing is that I don't want to tell her a lie. I don't even want to leave her to go and meet Sheila. No. I want to be with her. I want to be with her right there in bed. That's the way I feel right now. Funny. My man is even starting to dance at the thought of it. Stupid little man. How can he start dancing in public at the thought of having it with Tonia? Absurd. It's absurd even though we've been sexual strangers for months.

I cross my legs and wonder what to do with Sheila. I will most certainly not give her the thing. I would feel awful. It would be very dishonest now. I couldn't possibly do it. Oh! I know I will be terribly tempted. She's really sexy with these big, limpid, parrot-type, round eyes that speak to themselves when they want to speak to you and these virgin tits that you are afraid to touch for fear of being electrified. What excites me most about her is that she gets so carried away during the act that she comes spontaneously with a flood of tears and she cries like someone who is really being tortured. She goes on weeping for quite sometime even after the fire-works are over. That just about kills me. No kidding. It gives me real manly satisfaction to see those large-round-talking eyes ooze out wet love tears. Makes me feel like a real man. Anyway, it's all over now. No more love tears for me. Tonia needs me and I think I'll give it to her till our next serious quarrel.

I gulp my second beer, ask for the bill, give the barman ten shillings and as he hands me the change a heavy strong hand is placed on my shoulder from behind and the change drops on the counter. I turn back slowly and lo! I nearly piss on myself. That heavy hand on my shoulder squeezing me very hard but effortlessly is the hand of Asparagus.

Yanis is by his side and is looking at me like something the cat brought in. My mouth is open and my eyes are open and I even think that my ass is open. I could easily shit on myself. What a jolt! Asparagus long thick Greek fingers are massaging my shoulders blade seemingly softly but in reality very painfully. He is wearing a knowing mischievous and satanic smile. He looks innocent.

"Hello, Dodge," he says putting his other hand on my other shoulder and caressing me in a most painful manner. "How are you, Dodge." He is fixing me to the stool so that I can't get up while at the same time wearing this innocent smile so that nobody but me in the whole place knows what he is doing. God! He could have strangled me and nobody would have noticed anything peculiar or odd about the way he was kneading my shoulders around the neck. Clever bastard.

What I do is I decide that there's going to be no peace around here and that whichever way the war develops I am going to be the loser. These chaps are supposed to be getting out of port to-day and know damn well that all they can do is hurt me just to let off steam. What I do is I decide to fall off my stool 'cause it's the only way I can get off with Asparagus' hand pressing me down painfully and pinning me to the goddam stool. What I do is I let out some yell like a wrestler and at the same time shove back with my elbow and dig it right into the asparagus ribs. He lets out a painful laugh as I fall backwards between his legs and hit the ground with my shoulders. I throw a wild kick in the direction of his face but only manage to touch his chest. That was a very stupid thing to do 'cause I am practically under him and all he has to do is put his heavy boot somewhere on my groin but he doesn't. He lets me scram onto my feet and as I straighten out, he grabs me like a leaf and then drops me on his knee. That just about breaks my backbone so that when he picks me up again, pushes me a little way with his left palm and then rams ten tons of his right fist onto my jaw no part of my system is capable of lifting a finger. I remember the impact. It was ten times worse than a horse's kick. That's all I remember though; that impact. As I hit the floor I was already gone. The floor was like a cushion. Something unconsciously more welcome than the ten horses. I passed out outright into a dead swoon so I didn't even have time to curse before I was stretched. Damn all Greeks and their Asparagus.

Wednesday Afternoon

My head is beating a distant tom-tom and my eyelids weigh ten tons. There are bees on my back and my lower jaw feels like nothing I know 'cause it doesn't feel like my jaw at all. There are hands all over me supporting me but my knees are like jelly. I am conscious of being dragged onto my feet but it is a very far away feeling. It is as if I am being dragged by people who are a mile away. I am conscious of being shoved into a car which drives off with the sound of a very distant police siren some ten miles away coming to my ears. The siren is in rhythm with the tom-tom in my head. The sound grows fainter and fainter and I reckon I loose consciousness. When I try to open my eyes again, they actually open and I see doctor Kihagi standing over me. I am on a hospital bed and the tom-tom in my head is hardly audible. It's very far away. Almost gone.

I survey the surroundings and notice that I am not in any ward but rather in the doctor's examination room. That's where I am lying on his narrow bed. Julian and my old police friend Charles Masakalia are conversing in undertones a few feet from the foot of the bed. I close my eyes and try to talk to my brain. I am trying to recollect all the circumstances leading to my being here and it all comes back to me when I caress my jaw. It all comes back to me till the time I hit the floor in the blasted Bristol Bar.

"Looks like you are fully awake, Mr Kiunyu. How do you feel?" Doctor Kihagi asks me. I open my eyes but I can't open my jaw. I feel as if the lower and the upper jaw have been glued up somewhere right inside the mouth, behind the molars. I feel pain right at the back of the head when I try to open my mouth, so what I do is, I just nod my head.

"You'll be glad to know that you didn't sustain a fracture of the jaw, Mr. Kiunyu," the doctor says, "but you have an internal bruise". I wink my left eye with a slight nod to indicate that I understand. "It isn't anything really serious. It will cure itself normally. You should do fine with just a few pills to kill pain. Will you please try to open mouth?"

Masakalia and Julian move nearer as I struggle with my jaw. I try but completely fail to open my mouth. Doctor Kihagi puts his right hand on my lower jaw and his left hand over my face and then moves my jaw laterally from left to right causing me a lot of sharp pain. I let out a howl and he lets go.

"Did that hurt?" he asks.

"Terribly", I tell him.

"At least you can move your jaw now," he says smiling.

"Just as well doctor," Masakalia says," 'cause I have a few questions for which I'd like some answers. Is he fit to go home?" he asks.

"Sure," the doctor says. "He's discharged".

"When can I have the medical report?" Masakalia asks. "Can I have it right away? Mr. Kiunyu is coming with me to the police station. He has a complaint to make."

"But, of course. It isn't much of a report, as you are aware."

"It doesn't matter. A simple report is okay by me so long as it indicates that Mr. Kiunyu has a smashed jaw resulting from a fist fight." The doctor and the inspector walk out to the doctor's office and Julian comes to the head of the bed. I sit up and meet her stare.

"What happened?" she asks me. I don't feel like telling her anything incriminating, so I simply tell her that some drunken sailor chap hit me 'cause I sat on his bar stool when he was in the toilet.

"But the inspector was talking of a Greek captain."

"Oh, he did? I didn't know that the chap was a captain. Anyway, a captain is a sailor, isn't he?"

"Not exactly. They arrested the fellow."

"Oh, my God, so they did, eh? That's interesting."

"But the fellow nearly broke your jaw, why shouldn't he be arrested?"

"Of course he should be arrested," I tell her. She looks at her watch and opens her eyes wide.

"Good God" she exclaims. "It's ten after one. I should have been home hours ago. Can you drive me home?"

"I don't have my car."

"Of course, I forgot. I'll be on my way," and she walks out. I also walk out and wait for Masakalia, leaning against his car. He in turn comes out folding a piece of paper which he shoves into his jumper pocket. I feel bad because I know that Julian will recount everything to Tonia so I can't cover it up.

"OK, Dodge. We are going to the police station. You have a long story to tell me," Masakalia says. "I told you that I'll get you one of these days and I got you now. Breach of public peace — that's what I am charging you with. You fought in a public place."

"I didn't fight anybody, my dear Charles, I was clobbered. The chap just got in and gave it to me before I knew what was happening. I had nothing to do with the whole thing."

"I know. I got eye witnesses to testify to that fact but I am charging you all the same. How do you explain to a court of law that a chap just walked into a public place and smashed you on the jaw? It's simple. You simply carried an old private quarrel into a public place and thereby disturbed public peace. It's immaterial to me whether the chap hit you or you hit him. I got your Greek friend locked up on the same charge and I am going to lock you up too."

"You got to be kidding," I tell him.

"On the contrary, no. You are under arrest, Mr. Kiunyu."

"Oh no. But you can't . . ."

"Yes I can", he cuts me short. "Hop into the car".

We drive to the police station and Masakalia leads me to his private office where I make a statement. I tell the whole story as it happened but I don't seem to impress him about my innocence. He already knows that but he says that in his opinion, my innocence is not important. I try to remind him of this little bribe I gave him last night and that we are now friends et cetera, but instead he threatens to double my charge and warns me sternly about repeating old untrue stories. I imagine that he is kidding all along, till he presses a buzzer and two tough policemen walk in and he asks them to escort me to the cell. I am flabbergasted!

"But, Mr. Masakalia, you have no right to have me locked up. That is not the law. God. You haven't even charged me and even when you've charged me, I should be able to go out on bond".

"I know, Mr. Kiunyu. We are still investigating."

"You are not investigating. You are taking the law in your own hands. You are acting unlawfully."

"Take him in", he tells the two cops, and I am hustled out of the office into the basement of the police station where the cells are located. I curse like hell but when this big cop asks me whether I'd like my jaw smashed again, I shut up. I can't believe it. I can't believe that Masakalia can act in such an unlawful manner. I thought the bastard was now a friend. I thought we were friends of some sort 'cause he knows my crimes and I know his crimes. Damn, damn. How do you explain it? Gosh, the law in this country is no longer lawful. These police bastards can do anything they please. I am going to sue them. I am going to sue them for unlawful detention, but maybe I shouldn't. They might frame me thereafter on ten crimes I never committed. The bastards. How I hate cops.

I am locked into a dark cell that smells of stale urine. The only light is through a small hole in the door, dim and filtering from the corridor. God. What have I done to deserve this? Tonia is waiting for me for lunch and Sheila will be expecting me at the Rex at three. On top of all that, my car is abandoned outside the Bristol Bar and the bastards wouldn't even allow me to telephone my house. And what am I supposed to be doing in this goddam cell? Do I just keep standing or do I sit down, or do I lie on the hard cold cement? For how long am I going to be here? Damn, damn the cops. Damn the whole goddam cop tribe. I feel like strangling the whole blasted lot of them.

I am in the cell for uncountable hours when the big cop who esorted me in looks in through the hole in the door and coughs hoarsely. He then inserts a key in the door, pushes it open and asks me to follow him. He leads me to a room where his friend is sitting on a hard chair behind a worn out table and closes the door. He smiles at me and says, "Mr. Kiunyu, you are in big trouble."

"Go on", I tell him. I feel very angry. I look at my watch and notice that it's twenty to two. I'd only been in the cell for a matter of less than thirty minutes but it felt like thirty hours.

"Mr. Masakalia has gone for lunch," he tells me.

"Very natural," I tell him. "As a matter of fact, I need mine."

"Mr. Masakalia is not coming back after lunch. He is going to Nairobi. He will be back day after tomorrow."

"Oh, no. Are you trying to tell me that I am going to be in the cell till his return?" I feel like murder.

"Yes."

"What, in the name of all that opens and shuts, do you fellows think you are doing. How can you lock me up for nothing for two days? God! You are the biggest rogues from Mombasa to Kisumu and I am going to sue you like you have never been sued before. This is outrageous."

"Mr. Kiunyu, all we do is obey orders. Mr. Masakalia said to lock you up. The reasons are his own and not ours."

"So what did you get me out here for?" I ask angrily.

"To know whether you want to stay."

"What?"

"You see, Mr. Kiunyu, it's like this: we have nothing against you and we know that your being locked up is for the boss's personal reasons. As far as we are concerned, you can go out and enjoy yourself so long as you come back day after tomorrow before he comes back."

"Say that again." I can hardly believe my ears.

"I said it already," he tells me.

"But why should I come back at all, and why shouldn't you get sacked?"

"We'll do it like gentlemen. You just give two hundred shillings which we'll share equally and we let you out on your word of honour with a solemn promise that you'll be back here on Friday by eleven o'clock. If you are not back, we can, of course, come and fetch you."

"And how do you know that I wouldn't disappear and go up-country. How can you take such a risk?"

"If you pay two hundred shillings and swear on your honour that you'll be here on Friday, we are prepared to take the risk."

"Do you realize that this is corruption at its worst; at its cheapest level? How can you officers of the law set me free against your boss's' orders, and against your better judgement, just because of a few shillings? Do you realize the gravity of your proposition? You can't do such a thing. You represent the law."

"So don't teach us the law. Will you pay the two hundred shillings or will you stay in?"

"I will stay in," I tell him. "That will give me grounds to sue the whole lot of you. I shall, in the meantime, tell Mr. Masakalia of your proposition when he comes back on Friday. I still can't believe it."

"You dare do a thing like that and I'll break your neck," the big policeman warns me sternly. "We know you have already bribed Masakalia and we also know that he doesn't take hundreds. He takes thousands and he just received some from your Greek friends before he let them go. They had to get out of port and had to pay dear because every minute of their time counted. They are Greeks and they have gone. You are our brother and we are prepared to let you go for just two hundred. We are being kind. You are ruining it all. If you can bribe Masakalia who earns many times more than any of us, why can't you give us something small? Why?"

"But you'll get sacked. If he ever gets to know, you'll get the axe."

"And who is going to tell him?"

"Suppose I should die in my sleep to-night, how would you ever explain how I got there?"

"Leave that to us. Just give us two hundred bob. Everybody has to eat. Masakalia hasn't the family I have and if my children were dying of hunger, he wouldn't come to my rescue even if it was with bribe money that he never earned. How do you think I manage to feed a family of six children on a salary of three hundred shillings a month? Just tell me that, Mr. Kiunyu."

"It's none of my business how you feed your children. I am certain that you do not expect me to feed them for you. You are a man. On the question of two hundred shillings, I refuse. I get nothing for it but two risky days of freedom, while you earn one hundred shillings each in one day which you would normally earn in ten days. Two hundred shillings is too much. I could consider a hundred... fifty each."

"No, that's too small."

"Okay. I am prepared to stay in the cell until Friday". The truth of the matter is, I don't. I don't want to stay in the cell for one more minute but I am merely trying to beat down the price 'cause I can see that these chaps are in real need of some cash. In any case, when I get out, I do not intend to come in again on Friday. That would be condoning corruption. I'll be damned if I'll walk voluntarily into a police cell. They look at each other and the smaller one says, "We'll let you have twenty shillings for petrol so that leaves one hundred and eighty shillings. That's the limit." I decide I am on safe grounds, so I tell him flatly, "You accept one hundred shillings or you put me back into the cell."

"What is eighty shillings to you, Mr. Kiunyu, when you can give one thousand to Masakalia at the snap of his little finger? Pay us one eighty. It is fair."

"I said one hundred and not a penny more. We are wasting time."

"All right," the big one says. "No need pushing you. One hundred is too small but as you say, we are wasting time. But tell me, Mr. Kiunyu, would you pay two hundred if you didn't have to come back on Friday?"

"What do you mean?"

"Its like this, we destroy everything — tear up your statement et cetera, so there would be no record whatsoever. Would you pay two hundred?"

"Can you do that?" I ask him.

"Leave everything to us."

"But what about your boss? You'd lose your jobs."

"It can be arranged. Just leave it to us."

"I give up. Anything you say. Only one thing. If you should then re-arrest me or play any dirty game, I am going to parliament to complain. I'll sue the whole goddam police force."

"You said that before, Mr. Kiunyu. The deal is concluded. Two hundred and no more nonsense. Just cough it up, will you?"

"And you have to keep that bastard boss of yours out of my hair otherwise I'll expose you."

"Come, come, Mr. Kiunyu. Out with the money. You need not worry and don't think about exposure. The big law protectors have no ears for your type of complaint. They are the worst thieves."

"Oh, I see. So you accept that you are a smaller thief?"

"What do you want me to do with six children. You are being ridiculous. Who is the biggest thief in this country? Is it me? No. The biggest man is the biggest thief. We are just collecting crumbs and for that I could be sacrificed any day. Man, don't walk around with your eyes shut. I'll never be able to amass enough to buy a small farm in my life, but the big fish will have several large farms and several hotels and what have you. All I want is to feed my children."

"Do you think that I am one of those big fish? Why don't you extort your food from them?"

"OK, you are not a big fish. You are just a small time thief and we don't even arrest you for it. What are you complaining about?"

I pay them two hundred shillings and they show me the way out. As I go out, I expect them to re-arrest me but they don't. The whole set-up looks absolutely cock-eyed. I get out of the place and head for Bristol Bar to collect my car. It is not a long walk but the afternoon sun is raining down on my head and I am sweating profusely. Mombasa can be terribly hot and humid when it wants to be. This is one of the afternoons when it wants to be. I get to the Bristol Bar in fifteen minutes and right there inspecting my car, is Masakalia's assistant — I mean this chap who was taking measurements in our spare bedroom where Tonia hanged herself. I get a momentary fright 'cause I reckon that he is going to re-arrest me and I start cursing the whole police force under my breath. I hate them.

"Ah, I was waiting for you, Mr. Kiunyu. Thought I'd keep an eye on your bus while getting myself a drink. The boss is gone." I look at him and decide that I don't know what to think. Those cops back there at the police station had said the same thing. "The boss is gone." So what the heck did it matter to me whether he was gone or dead.

"You took a long time coming," he adds. "I've already had two beers." I feel bewildered. I just stare at him and shrug my shoulders.

"So?"

"Well, I was waiting, hoping to catch you when you got here. Thought I could touch you for a drink for services rendered." I was completely bewildered.

"How did you know that I was going to get here? What services are you talking about?"

"Well, of course, you wouldn't know but I am the one that prevailed over Masakalia to set you free. In a way, yes. I mean, he only intended to have you in until six and then release you after a bit of discomfort, but I am the one that prevailed on him to release you immediately. I personally telephoned the police station from his house and asked them to release you immediately and unconditionally, and I instructed them to tell you to meet me here. I was wondering what was keeping you so long." I scratch my head and decide that everybody is trying to use me. I've never heard such stuff before. I don't even know what to think. I can't believe anything.

"Are you trying to tell me that Masakalia gave instructions that I should be released and that you communicated those instructions to your constables at the police station, and that I am officially released, and that you were merely waiting for me for a drink? Is that what you are saying?"

"What is wrong with that? How else would you explain the circumstances?"

"Why was I arrested in the first instance?"

"Don't ask me. I wasn't there. All I know is that — and please don't quote me — Masakalia wanted to give you a small lesson. You are always involving the police in one thing or other, so why shouldn't you taste a bit of their hospitality? That is the way Masakalia explained it."

"I see. Now I see a lot. You are a miserable lot, the whole lot of you. You hound people for nothing. You should all be sacked." I am very angry.

"Ah, ah. Not so goddam loud for chrissake. I did you a good turn and all I get is words thrown at me. Why do you think we did not prosecute your wife for attempted suicide. It's because my calculations showed that she couldn't have done it. I was prepared to swear on that in a court of law or throw a lot of doubt and when I now plead that you be released and for nothing at all, 'cause you never did a thing for me, you start shouting calling me and my lot miserable. Why don't you open your eyes?"

"Gosh. One of your constables asked me the same question. 'Why don't you open your eyes?' Tell you what, I am sorry if you feel I am ungrateful. I have nothing against you personally — but, there's something wrong with the whole goddam police force."

"OK, suppose we talk about that over a drink. I hate to say so, but I am really broke. You don't have to buy me one if you don't want to. I have credit facilities here at the Bristol but the amount I already owe scares me."

"Look, I'd like to buy you a drink but I haven't eaten. I'd like to dash home and eat something.

"I understand. OK, another time then." The truth of the matter is I'd like a drink myself but I don't want to show my face at the Bristol. My jaw is swollen where Asparagus landed his punch and I don't feel so good. At the same time, I'd like to buy this guy a drink because I reckon that he is only half dishonest. His measurements showing that Tonia could not have hanged herself from the window are wrong though. That's where she must have hanged herself from. His constables just robbed me of two hundred shillings for nothing and I am not feeling very inclined to cop company, but this chap is sort of half decent, if you see what I mean. So what I do is, I finally decide to swallow one beer, 'cause there isn't any at home and Asparagus stopped me going to the supermarket. It's shut now. It's lunch break. Tonia must be wondering where I am 'cause I promised to eat her lunch.

We get into the bar and I ask for two cold pilsners. I pay for them on the spot and proceed to drain my bottle despite my paining jaws, while this police chap is waiting for a glass. I don't remember his name. It's either Charlie or John or something, but I really don't want to ask him to remind me. The barman gives me my change and proceeds to ask me a lot of questions which I decline to answer 'cause I am holding the bottle tight to my mouth. He's talking about all sorts of things that happened after I was floored and I feel like hitting him because I don't want all and sundry to know that I was floored.

What I do is, I don't pocket the change. I push it towards Charlie or John or whatever his name is and then say good-bye. Boy, I was thirsty. Charlie or John hasn't as much as tasted his bottle when I am through mine and off through the door. I get the car started and drive directly home. I am hoping that Julian has talked to Tonia already, in which case, all I have to do is to fill in the details, instead of having to break the news as an explanation of my lateness.

As I walk upstairs into the lounge, I am already feeling ashamed. I am ashamed. I am ashamed for having been so dumb as to allow two dumb cops to cheat me in broad day-light. I should have seen their game right through. It was as transparent as nylon. The minute they told me the Greeks had been released on bribe and not bond, I should have seen the catch. I should have known that there was no case.

I am almost as dumb as the cops, if not worse. They robbed me under my very nose. Blast them.

Tonia is not in the house although the car is down in the garage. I find a note on the coffee table saying that she has walked over to see Julian and she'll be back presently. I look at the note and shrug my shoulders. Maybe it's just as well she's not at home. I'll give myself lunch and leave her a note saying that I have eaten and that I'll be back presently. It's now going towards two thirty and I have to be at the Rex at three. I got to hurry.

What I do is, I strip and rush to the bathroom. I feel sticky and stinking so I reckon I'll wash off the cell smell before I see Sheila. I take a quick cold bath, submerging my whole head completely under water and hoping that the swelling on my jaw will subside somewhat.

I am out of the bath in about five minutes and dressed in another five. I take a look at myself in the mirror and decide that I don't look too bad. I move downstairs to the kitchen, open the oven and my nostrils are assailed by a very appetizing smell of chicken curry. I pull the dish out and proceed to fill a bowl with rice and curry. I eat with hands, scooping large mouthfuls, but I can't crack chicken bones on account of my jaw. When I am through with the eats, I wash my hands and go upstairs again where I proceed to clean my teeth after which I scribble this little note for Tonia telling her that it was a wonderful lunch and that I'll be back as soon as I can. It's seven minutes to three. It takes less than five from Cliff avenue to the Rex. I am OK, for time. I dash into the bedroom and dial the Rex. When the receptionist answers, I tell him to put me through to Mrs. Shah's room. He tells me that Mrs. Shah is just registering at the counter so would I speak to her right there. He passes the receiver over to Sheila.

"Hi, Sheila. It's Dodge I am on my way. What's the room number?"

"Just hold on," she tells me and I hear her talking to the receptionist. She then comes on the line again and says, "One forty-five. Don't delay," and she hangs up.

I hang up too and scram out fast. I would be absolutely dismayed if Tonia was to show up now. I get into the car and drive off slowly contemplating the events of the past few hours. I am no longer angry with the cops. They have to subsist, the poor bleeders. I suppose the cold bath and chicken curry have done me some good. I am not feeling bad at all. Not at all. I feel pretty fine as a matter of fact.

I get to the Rex, park the car, lock it and get into the hotel lounge. I don't say a word to anybody. I just make for the staircase and disappear from the receptionist's piercing eyes. Room one forty-five is on first floor on the left hand wing. I tap gently on the door, turn the nob, open the door, slip in and lock the door behind me. Sheila is at the window facing outside and she doesn't turn till I've locked the door behind me. I stand right there by the door and stare at her. My, my. She's looking like a naughty Indian princess that wouldn't sing to her lover but would gladly tickle his balls when the grandmother was not watching. She just looks like herself-eyes and all, but she's wearing this sari that makes her look all different.

"Hi, Sheila. God, you are looking like you are going big places. How are you?" I advance towards her, hold both her hands in mine and kiss her on the cheek. She doesn't answer me. She just talks to me with her eyes.

"What happened to you? Have you been fighting? Your cheek is swollen."

"You wouldn't believe it, Sheila but I was hit by a Greek engineer. I didn't have a quarrel with him either. He hit me on behalf of his captain. Anyway, forget it. Such things happen to men." I pull her gently and we sit on the bed.

"I think I am beginning to believe Khimji. During lunch he was rattling about you robbing a Greek captain and then robbing him. What is it all about, Dodge? Khimji is very angry with you. I've never seen him in such a temper. He had income tax inspectors hounding him the whole morning and he was blaming you for everything. What is there between you and my brother, our affair aside?"

I don't very much like this opening to our secret meeting and I have no intention whatsoever of discussing my past buccaneering enterprises with Sheila or with anybody else for that matter. I have no intention of resuming our old intimate affair with Sheila but neither have I the intention of being unfriendly. All that I really want to know is what evil Khimji is planning for me and at the same time, to reassure Sheila of my general goodness of heart and my sympathies for what has happened between her and him because I am the cause.

"You know your brother better than I do, Sheila. Now that he has an inkling of our affair, he will heap gobblin on me and he will heap gobblin on you. You know that we've been having some sort of occasional business deals, your brother and I, but what you couldn't possibly know is that he's been cheating me on these deals. I don't have his business experience. You know he has no scruples when it comes to money. When I discovered what he was doing to me, I simply decided to beat him at his own game, openly. I withheld some money which he was expecting from me and told him to his face that he could go jump into the sea. I wasn't paying it on account that he cheated me before. That is the only quarrel between me and your brother right now. Anything else is invented."

"Oh, I see. He was raving about you having bought a new car with his money."

"Do you believe him?"

"I don't know and I also don't know why he's planning to ruin you. He told me he'll ruin you. He means to hurt you, Dod. I overheard him on the phone. He was telling somebody to smash your car."

"That would be very silly. The car is fully insured."

"I think that he's also got people to beat you up. You see, when he was raving at me, he kept talking about the things that money can do and that he'll reduce himself to a Bombay beggar if that is how much it will cost to have you castrated. He was very furious."

"He said that? Did he say that he wants me castrated?" She nods her head. I hold her hand and stare her right in the eyes. I ask her again.

"Did he say that he's going to hire people to castrate me?"

"He repeated it several times. I got terribly scared because I know his persistence. I know he means it. That's why I had to get in touch with you. You should be on your guard, Dod. He is a very evil man, my brother. The way he was carrying on this afternoon left no doubt in my mind. He means to hurt you."

"How does he know that you wouldn't tell me and that I can subsequently go to the police?"

"He as much as told me to yell it at you if I cared. He said he'd even told you."

"Jesus!"

"I told you he is evil. God. You don't know what insults I had to bear myself. You can't imagine it. He's absolutely horrid. I ran away from his presence but he kept following me, flinging insults till I had to lock myself up in my room and he didn't stop there either. He stood there, outside the door and said the rudest thing you imagine. I can't even repeat it."

"It must have been real bad."

"You are telling me. Do you know what he hurled at me through the closed door, — he told me; 'Go and have your filthy dog cunt fucked black and inside out while you have the whoring chance 'cause when I am through with him, you can only lick his dead testicles like a mother cow.' Can you imagine my own brother saying that to me?"

I am starting to get worried. This is no joke. Khimji means to set some thugs on me and he knows damn well that there is nothing I can do 'cause I can't go to the police. The only thing I can do is have my own thugs as body-guards but that would be very disagreable to me. I can't have people tagging after me and besides, it's damn expensive even if all I had to pay for was drinks. What the hell does he think he is? An American gangster or something? There's one thing that's not going to happen to me though. Nobody is going to castrate me. Nobody. I'll have to be dead before that happens to me. Jesus. I must do something about Khimji. Getting him hounded for income tax is not enough. It's gonna be something physical and painful. Something that will instil holy fear in him. Something that will hurt him and scare him the way he's got me scared. Sweet Jesus. Suppose he should actually manage to get me castrated, what then? What can I do? He can bribe the police with as much as twenty thousand shillings to drop the case, if there was a case, that is. Oh, the bastard.

"What will you do, Dod? What shall I do? What shall we do? You are responsible for all this mess, you know? You've caused me a lot of trouble for absolutely nothing?"

"I know, Sheila. I'll accept all the blame. Honest to goodness, I don't know what to do. The fellow is your brother, you know. I could not foresee the current developments."

"But why did you have to start it all? What prompted you even to mention my name to Khimji? Why, Dod? What were the circumstances? What was this disagreement you had with Khimji before the police? What was it all about and how did my name come into it?" She's angry.

"I don't understand it myself. Honest."

"What do you mean by that? You are the cause of everything. If you'd not dragged me into it, Khimji would never have known a thing. Even if he heard from some doctor that you'd made some Indian girl pregnant, he couldn't have connected the incident with me. As it is, you'd already made an allusion to our affair. Even though you made that allusion as a denial, it doesn't make much difference since you'd not been accused. It amounted to a confession. You'd no business whatsoever mixing my name in whatever you and Khimji were quarrelling about. Dod, it wasn't fair. Not if you respected me. Why? Why do you have to mess up my life?"

Sheila is working herself up into a rage. I am perplexed. I thought this would be a meeting of two unhappy people consoling each other but I am wrong. She doesn't see it that way. We are not two unhappy people. No. She is the unhappy one and I am the cause. I am not exactly prepared for this role although in a way she's damn right. I didn't mean it, or course. I mean, I didn't mean to hurt her or land her into any trouble but I've ended up doing exactly that. The harm is already done. Gosh. I feel bad. I am even starting to wonder whether I should have kept the appointment at all. All I've got as result is one big hell of a scare about my balls and a guilty conscience about mixing up Sheila with the Kiunyu/Khimji unofficial conflict. I am an ass.

"I am really sorry, Sheila. Now that I look back on events, I think I behaved like an ass, but I had no ill intentions or lack of respect for your person. How can I fail to respect you?"

"Don't ask me how," she snaps. "You've gone and done it, Dod. You don't even realize the gravity of it all. I have to leave home. I have to run away. What do you think will become of me? Why do I have to run away from home? Do you know why? It's because of you. It's all because of you. Why is my own brother insulting me like a whore? It's because of you. Yes. You and your mouth and your dishonest ways. Yes. You and your great respect for me."

"Oh, my God. Sheila, I can assure you on my word of honour. . . ."

"Ha. Are you talking about honour?" She interrupts me with a sneer. "So what is your word of honour? Gloating to your African police brother that you made love to an Indian girl. Is that your word of honour? I thought it was a discreet affair between two people who wanted to hide their beautiful emotions from all and sundry because you are married and I am an Indian. I wouldn't have told a dead friend about it, but what about you? How many of your African friends know that you've been making love to an Indian girl? How many? Is that your word of honour?"

"For God's sake, Sheila stop shouting. You don't have to shout because I am only a foot away from you. Please whisper things."

"Yeah. I know. I shouldn't shout," she hisses. "I shouldn't say anything. I should take it all lying down. Oh, yes. After all I am an Indian. I can be deported by your brothers if you gave them a bribe. I shouldn't criticize your behaviour. Yes. I should keep quiet and listen to you. Fine. I am quiet now. I am not shouting. Talk. Tell me why? Just tell me why you'd to open our closed book?"

I am beat. I just give up. Sheila has worked herself up into such a rage that I don't think it's worthwhile trying to explain anything. Her talking eyes are not talking any more. They are hard. The naughty Indian princess has disappeared. Right now, she's pacing the room, cracking her fingers. I am cracking my fingers too but I am still sitting on the bed.

"Why. . .?" she shouts all of a sudden. "We are quits. We've been quits for a long time now. It was my decision. I couldn't see a logical end to our affair. It was stupid to start it in the first instance. I was a fool but I paid for my sins. I had an abortion. I had an abortion when I should have been a virgin. Do you by any chance understand that? Do you understand any Indian custom? You don't know what I had to sacrifice in my conscience. You'll never understand. I sacrificed a lot but I paid for it. When I paid for it, I put an end to it. That's why we are quits. Why? Why after all that. . . why after we've not seen each other or entertained ideas of seeing each other for a long time now. . . why did you have to ruin all that I was trying to mend? Why?"

"Listen, Sheila. No cause on my part will mend what is ruined. It's not important any more. What we should try to do is look at the circumstances and see what can be salvaged and how. The question is how and not why. Come and sit down Sheila and please don't let us be angry with each other. For any harm to your person and your future that is directly attributable to me, I offer my sincere apologies. Honestly, I offer my throat."

"And great help that would be — your throat. The only snag is that your throat wouldn't be much use to me when I leave Mombasa and go to Nairobi to start a new life away from filth like you and my brother and your crooked ways. At least, he doesn't pretend. He's bad through and through but you are worse. You pretend to be good while you are just as bad, or worse."

"Really, Sheila, I think that we have said all that there is to be said. If we continue in this vein, I don't see where that will land either you or me. Let's call it off as friends. I mean it really. There is nothing I can do right now to put things right. The circumstances are all wrong. I am extremely sorry, believe me, please."

Sheila moves over, rests her right foot on the bed frame and with hands akimbo, continues to heap all sorts of goblin on my black soul. She accuses me of being a thief, an irresponsible drunkard who never did anything serious except being unfaithful to his wife and who takes advantage to destroy anything that is good in others. She accuses the African race and its clients of trying to emerge from the mud, from whence it came and where it shall return, et cetera, et cetera. I don't understand the meaning of it all but all the same, I am getting damn angry. I can only stomach high verbal pressure up to a certain point. I have reached that point. I have reached that point because I realize what a fool I've been. I've been a fool because now I know for sure that she arranged the meeting so that she can lash out at me and my race and not to warn me against her brother. Everybody is fooling me today. This is her moment for letting off steam.

I decide that I've had enough for one day. What I do is, I stand up, grab Sheila by the shoulders and shake her violently without saying a word. She stops prattling. She stares at me in complete surprise as if to ask, how dare you touch me, you of the untouchable caste? I then hurl her on to the bed full length and stand just as she was standing — right foot on the bed frame and hands akimbo. I am furious. She bares her teeth at me and covers her exposed thighs. I don't let her speak.

"Listen, girl," I tell her breathlessly. "I think you've said all you had to say. You are not looking for any solution to anything so don't talk to me about your plight which you make sound like a mountain when it's in reality, a mere mole hill. Baaaah! Oh no. No more. What the blinking shit do you think you are giving me hell for? Do I have to take it simply because I don't understand your tradition? No! Negative. This is just a simple case where a grown up man meets a grown up girl through her brother, screws her a few times in due course and the brother gets to know about it much later when the two are not even screwing anymore. It's simple and it happens all the time all the world over. Why the hell should you think you are so different just because you are an Indian and I am an African? You are a goddam racist."

She doesn't answer. She just looks at me and says, "Go on. You are telling me things you never told me before." She is sneering at me in a most despising manner. I am getting terribly worked up myself. All of a sudden, I feel like slapping her. What is she anyway? She's just a woman like any other. She's no different from anybody I've screwed except that she's Indian and she cries at orgasm. I get this great urge to beat her up just to see her cry. I've seen her love tears but I've never seen her pain tears.

What I do though, is, I don't beat her. I don't beat her because I know I've wronged her, only she wouldn't listen to my apologies. I don't beat her also because she's a woman to me and not just another Indian. When you've had it with a woman a couple of times, you don't notice her colour or religion except of course, in public. The other reason why I don't beat her is on account that she's stopped baring her teeth at me and looking like a tigress. She's putting back some princess in place and is starting to talk with her eyes and not her mouth. I decide that this is a good moment to get the hell out of here. At least, we should part in peace. I force myself to make a kind little speech.

"Okay, Sheila," I tell her. "I am really sorry whether you believe me or not, but I feel like you, that we were made to go and live different ways. Thank you for the kind warning about some harm that might be coming my way, I really appreciate your concern about my health. It's very kind of you. I feel that I owe you a lot for the trouble you took and would be ready to render you a helping hand in return if you'd indicate how. Please don't let us quarrel anymore. It wouldn't get either you or me anywhere. Please. You got me angry when the last thing I want to do is get angry with you. I am sorry and if you want me to repeat it again, I shall. For the time being, I don't really think that there's something worthwhile to be added and I was wondering whether, with your permission, I could take my leave."

"Yes, Dod. You have my permission. Thank you very much for coming but you may leave now." The way she says it gets me so pissed that I regret for not having given her one little wallop just to remind her that she had no right to think that I came from mud and shall return to mud. Where the hell did she come from? From white-wash?

"Don't stare at me; I said you may go," she shouts. "Your wife is waiting. Don't you understand what it means to be married?"

"I know, you Indian bitch!" I yell back as I turn the handle. I open the door but then close it because there are these footsteps approaching and I don't care to be seen by anybody while getting out of this joint. I am so mad at Sheilla that I don't even look at her again. I just stand facing the door with my back at her. The steps get past and stop. There are two people. I reckon it's man and wife. They are whispering. I imagine that they are going to get into the room next door but they don't. They just stand out there. I turn round to make a sign to Sheila but I don't have to. She standing right behind me.

"Sorry, but there are some folks out in the corridor," I whisper."
"It wouldn't be prudent to. . ."

"So what." She shouts. "They are not tigers. Get out!" She takes one step forward, yanks the door open and forcibly pushes me out. God, God, God! Blasted Jesus Christ. Do you know who is directly in front of me outside the door? Do you know into whose arms I fall? I fall right into Khimji's open arms. The mental shock is tremendous. It's tremendous because right there next to Khimji is Tonia! I cannot tell you how I feel 'cause I can't tell you. I just can't tell you. I can't tell you anything. I am half dead. I am so dead that when Khimji pushes me away right back through the door onto Sheila's surprised arms, I am not conscious of whether I am going backwards or sideways. God — Oh, God. What a bloody blinking embarassing mess. I want to be twenty feet underground. I want to melt into thin air.

It all happens very quickly. Khimji makes another push and we find ourselves in the middle of the room. He marches in dragging Tonia along and closes the door. We are like two armies facing each other, only my side has no guns. Sheila and I have no guns. We are completely disarmed. I expect her to drop and faint but she doesn't. She even recovers faster than I do. I am almost pissing inside my pants but she stands her ground.

"You see," Khimji gloats. "I told you we'd get them, Mrs. Kiunyu. Here they are now right in your very eyes. They have been here since three. I told you, I had them watched." Tonia doesn't say anything. I think she's more shocked than I am. She just looks like a stationary piece of flesh. I feel so bad, so absolutely bad that the momentary fear and shock evaporate. All I am left with is hate for Khimji. Oh, how I hate him. How dare he drag Tonia along to witness such a thing? How dare he if he's a man? Would you drag a lady along just to show her what her husband was doing to your sister? Would you? Would you in your right mind expose your sister to such shame? How dare he drag Tonia into all this? Oh, bastard! Fucking, shitting bastard of an Indian. I have no words though. I am tongue-tied. I am mute. Khimji pouts at Sheila and says in a jeering tone:

"I knew you'd be whoring like I told you. I overheard you this morning. I knew you couldn't help it. You are just a whoring cow and I disown you as a sister." Sheila moves to the window and I am completely surprised that she can behave so calmly. I am still in cold sweat. Tonia is also mute and I decide that the Indians are one up on us. Trouble is I have no words. I can't say a thing. Khimji seems to be the only one with words. He is smiling happily.

"I told you, Mrs. Kiunyu, that I have nothing against your husband as a person. What I object to is all the wrongs he's doing me after I've been so kind to him. I've done him no harm but just see what he's done to me. First, he robs my money, secondly, he sets the police on me and I have to pay money. Not only that. He set the income tax bleeders on me and they were hounding me the whole of this morning. It costs money, Mrs. Kiunyu. Those buggers wouldn't take anything less than three thousand shillings in way of a bribe and I had to pay. Why? Just because of your husband. He's right there in front of you. Ask him. I don't mind all that though. That's money and my business is money. What I can't stand is what he's doing to my sister. He has ruined her life. He's ruined her completely. He's already got her pregnant I don't know how many times and he keeps paying for the abortions. Terrible. Your husband is a terrible man. He should be castrated. You wouldn't believe me when I talked to you over the phone — but ask him now. I tell you, they have been fornicating since three o'clock; haven't you, you bastard?"

I don't know what to do exactly. Right now I am not prepared for words but I am ready for violence. The only trouble is I don't know who to hit. I'd like to hit them all, including Tonia. She's got no business running around to find me out. The tragedy of the matter is that we didn't even screw, Sheila and I. We should have done it 'cause that way it would be easier to explain things. That way you just say yes and take the consequences. It's easier. You can confess and ask for forgiveness. You can repent. You'll be pardoned or condemned. Trouble is, how do you explain that you haven't been doing a thing except quarrelling. Who is going to believe you? Heck. I just decide to fight Khimji. I have to. I just hope he wouldn't smash me on this jaw that has the remains of Asparagus.

I move towards him flexing my muscles just to make sure that my system has gone back to normal. I move casually so that he doesn't suspect my motive but Tonia does. She moves forward in front of Khimji and gives me the hardest slap in Kenya, and on my wrong jaw.

It hurts so bad, so terribly bad that I reel back holding the poor jaw in place with my right hand and fall right on the bed. It's only a matter of a minute since the whole hullaballo started but it looks like hours. It also looks like everybody knows exactly what to do except me. Gosh. Tonia stands over me and says very slowly and deliberately, "I am sorry for the embarrassment, Dod. It's not precisely my idea of searching for family happiness. Now that the cat is out of the bag in a way that can't be contested, all that I can say is that you'll never tell me a lie again 'cause you wouldn't be telling me anything from now on. If I ever suspected you before, I did you injustice. I suspected you with cheap street women of no consequence. It didn't occur to me that you could be carrying on with young, rich and elegant Indians that could be taken for ladies from the outside. I don't think you've done very badly in the choice of your bedmates. Congratulations." She whirls round to face Khimji who is chuckling to himself at the scene.

"As for you, Mr. Khimji, all I can say is thank you very much for your pains in escorting me to the scene of crime. It was very considerate of you but I would have preferred more than my life to have no knowledge of it. If you've done anything for me, it is to ruin my life. You've ruined everything for me. You've done me such irreparable harm that I have no more words for you. You conducted me to my doom." She's almost crying. She makes for the door and I get off the bed. At the door, she whirls back again and stares at Sheila. She stares at her for one full five seconds. Sheila stares back. They are staring at each other.

"As for you, Miss Khimji," Tonia says tersely, "I voluntarily give you my husband. I have no more use for him and I am sure you can use him. I'll only ask you one little favour; please use him well and in the event that I cite your name in a divorce suit, I hope that you'd collaborate. I, in turn, promise not to interfere in your affair with Dod."

"Please listen," I blurt out. "Let's explain this thing right here and now." At last, I've got words. I understand. Khimji is not worried about his sister right now. What he wants is to break my home and he's damn well done it.

"What do you want to explain that is not already explained?" Khimji asks me. "All we came for is to prove that you leave your wife and come out to fornicate with my sister. What do you want to explain;

the details?" He laughs like a hyena.

Tonia opens the door and walks out followed by Sheila. Khimji follows and I find myself following him out of the cursed room.

"I warned you," he says as we walk downstairs. I follow him cursing till we are almost near the reception desk. He doesn't curse back. He just walks briskly in front of me as if I was not talking to him at all. We go out past the reception desk quietly and when we get onto the street he dashes to his car and I just stand there and stare. Tonia is walking down Kilindini road towards the roundabout of Nkrumah/Salim rod. Sheila is walking in the opposite direction. I light myself a cigarette and fix my eyes on Tonia as she walks away. Poor girl. I feel so guilty about it all. She doesn't deserve that kind of Indian confrontation. Khimji should be castrated for bringing her in. I have to do something about Khimji. Gosh, I am confused.

I cross the street and make for my car. Jesus Christ! What is this again? Am I seeing things or is it really true? You know what is happening? Well, I guess not. What is happening is that my car is sitting on the rims. All the four tyres have been completely deflated and thousands of pieces of what used to be the wind-screen are sitting on the front seats of the car. I am so absolutely overwhelmed that all I do is hold my head with both hands and stare at the mess. My brain is tickling only in one direction — Khimji. This must be the work of Khimji or his thugs. What the blinking hell am I to do with this Indian? Damn. And there are no witnesses.

What I do is I examine the tyres and notice that not only are they deflated but whoever did so threw away the valves so I can't inflate them even if I borrowed a portable pump. I reckon I am angry with the car too. It's just sitting there like a tired donkey that is immune to flogging. What I do is I get the door open, sweep off the windscreen from the driver's seat and start reversing the car. There's this Agip Service station about a hundred yards behind and I don't give a damn right now what happens to the tyres and tubes and rims. I just reverse the car slowly, going toklo, toklo. I am lucky because there's not much traffic at this hour. I reverse the car right by the air-pressure machine as the service station attendants stare at the limping car in surprise. I get out and manage a smile.

"This car is lame in both the front and the hind legs, can you chaps do something about it?" I ask.

"What happened?" one of them asks.

"Some chap broke them. He even threw away the wheel caps. You'll have to get me four new valves."

"But, sir, was it an accident? I mean the windscreen sir."

"No, it was deliberate action. Some chap didn't like the car so he bashed in the wind-braker and deflated the rollers."

"Is it your car, sir."

"I think so. How about putting some air into these tyres. I want to catch up with the chap."

"The tubes may be gone and if they are not, they'll go pretty soon. You shouldn't have driven on rims."

"I know. Just try and fill them up and then we'll see how they'll take it."

The chap proceeds to inflate the tyres after fitting new valves and to my surprise the car manages to stand up. He then drives it to the greasing bay, sprays the tyres with water and then proceeds to examine them for possible air leaks. There are none. He then gets this pressure hose and blows the windscreen pieces off the seats. I pay him, thank him and then drive straight home.

All the way I was looking for signs of Tonia but she isn't anywhere to be seen. She is not at home either. I hang around for some ten stupid minutes and then decide to take a walk to the Railway Club for a little wetting. I'll get the wind-screen fixed tomorrow but not today. Right now I am thirsty and I need a walk. By the time I get to the Railway Club I am dripping with sweat. It's after four but the Mombasa sun is very persistent today. There are a lot of cars parked outside so I reckon that there are a lot of mugs on the booze this afternoon.

I get into the Club and I can see straight away that I was right about a lot of mugs on the booze. The place is full and there's a lot of drunken noise from all corners. All the stools are taken. People are standing about with glasses or bottles in their hands. There's a lot of hi, Dodge, hello, Mr. Kiunyu, et cetera and shaking of hands here and there. My three navy friends are right on the other side and Jim is waving his hand at me. I ask the barman for a pilsner, a very cold one, and then move over to join the navy chaps.

"Dodge, old chap", Jim cries, "where have you been, old chap and who hit you on the cheek? You need a bodyguard and I appoint myself one." We exchange pleasantries and I am in the middle of telling them some made up story to account for my swollen cheek when a hand is placed on my shoulder from behind. I whirl back and come face to face with Masakalia. God. I nearly smack him on the head with the bottle of pilsner I am holding in my hand but I control my emotions. The goddam fellow told everybody to tell me that he'd gone to Nairobi and had me locked up while he was enjoying himself on Greek money right here in the Club where he's not even a member. What a filthy cheating bastard.

"Hi Dodge. I didn't think you'd come out so early. What happened?" I don't answer him. I don't answer him because I have some bitter spittle in my mouth and I want to crash it on his face. How dare he? If he wasn't a policeman he would be on the ground by now.

"OK, Dodge. No hard feelings. I didn't mean any harm or anything, so how about buying me a drink? Let's bury the past."

"I ain't got no Greek money so why don't you address yourself directly to the Greeks?" I hiss between my teeth, keeping my voice low so that the other mugs don't hear.

"They are no longer in town Dodge. Be a friend. I said that we forget the past. Forget all the blinking past."

"Fine, and in so doing I shall also forget that I ever met you. Just forget that you know me, will you?"

"You don't seem to understand what I mean. If it's not so much of a bother would you like to come outside for a while. I have something important for you."

"Keep it," I tell him.

"No kidding. This is important. I can't explain here. Come out for a while." I decide that I might as well listen to him 'cause if I don't he can always make me listen at the police station. I tell my friends that I'll be back soon and then follow Masakalia out. He leads me right round the block to a quiet corner where we sit under a tree. I've still got my bottle of pilsner which is now half gone and I continue to sip slowly as Masakalia unfolds his story.

"I got the whole truth from the Greek chaps about your involvement in foreign currency black-marketeering. The captain signed a whole statement before I let him go. I now have enough evidence to book you on that serious charge of contravention of exchange regulations."

I look at him with disbelief in my eyes. I shake my head without a word and finally ask him to continue.

"Madhivani was arrested at the Nairobi airport yesterday. He had a lot of foreign currency bills on his person. I have been asked to investigate from this end to determine the organisation of the currency smuggling ring. The Government is very concerned about this offence. The chief of the C.I.D. is coming down tomorrow. He's bringing along three of his chaps who are going to help in the investigations or rather I am going to help them because they have more powers in the matter than I'll have. The idea is to comb the whole town and book known and suspected currency buccaneers and I am afraid that you'll figure in that list. This is the important thing I had to tell you."

"And what do you want me to do about it?"

"Two thousand shillings — that's what you may have to pay to keep your name off the list. I shall not be able to give a hundred percent guarantee on the matter but you'll be half-way protected at least. That's all I can guarantee."

"And who is going to protect me?"

"Nobody in particular. The two thousand shillings will do it."

"If you'd thought of protection, why then did you have to get an incriminating statement from the Greeks?"

"That's just in case you don't pay up."

"So if I don't pay up you'll use that statement against me?"

"If you don't pay up there's no reason why you shouldn't be arrested along with others and if you are arrested, it will be much easier for us if we have something tangible against you."

"And how will you explain the presence of that statement since it amounts to a confession from a thief who you let escape?"

"There's nothing in the statement to show that the Greeks were involved. It's merely a confidential statement from an informant. It is like an anonymous tip except that the informant in this particular case was obliging enough to sign a statement. In any case, the statement is not all that important. I wouldn't need it to get you arrested."

"I see. How much money did you get from the Greeks?"

"My dear fellow, I don't have the foggiest idea what you are talking about."

"You know damn well what I am talking about. I was going to take those Greeks to court for causing actual bodily harm to my person, but you wheedled me off the track by accusing me of disturbance of public peace so that you could release the Greeks on bribe before I lodged the complaint. How much did they pay to stop you from charging them?"

"That's none of your business my dear fellow." I can see that he is getting angry.

"You know what? You are a bloody, greedy thief." I tell him.

"Whatever you think wouldn't help you. We are talking about two thousand shillings and you know damn well that you have to pay."

"And suppose I don't pay?"

"The only way I could help you is giving you two days to run out of the country. You get out and stay out. Why wouldn't you pay any way. It is not your goddam money. It is stolen money for which you should be in jail now. The only reason why you are not in jail is me, so why shouldn't I share a small portion of your loot?"

"You are a crook."

"But so are you, my dear Dodge. I never take money from honest people. I only take it from crooks."

"And you protect them thereafter for a short while, but when you need some more, you corner them again. You are a very good protector of the law."

"What do you want me to do? I can't protect the law alone. The law makers in this country are the biggest thieves and receive the fattest bribes. If an Attorney-General can accept gifts, why shouldn't I? If my police Commissioner can take a bribe, why shouldn't I? Who is taking bribes in this country? It's not me. I only go for small sums from small time crooks because I actually sympathize with the goddam crooks. It is not their fault. They are pushed into crime by circumstances. It is a general sickness starting right from the top and decreasing proportionately downwards. In other words, my dear Dodge, the bigger you are, the bigger the thief. I am only a small time Police Inspector. I am not a Minister or a brother to any of the big fish. My crimes are small. I can't grab big things."

"Why don't you get your money from the bloody Indians? They have the money. Why do you have to pester me after you were paid handsomely by these Greeks? Do you think that I pick my money from bushes? Man, I don't have the money. You are trying to grab just like those big fish you are condemning. You are just as bad or worse. I don't have the money I tell you, and besides, I have quit and you know it. What do you think I'll be eating tomorrow? If you want money my friend, just go and blackmail Indians. That way you'll have plenty. I am tired and sick of the way you are hounding me all over the place. I am sick and I won't take any more of it.

"You'll be more sick in prison, my dear Mr. Kiunyu."

"I am not going to any goddam prison 'cause I have quit that black business and I am not engaging in anything unlawful. It's absurd."

"I agree with you Dodge. It sounds absurd but you can take it from me that there is this two thousand shillings that stands between you and this C.I.D. team that's coming down tomorrow. You can also take it from me that you are going to end up in prison. Some people have to be sacrificed so that the big fish can steal in peace. Who are the biggest foreign currency thieves? It's the big men, the ministers and their cronies. They are not small time crooks like you. No. They actually have bank accounts in foreign countries. Millions and millions of shillings smuggled out with the consent of the law because those chaps are the law itself. All their crimes are within the law but yours are outside the law. That's why you have to pay. That is the reason why you and your lot have to be sacrificed to give a semblance of government vigilance. You have to pay."

"Over my dead body."

"It's your funeral then, my dear Dodge. Where do you think you are? You are in Kenya. Are you blind to what is going on? Are you blind? Don't you know what is happening? Gosh! You are walking through life with blinkers on. Look at this case of ivory. The day they were sentencing a chap to seven years imprisonment for illegal possession of game trophies, a lorry full of illegal ivory, rhino horns and hippo teeth was being given police escort to the airport. Whom do you think the goddam stuff belonged to? To my brother? Ha, you have to know Kenya. The chap who got seven years was a permanent collector for the chap who was having his illegal stuff escorted by the police to the airport. He was sacrificed.

"Do you by any chance think that Madhivani will go to jail? That case will be withdrawn before it is halfway through. He'll bribe his way through but he'll bribe big fish with big money and get his break. Some poor people have to be put in jail in his place. That's how we operate. I am trying to give you the same break for a song and instead of being thankful you call me an extortionist. You are ungrateful."

"I don't have the money and if I had, I wouldn't pay. I tell you I am sick of the whole bribing system. I prefer to go to the goddam jail. Why can't you protect me without this bribing nonsense? I have already bribed you once."

"That would be upsetting the whole order of operation. You have to pay for favours. There's nothing for free these days and you know it. I am part of the system you know."

"Get damned, you and your system. I've already been robbed by your chaps today and I swear to God that I am not parting with a damn cent. You can set the whole of your goddam rotten law against me but all you'll get is my blood or my dead body. Not one single cent. That's final. I've had enough of you, blasted bleeders. That is my decision now and I shall die with it, so help me God. As for you, you can go jump off the Likoni Ferry or simply melt for all I care." I see his eyes harden and his lips twitch with the hard determination of hate.

"In that case I swear on my sacred honour that you'll see the end of tomorrow behind bars," he says sternly. "With all your newly acquired holy airs, you are of no use to me or anybody, so I'll have you buried in prison without the slightest conscience. To me, you are a man who refused to work and develop the nation. You are useless to society. Your contribution will not be missed when you languish in prison. It's the best working ground for you and I'll send you there, so help me God — if just to teach you a lesson. Don't you realise that if all the small time crooks were to quit and become arrogant like you, we small policemen would starve?"

I consider the whole situation and decide that given all the goddam unlawlessness in the country this chap can and will actually put me in jail. It doesn't have to be on this currency business but on anything that he can cook up and frame me. It also occurs to me that since Khimji is after my blood, I would have no recourse to justice or redress 'cause Masakalia would be very willing to receive a handout from Khimji to foil any complaint from me. The way I see it is that I'll end up in jail whether I am guilty or innocent. If I am attacked by Khimji's thugs and I fight back in self defence, I am the one that will go to jail. If I stay at home and lock myself up, Masakalia will drag me out as part of this hunt for currency buccaneers. If I run away from Mombasa, it will be an admission of guilt and they'll hound me and sacrifice me.

Any old buccaneer that is not prepared to pay Masakalia is also likely to end up the same way. I can't go to the law because Masakalia is the law around here. I can't go to his bosses because that is just as bad as going to a thief to accuse a thief. What the goddam hell do I do if I don't want to cough up the money?

All of a sudden I see red. I see the end of the world. I am so angry that I could murder somebody. What do you do in a situation where you don't know where to go to seek justice? Do you just hit your head against the wall or do you simply hang yourself? All of a sudden I feel myself invaded by such intense hopelessness and hate that, on the spur of the moment and without any thought, I raise my bottle of beer and crash it with all my force up on Masakalia's head. I hit him so hard that the bottle breaks right to the neck and he lurches and colapses to the ground. There's so much blood gushing out of the top of his head that the sight of it nearly freezes and roots me to the ground.

I am momentarily numb. I am not thinking. I do not understand the significance of anything. Everything is dead except for that river of blood gushing out of Masakalia's head. Time is standing still. It is standing still till Masakalia starts to moan in his swoon. I recollect myself and start moving away from the scene and the club. I am moving away in the opposite direction. It's as if I am moving away from myself. Simply moving away. Away. That's all there's in my subconscious. To move away.

I don't know for how long I was moving for I was not conscious of actual movement. It was only after I passed the Mombasa Secretarial College that I was conscious that I was moving towards Kilindini road. I became conscious because there were these boys and girls chatting and laughing in pairs just outside the college. They represent life. The futility of life. The emptiness of the future. How absurd. Little do they know that they are just going to become toys for the children of mother power. Yes, guitar strings to be played to the tune of dictatorial democracy by righteous thieves. Yes. And where am I going. Where can I go? Where should I be going? I don't know. All I know is that I move till I hit Kilindini road. An idea hits me in a flash. Room one hundred and forty-five at the Rex — Why not go there? It's paid for the day and it's vacant. Why not get back there and think?

I turn left and make for the Rex. I get in and walk straight up.

There's nobody at the reception. I am hoping that nobody has been in to tidy up since we left and I am goddam right. I simply get into the room and turn the key in the lock. Nobody has seen me. I then jump on the bed and lie on my back. I reckon that I don't have much time to rest on comfortable beds in the coming few years. They'll be looking for me all over town to-night. It will be an undeniable charge of violence and causing actual bodily harm to the person of a police officer in the normal course of performing his duties and I know damn well that any attempt to put up a defence will be wasted effort. I am condemned before I go to court. I will put up a defence though. I'll talk about the whole goddam bribing business; not to get an acquittal, no. I will be condemned irrespective but simply to let the rudy judges know what I think about the law and its unlawful guardians. When I've got it all out of my chest, no local newspaper will dare print my defence 'cause I am going talk about things that the ordinary public would like to hear.

In a way, it is probably not all that bad after all. Masakalia was going to put me in jail anyway and I would have gone in with a lot of bitterness. I would have gone to jail for nothing. Now I'll go in for something. I will suffer for a cause. Now I can hurl my guilt at the judge and explain the circumstances. Yes. I know I have committed a serious crime. I have bled the skull of the law. I have smashed the dome of the cathedral that protects the holy wealth of our self-appointed gods. Yeah, I have spilt some blood of one of the children of the vicious law goddess and there's no way I can escape her claws. The vicious retaliating claws of the law, that's what I am waiting for. By the grace of the Almighty, I'll have this last night in comfort before those talons are embedded in my neck. Damn the law and its talons. But tell me my dear God; tell me why I shouldn't fight the law. Tell me why I shouldn't walk to the police station and set the whole place on fire. Why shouldn't I do it since I am already condemned? Tell me. Tell me also about Tonia. What in the name of your son Jesus, do you think is going to happen to her. Can you hear me, Old Chap?

FIVE

Thursday

Take some advise from me soldier. Never hit a cop. It don't matter how right you are but the bastard is the law itself and the law has a thick skull. You can't crack it. Anytime you hit the law it bounces back and hits you harder. You can't even bribe another cop to get you out of the mess 'cause when you hit a cop, the whole tribe comes out together against you like brothers should. They become real brothers-in-law.

Me, I have been an ass. Bleeding Masakalia on the skull is the most stupid thing I've ever done in my life. That's what I am thinking about right in this hotel room at the Rex. Now I can think. I've rested my silly bones for a whole long night so I can reflect with a clear mind. The reason why I am an ass is that all my goddam plans will now go to the dogs. The minute I am out of this room whether on my own steam or under police steam, I'll only have one place to go. They'll lock me up in the darkest cell. The implications are devastating. I am completely doomed. I am doomed for ever. I am so angry with myself that if I had a knife, I'd cut my own throat. I had a hell of time trying to sleep the whole of last night. I don't think that I slept for over one hour. I am still tired and sleepy. I have been thinking about this whole thing and I think I have hit on a madman plan.

The madman plan I have is too simple to be true. Maybe I am mad anyway. What I have decided to do is go into hiding right here in this hotel room 'cause I reckon that it is the last place they'll suspect after yesterday's incident with Sheila, Tonia and Khimji. To the best of my knowledge, no one saw me getting in here. Maybe I am wrong but I didn't notice anybody notice me. It would be unfortunate if Khimji had somebody shadowing me, but I am convinced he hadn't. I feel certain that he's satisfied with the damage he inflicted on me so he's having a laugh until when he'll probably think up something different but I wouldn't be there for his thugs to shadow me.

The way I see it is this: the cops will start combing the whole town for my blood but I think it is very unlikely that they'll think of looking in here. Tonia, Sheila and Khimji saw me last getting out of the Rex. The next person will be the petrol station Assistant who inflated my tires and saw me drive off. From there, they'll find my car at home and at the Club, they'll find out that I had a drink with the navy chaps and that Masakalia called me out. Then, when he recovers consciousness, Masakalia will tell them that I hit him unconscious and that's all he remembers. From there, they have then to track me down. As I walked away from the Club, I didn't have my eyes with me so I don't know who saw me walking away but since nobody talked to me all along, it's reasonable guess that nobody took much notice of my walking self. At least nobody followed me. If somebody saw me, all he or she could say is the direction I took. That's all. Them cops will have to figure it out themselves.

I was quite careful when I got to the Rex. I don't think that anybody saw me get in or pay the necessary attention to the fact. Having had a hell of a row here, nobody would expect me to come back. The room is not mine. It's in the name of Mrs. Shah. Even if the cops were checking all hotels, there would be no way of finding out short of bursting into every hotel room around town. They can't possibly do that. So what I've got to do is sit tight right here in the room without showing my head out of the window. The way I've got to do it is, I'll ring the receptionist and tell him that Mrs. Shah requires the room for two more days. Then I'll ask him to send up some room service chap with a couple of beers and my brunch. When the room service chap shows up I'll pay him for the services and give him the money for two nights' lodging and ask him to bring the receipt up. It would be in the name of Mrs. Shah and of course he'll naturally assume that I am waiting for the lady for an illegal screw. I don't frequent the the Rex so I don't expect any of them waiters to place me. Anyway it's going to eight o'clock so what I do is I lift the phone and ask for the reception.

"Hello, this is room 145".

"Yep," the guy says in a crisp busy voice.

"Mrs. Shah wants the room until Saturday."

"Saturday morning or later."

"Saturday morning."

"Just hold up the line please." I can hear him rifling through some papers and then he comes back on the phone.

"The room is single and it's paid for one night."

"Yes. She now wants to extend that to Saturday morning."

"Double or single?"

"Double". I reply without thinking. I hadn't thought of that one but I reckon that if the room is booked double those chaps will think that the room is hired for some double action and wouldn't think of anything else. They have a one track mind.

"O.K. it's booked", he says and is going to replace the receiver when I yell, "I'd like some room service. Can you send somebody up?"

"Ring up room service," he says and hangs up. I notice that room service is indicated against number six on the telephone dial so I dial six and ask them to bring me up some three beers and dinner. The chap asks me what I want to eat and I tell him I don't know so he reads out the menu aloud. I settle for simple fish and chips and he tells me that it'll be up right away and I hang up. I run my fingers through my hair, stretch myself and then walk to the door and unlock it. This is self-imprisonment.

In ten minutes' time there's a knock at the door. I open it and the waiter walks in carrying a huge wooden tray. He passes me without as much as looking at me and proceeds to the little table where he deposits all the contents of his tray. He then holds out the bill and asks me whether I am signing or paying cash. I say I am paying cash and I proceed to peel out the money. He's a very odd fellow, this waiter. He's of Arab extraction. He must be about sixty 'cause he has very few teeth left. Very odd. If I was running a hotel of my own, I would never have a toothless chap as a waiter. If the chap was real good and I needed him that bad, I would at least buy him a set of false teeth. Anyway, the bill is only seventeen shillings so I give him twenty and ask him to keep the change. I then place three fivers on his tray and he opens his mouth. It's a funny mouth.

"It's O.K." I tell him. "It's for the room. Give it to the receptionist downstairs and please bring up the receipt — and please bring along some tomato ketchup while you are at it." He bows and walks out without saying a word. I ring up the receptionist again and tell him that there is this waiter bringing down some room money for the two extra nights and ask him to make a receipt. He says it will be two hundred and sixty shillings and I tell him its O.K. and that I gave the chap three hundred and that he could credit the whole lot to the account 'cause *we* don't expect any balance by the time we leave. He says O.K. and I hang up.

The waiter comes back with the ketchup and the receipt and I give him another shilling. He doesn't even thank me. He just nods, pockets the shilling and then makes a stiff bow as he walks out. A very odd chap. I lock the door and proceed to the little table and straight away attack the food. There's no beer opener in the room so what I do is, I use one bottle to open the other. Very tricky business if you don't know how. When I've gone through the fish and chips, I decide to call Tonia. She'll be wondering what happened to me. I know she'd like me to call her so that she can tell me off. If I don't call her she'll be hurt and worried even though the minute I say hello she'll start blasting me. Now that I have something in my stomach, I suppose I can take it. The phone is by the bed, so I transport myself on the bed and still sipping at my beer from the bottle, I ask for the number. They put me through but there's no answer. The phone rings a long time but nobody picks it. I hang up and then ask for Dr. Kihagi's number.

"Hello. Dr. Kihagi's residence."

"Hello Julian, this is Kiunyu, I was wondering. . ."

"You." She exclaims. "Where are you?"

"Listen Julian," I cut her short. "I just telephoned the house and Tonia wasn't there so I was wondering whether she's with you." I hear her hiss and then call out, "It's Dodge". Then there is a silent moment and I hear Tonia's cool and calculated voice:

"Yes, what do you want?"

"Look Tonia, I am calling from Voi. I am on my way to Nairobi. Something happened but I can't explain it on the phone. It's important that I dash to Nairobi. I'll be back Sunday."

"So what has that got to do with me; your running away to Nairobi with your Indian? Do you expect it to interest me?"

"Please, please Tonia, I beg you on my word of honour I'll explain all. . ."

"No. It will not be necessary. You don't have to tell me what you are doing. Tell it to the police. They are looking for you."

"OK, Tonia, please do me one favour though. Please don't tell the police that I've gone to Nairobi."

"I am extremely sorry but I'll tell no lies for you or anybody. Please leave me alone," and she hangs up.

Whenever I have a verbal disagreement with Tonia, it depresses me so much that from a very happy man I can become an extremely angry person. She has a way of putting the bad mood on me. I suppose it's simply because she's my wife 'cause if some other bitch blasted me, I wouldn't get into this sort of mood. Or maybe it's just the way she does it, cool and calm. Anyway, that little telephone conversation has left me deflated and depressed. I am wearing an angry face. I can see her sitting there pouring all her sorrow to Julian who would confirm that I am a completely worthless person. I can just about see them sitting there drinking tea or something and talking about me. Blast them.

What I do is, I decide to take off steam on somebody else. I decide to put a little scare on Khimji just for the heck of it. The fellow must be gloting over his sins right now so maybe I should disturb him a little. I ask for his number and he comes on the line. If Sheila had picked up the phone I would have been at a loss somewhat, so I am relieved when I hear Khimji's voice.

"Hello, Khimji here."

"Listen you Indian bastard, you are dead."

"Ha! Dodge my man. Glad to hear from you. How is your opinionated wife?" He laughs.

"I am not kidding man. I am calling you from Voi on my way to Nairobi where I am going to procure myself a gun. I expect to be back on Sunday and before the end of the week you'll be dead. I'll shoot you six times in the stomach right in the open 'cause I don't care if I hang. You ruined my life you bastard. So I'll shoot you in such a way that you'll die slowly after which I'll surrender myself for hanging. There are no two ways about it. You are dead."

"You are mad. What do you think. . ."

"Dig yourself a hole," I cut him short. "Also you can burn all your money 'cause you won't be needing it in hell. I can promise you that if you are not dead by Thursday next week, you'll be in hospital dying. I don't think I'll miss you with six shots. Wish me luck," and I hang up before he can say anything. I don't think he'll believe me but he will sure be uneasy. He might even go to the police for protection and that's exactly what I want. I want them cops to think I've gone to

Nairobi. That way, they wouldn't be looking for me around here. We'll see.

I proceed to the toilet, enjoy a long leak and then come back and open. All of a sudden I want to know whether they've transported Masakalia to the General Hospital or whether he is in a private clinic. I decide to ring the hospital and find out what is happening around there. When I get through I ask this nurse that answers the phone Masakalia's general condition and in what ward they've put him.

"Can I come and visit him?" I ask her.

"Who is speaking?" she asks me.

"His brother," I tell her.

"Which one?"

"The second brother. I got the news a while ago that he is wounded."

"Who gave you the news?"

"The police."

"Where are you calling from?"

"From Voi."

"Please hold on." I hold on for about two minutes and then she comes back on the line.

"Please come at once sir."

"What is happening?" I ask anxiously.

"Your brother is dying. He can't possibly survive. There's a piece of broken glass lodged in his skull. Hurry up. He may be dead before you get here. The doctor has given up. He's practically dead. Hurry up."

My bottle of beer drops to the floor and I replace the receiver even without knowing what I am doing. What!. . . Ah. . .ooh dear. I don't know anything any more. I don't know anything. How? It's not true. How can Masakalia be dying? I just hit him with a half empty bottle of beer — so why should he die? No. I am paralysed. Completely numb. I thought I was doomed but I was only half doomed. Now I am gone. No salvation whatsoever. Ha. So Masakalia is practically dead. He'll be completely dead in a few moments. What about me? I have to hang, haven't I? Oh, sweet Jesus, do something for me. Please do.

All of sudden I get angry with Masakalia. Why the hell does he have to die at my hands. Why? I am cursing under my breath. My whole body is a frigid mass. "Why should you decide to die, you bastard? You know damn well I didn't mean to kill you. I just hit you 'cause you were pestering the hell out of my life and I was getting sick of the whole thing. I hit you on the spur of the moment, but Jesus knows I didn't even plan to hit you. I just hit you. That's all I did. Your dying will be your own blinking choice. I am not responsible. Do you by any chance realize what a bloody mess you have landed me into? Do you? Why do you want to die? What are you dying for? For what reason or motive? I know why, you bastard. You simply want to see me hang. That's what you want. And what did I do to you — eh? Tell me. What did I ever do to you? Nothing. So why die on me? If you want to die, why drag me along? If you are tired of living, why not simply give up the ghost in your sleep and leave us in peace?"

I feel so hot that I think I am going to catch fire. Maybe I've developed instant fever. My blood pressure is high. I can hear my heart clearly. It sounds like a water pump. It's not even a pump. What I mean is, this crude gadget they call a battering ram. It is ramming and battering my whole system so much that I feel like I am going to disintegrate altogether. Gosh, I am hot. My second bottle of beer has spilled all over the carpet so what I do is I grab the third bottle, open it with my teeth and pour it all over my head. The frothing stuff flows all over my face and its only after I've emptied the whole bottle over my head that I realise that I've done another silly thing 'cause I could just as well have put my head under the shower and the cooling would have been more effective. Anyway I am all wet with beer — right through the shirt to my trousers and quite a bit of it has spilled on the floor. I am mad. Does a madman ever know that he's mad? Suppose I was really loony, would I know?

What I do is I take off my shirt and trousers and spread them on the floor to dry. The shirt is much wetter than the trouser and all of a sudden I get this great urge to piss on the trouser to make it equally wet. I am mad. What I do is I slap myself very hard on the thigh but I feel nothing. So what I do next is I go to the bathroom and stand under the shower pants and all. Finally I take off my pants and use them to scrub my back. I then rinse them hang them on the towel rack, dry myself and walk back into the room stark naked. And out of sheer madness. I piss on the carpet. As I do so, I examine my little shrunken penis and feel very sorry for it. It has to die too. It will hang with me.

Out of the blues, I start crying. I don't know what I am crying for, but I just cry. To my surprise I am enjoying it. I am enjoying my tears. They are wet and warm. Perhaps I am crying for the whole world. Crying 'cause I have to leave it behind. It won't be a long time now when I have to say good-bye to it. So maybe I am crying for myself and cheating myself that I am crying for the world. Who knows? Maybe I am scared of hanging after all. I am scared. Yes, I am. Now that I am sure to hang, I am scared. God; I am scared. Now I can see it all. No conjecture. My end is a reality all because of this bastard, Masakalia, who I never intended to kill and who is by now dead. Blast him. The trouble is I am not even sorry because I never intended to have him die. I hold him responsible for his own death and blame him for my eminent hanging. Not even God can help me, no — or can you, dear God?

Who can help me? Who will cry when I am hanged? Will Tonia cry? I don't know. She may cry and be unconsciously, inwardly happy. Inwardly, it will be good riddance. Maybe she'll never cry sincere tears. Who else? There's nobody else.

I try to stop the tears but they don't stop. They pour down my cheeks profusely. I am wetting the sheets and my nose is a mess. I feel lonely and abandoned. I have no friends. No real friends. I have no friends that would shed genuine tears at my death. Anyway there are no public funerals for those condemned to death in a court of law so perhaps those who would cry would not feel the impact. Those prison authorities just bury you in some hole within the prison grounds and if you are lucky, the news of your hanging is printed in some hidden corner of the local news paper. That is the end of it.

No orbituary or memorial service thereafter. I've never heard of a memorial service for anybody who'd been condemned to death by the courts. The church also condemns you to perpetual oblivion. That's me. I shall be hanged and I shall be forgotten. Not even the worms that shall feed on me will remember me. Nobody shall remember me kindly for I don't think that I've been much good to anybody in particular. Through no design on my part, I have been bad all through.

Lord, I feel bad. I feel so sad. Yes, I feel bad. Very bad. My heart is heavy. I am carrying ten tons of a sad heavy load. Who would dare share the load with me? Who would dare comfort a murderer? "Would you, my dear Tonia? No I know you wouldn't like me to hang but I also know that you'd wash your hand of the filth and the smear that the prosecutor heaps on the head of the accused. And you navy chaps that have shared my spoils, joys and sorrows over the everlasting pint of beer, would you help me shoulder my present load? No. You cannot. You dare not. You are decent Officers of the National Defence. Yes. You are gentlemen. You couldn't possibly allow yourself to be mixed up with a murderer even when the murderer is no other than your poor friend Dodge. I forgive you gentlemen. It's not your fault. We must all follow the dictates of Society. So don't pity me. I ask of nobody to shed a tear for me. If there are tears to be shed, I'll shed them myself. I am alone and solely responsible for the sad events of the day. I am responsible for my neck."

Do I understand it all? Do I? It is possible to think of hanging especially when it's other people's necks but my own neck — have I grasped the meaning of it all? How shall I feel the morning they wake me up and escort me to the hanging chamber? Is it a chamber anyway? How do they do it? All I've heard is that they take you to some place, and make you stand on a trap door while they put the noose around your neck, then they release the trap door and you drop through space up the length of the rope just a few feet before you hit the ground. That simply snaps your neck in an instant. No pain. That's what I have heard. So maybe it wouldn't be all that bad especially if they drugged one a little just before the event.

Anyway, we shall see. It should be quite an experience I must say that Masakalia is to blame for every bit of it. The bastard. Going around pretending to be tough and it only required just one little bash on his soft skull for him to die. Ha! I just can't feel sorry for the blighter. He'd absolutely no business dying and putting me in this sort of mess. Absolutely none. He deserves to be eaten by the worms. Oh, how I hate him. I hate him to my last dying breath. I shall hate him till death. I shall curse him when they put the noose around my neck. I shall curse him as they release the trap door and I drop through a void to my death. I shall hate him as much as I hate myself right now. Oh, I hate myself. I hate the world and all that is on it — cows, beasts, birds, dishonest people and even the fish of the sea. When I am dead, they'll all go on living happily. No tears for me. I hate you all. You are all Masakalias and you shall die. You shall follow me and maybe when you die, nobody shall cry for you. Gosh. I think I am mad. I must stop crying. Help me Jesus.

The way things are right now, there's no point hiding in this joint anymore. I might as well walk to the police station and give myself up. Julius Ceasar said something about cowards dying many times before their deaths and I reckon that the longer I stay around the more times I'll die. I have to get the hell out and at least make my will. I don't have much to will to anybody but I wouldn't like them bastards grabbing everything as death duties. Can they do that? Do they charge your heirs death duties when they hang you or is the duty only applicable to those dying in another fashion. Damn if I know. I would most certainly like to clear the point with a lawyer.

I do not intend to hire any lawyer for my defence. That would be money wasted. What I'll do therefore is, I'll turn everything over to Tonia before I am arrested. After all, she is my only heir. Come to think of it, I would have a real problem disposing of anything I have if she weren't around because there's nobody in this whole wide world who would qualify for a cent from me. My mother has been dead since I was around ten and my father died as a prison inmate just a couple of minutes after I knew him for the first time. I have no brothers and sisters and no relatives I know of. My grandmother died a fortnight before I got to Kaheti to visit her and I have never heard of a grandfather either on my father's or mother's side. Tonia is my only relative in the sense that we grew up together as kids. Her mother was a prostitute and my mother was a prostitute and when mother died Miriam, Tonia's mother, took me over and brought me up until she sent me away to my granny at Kaheti and who as I said earlier was already two weeks dead and buried. Anyway, to hell with the past. I don't think that I have one sweet memory of my miserable youth. To hell with it.

I decide that I don't have to go into the nonsense of writing up a testament because that would be another bit of wasted energy. All I have to do is to make a cheque for Tonia for every penny I have in the Bank and then transfer the ownership of the new car into her name. She can use the money I hid in the can behind the fridge for getting the windscreen re-installed and the balance for paying for my coffin. I am going to insist that I be buried in a proper coffin. That will be my only plea after the judgement is read. I do not see why the rudy judge should object, especially given the fact that the coffin will be provided free and at no charge to Government. I would most certainly object to being buried in a coffin provided by the Government. Whoever would be charged with the procurement of the coffin would probably eat half the money and get you buried in a cheap container that would not hold away the worms for a short month. Me, I always dream of solid coffins.

What I do is, I dial home and Tonia picks up the phone immediately. She's still on this long sick-leave that Dr. Kihagi gave her.

"Hello Tonia. This is Dodge. Are you alone? There's something I want you to do for me right away."

"We are quits you bastard, so how can you start telling me of things I have to do for you? You have a large population in Nairobi so why don't you use it — or where are you? You couldn't possibly have arrived in Nairobi so soon."

"Listen Tonia, please. . ."

"No I will not listen to you, Mr. Kiunyu and please understand that there's no point trying to talk to me now or anytime in the house or on the phone. I will not listen to you at all. If you telephone and I recognize your voice, I'll simply bang down the telephone like I am going to do right now," and she banged it down hard.

Well, I got it coming to me but I do not blame her. If she'd given me the time to explain the Sheila thing and my present predicament then perhaps she'd understand. Trouble is she doesn't give me the time. I do not blame her. I am all to blame. If I were in her shoes, perhaps I'd be pissed up too. The only problem is that I have to do something about the whole situation whether she's pissed or not. I have to talk to a friend that she can listen to but then who?

I eliminate all my drinking friends on the grounds that Tonia wouldn't listen to them and to my surprise I discover that there is no friend I can use except Dr. Kihagi and he isn't even a friend. The fellow doesn't like me but I am sure that Tonia would listen to him on account of her deep friendship with Julian. Problem is I can't trust Dr. Kihagi. He is more likely to go shooting his mouth to the cops instead of coming to my help. I have to trick him into silence. It's almost twelve thirty and maybe I can catch him at the hospital before he goes for lunch.

I get through to the hospital and ask for Dr. Kihagi. The operator asks who I am and I tell him that I am Dr. Koinange calling long distance from Nairobi so would she get snappy and connect me to Dr. Kihagi. He comes on the line almost immediately.

"Hello, Dr. Koinange, Kihagi here."

"Listen, Dr. Kihagi. This is not Dr. Koinange, it's Dodge."

"What!"

"Listen, I just told your operator a story so that we could be connected quickly. It's very urgent."

"Is that you Dodge Kiunyu?"

"Yes of course, who else do you want me to be. Listen, I am in a little jam and I think you are the only one who can help Tonia at the moment."

"Hey, what is this? You are a wanted man and we are all wondering where..."

"Please, please," I cut him short. "Listen first. It's about Tonia. I just talked to her and I am afraid she might hang herself again. That is why I want your help."

"What are you talking about? You are in Nairobi, aren't you?"

"Can I trust you?"

"Say that again."

"I asked you whether I could trust you."

"Well, well, well and since when did we start having confidences. I don't trust you and I am not going to get myself mixed up in your personal life at this moment. Sorry but I have work to do. As for Tonia, I think she's OK, if you'd stop pulling her down and getting her mixed up in your disorganised existence. You know, I think you are one of the most...."

"Please cut it off doctor. I understand you. Just in case you were wondering, I am right here in Mombasa. Didn't make it to Nairobi. I am going to be arrested pretty shortly and I just thought before the law descends on me, I could persuade you to do just a little favour for Tonia and also collect four bottles of whisky I have right here before the police get me and share the drinks. Two of the drinks were meant for you but in the circumstances, you can have all the four bottles." I hear him hesitate for a split second and then he says, "How much do I pay you?"

"In the circumstances they are all free." I hear him lick his lips. "And how am I supposed to collect them?"

"First thing is not to say that you are coming to see me otherwise the police are likely to get wind of it, in which case me and the whisky might disappear at the same time. Second thing is, you pass by the Transport office before they close and collect for me a blank vehicle transfer form. You bring along with you some paper and an envelope for me to drop a line to Tonia. You will find me in room 145 at the Rex and please don't bother to get yourself announced. Just walk right in and please, no word to a soul."

"O.K., I am on my way," he says and hangs up. I feel relieved. I don't fancy them cops grabbing me and locking me in for ever before I have a chance to speak to a free person even when the fellow is no other than Dr. Kihagi. He really must love his whisky. Of course he will be very mad when he finds no whisky but all I really need is the time to write a cheque for Tonia, sign the vehicle transfer form and write a small note to Tonia letting her know that being the only sort of relation I have on earth, I shall continue to think kindly of her even at death, and explaining about the curry-can behind the fridge and my coffin. That's all. I'll see to it that by the time he realises that there is no whisky I should be through and I can't see him refusing to take the note to Tonia. Then we shall walk out together and I'll head for the police station while he heads for Cliff Avenue. That will be the beginning of the end. My end.

Now that I've come round to accepting that the end is round the corner, I don't feel so bad. As a matter of fact, I feel some sort of relief. What the heck is life all about anyway? Isn't it simply being born, living and dying? Even God doesn't seem capable of changing this eternal pattern, so why fret? Isn't dying simply like saying goodbye to somebody you love and whom you are sure you will never see again? What is the difference between the fellow who says goodbye to his parents, brothers, sisters, kin and community and sails to a far away undiscovered country from whence he can't return or see his home country folks for ever and the fellow who simply says goodbye to the mother earth and sails to heaven or hell? I reckon that the difference is the same. All is not lost.

What I do is, I ring room service and ask for two beers. If Dr. Kihagi can't have his whisky maybe he wouldn't mind a beer. At least I have to be hospitable. It may be my last act of hospitality. They are very quick with the order. It is the same toothless waiter whom I pay and ask to keep the change. I don't lock the door after he's gone 'cause I am waiting for Dr. Kihagi any minute. I decide to start on my beer 'cause there's no reason why it should be getting warm while I am waiting. The beer tastes good.

I am feeling rather well so I decide to give Tonia a ring just for the heck of it. Now that I'll be dying, I do love her rather a lot. I don't know why, but I do feel that I would like to kiss and hug her goodbye. I should be in her arms when the police come to grab me and she should fight them and claw at them just to show that she does care. Anyway, that's all wishfull thinking. It's self pity. I am simply afraid of dying unloved. Anyway, I feel like giving her a ring and I do. The phone rings for a long time but nobody picks it up. I replace the receiver with a curse. I am taking a long sip from the bottle when the phone rings. I am momentarily startled 'cause nobody is supposed to be ringing me for the obvious reason that nobody is supposed to know that I am around in this joint. I decide that it must be the reception chaps — or could it be Dr. Kihagi? Anyway I pick up the phone and say:

"Room 145, hello."

"Oh, hello. Is that you Dodge? This is Sheila."

I am so stunned that I nearly bolt. How on fucking shit earth could she have known that I am here? All of a sudden I am afraid. I hate complications.

"Sheila — how in the name of all that opens and shuts did you find out that I was here?"

"I didn't, Dodge. It was Khimji who found out."

"What..."

"Listen Dodge. This is urgent. I don't know how, but Khimji has found out that you are confined in the same room where he found us. I overheard him when he was talking to one of his hired thugs. He was very happy about the discovery. He and three of his thugs are already on the way there. The main idea is to beat you up thoroughly so that Khimji can get his own personal satisfaction and then hand you over to the police so that he can get into their good books. They are looking for you all over the place you know. Anyway, now you know. You've to get out of there fast. You may not have much time. I heard Khimji talk of castration. Do something fast."

"OK. Thank you very much Sheila. I am saying this from the very bottom of my heart. I really do appreciate the tip. If I should ever get out of this mess. I shall show you personally how much I appreciate and how apologetic I am about what happened yesterday. Bye for now and please..."

I do not finish the sentence. The door is flung open and Khimji followed by his three assistants troop in breathlessly. I panic. The phone drops out of my hand and my mouth just stays open. They are all looking murderous. I decide that I am licked. I am also inwardly annoyed. I have no serious quarrel with these hooligans and here they come to foil my plans about giving myself up to the police. Anyway, I have no time to reflect. It's all too sudden. The three thugs with Khimji look like real thugs. Bloody bleeders. They are waiting for orders from Khimji and then they will pounce on me like vultures. They all advance quickly and surround me. Khimji holds his hand to stop the thugs from attacking me and then sneers at me with malice mixed in a wry smile. He says, "It's all over now, you whore. I've come to finish you up. So you've been hiding here and cheating the world that you are in Nairobi. Well, I found out. I am cleverer than the police. I will have you castrated like I said before and then I'll call in the police to..."

He doesn't finish. The door opens and Dr. Kihagi puts his head in. At seeing the assembly he frowns and like a true gentleman he enquires, "May I come in?" and I say yes and he walks in. I can see that he is very puzzled and I can also see that Khimji and his thugs are also puzzled. I take advantage of the situation and say breathlessly;

"Prepare for war. These are all thugs. They've just forced their way in and they mean to hurt me." I then turn to Khimji and say: "Mr. Kihagi is a Police Officer."

I can see more puzzlement on all faces and my mind is working very fast just to figure out how the situation can be righted but I haven't got much of a chance. Khimji looks at Dr. Kihagi and frowns.

"What Police Officer are you talking about? This is your doctor friend." Then he turns to Dr. Kihagi.

"Doctor, what is your connection with this matter? Mr. Kiunyu is a wanted criminal and I intend to hand him over to the police. What is your angle in the matter? What is your business with this man?" I can see Khimji's thugs getting murderous again and my poor doctor friend is quite at a loss for words. He finally manages to blurt out, "I have come to consult Mr. Kiunyu on a very delicate issue which is none of your business. Who are you, anyway, and who are these people with you?"

"That's none of your business either," Khimji snarls at him. "You get out of here fast or you just stand there like the rock of ages and watch us drag your friend to the police station. We are taking him there by force. Get him boys," he shouts at his thugs.

Things are happening too fast. In a flash of a second I decide to fight it out to the bitter end. The thugs come for me and in the same split second I grab the full bottle of beer that is just within reach and as I smash it with a backward swing on the nose of one of the thugs behind me, I make a mad dive right onto Khimji's belly and I hear Dr. Kihagi yell. "I'll call the police!" As Khimji and I hit the ground, I get a horse kick in the ribs that sends me rolling like a log and thereby tripping one of the thugs who falls on his advancing friend and as the two disentangle, I spring to my feet. It all happens too quickly. As I spring up, Dr. Kihagi cries out, "Help! Help! Help!" and I see him land a mighty kick on Khimji who is struggling to get up and then smash a terrific left punch on one of the thug's jaw.

There's general confusion. The thug who received my bottle on his breather is completely out, bleeding on the floor. Khimji is struggling for the second time to get onto his feet. Dr. Kihagi is swinging a right at the other thug and I am making a dash for the other bottle of beer. Before I grab it, there is a terrific whack on the side of my left jaw and as I reel sideways, I see the flash of a knife's blade but because I am already off balance, there is no way I can avoid it.

The blinking bastard of a thug drove the knife so hard into my ribs that the impact was like a blow instead of a stab. The searing pain made me yell to heaven and as I staggered, I felt a mighty kick on my balls and as I folded up with pain, I received a knee lift on the chin that made me see a million stars as I fell to the ground. Darkness was coming. The last thing I saw with my strained eyes was a knife blade being driven into Dr. Kihagi's stomach twice in succession. He reeled and fell heavily on me. After that, everything was complete darkness. Heavenly oblivion.

SIX

Friday

"Are you awake now, Mr. Kiunyu?" I hear a distant female voice ask. I try to open my half-open eyes a little bit more but they don't open. Instead they close completely. I feel as if I am sinking again. Then I feel hands lift me and some searing pain cut across my groin. I let out a muffled howl as I feel my buttocks rest on something cold. I hear the same distant female voice

"You will be alright, Mr. Kiunyu. We are merely putting the bed-pan in place." I have neither the mind nor the strength to figure out what is going on so I reckon I just go back to sleep because when I wake up again, there is no bed-pan under my buttocks. I can dimly see that there is a fellow by my bedside feeling me all over. He is wearing a doctor's uniform. The whole thing hasn't registered in my mind so I merely focus my eyes on him the way a hare sleeps with its eyes open. I can see him looking at me but I can't determine whether he is looking at me or merely focussing. It's just a state of mind. Maybe I am the one looking at him.

"You are awake again?" he asks and I wink my eye at him. It's just about all I can do at the moment. I can see shapes but I can't do a thing. I can't move.

"You know you are in hospital, don't you?" and I wink again.

"Any idea how long you've been here?" I move my lips to indicate no and indifference at the same time.

"Well, you've been here since yesterday afternoon and it's time you got completely conscious and awake. There appears to be no medical reason why you should be in a coma at all. Your injuries are superficial. Your system is fighting against recovery and if you don't wake up completely from now on, I'll give you something that will cause you so much pain that you wouldn't be able to sleep again. Get me?" he snaps and I wink.

Even with my half-open eyes, I can see that he is angry with something and if that something is me, then it's too bad because I feel my eyes closing again. I must be doped or something. My eyelids won't open up completely no matter how much facial effort I expend, so I resign myself to sweet slumber and completely ignore the doctor's threat. Sleep is sweet. It's all over me. As I abandon myself to heaven, oblivion and death, I hear a distant voice curse, "The blinking bastard." And then I hear no more. When I come to again somebody is trying to move me around for reasons I cannot fathom till I feel a sharp pain in the groin and open my eyes.

"You have to raise yourself onto the bedpan, Mr. Kiunyu. I can't do it alone," a female voice is saying. "C'mon, you are awake. I'll help you." My eyes open wide and I see the nurse clearly. I notice that it's the same that was on duty when I brought Tonia into hospital after she'd hanged herself. My mind is clear now. I can see things clearly. I can now remember things. I am fully awake. Jesus I am awake. It all comes back to me in a flash from the minute I hit Masakalia on the head to the minute one of Khimji's thugs stabbed me. The whole mess comes back to me and I begin to sweat. At the same time, a sharp pain flashes from the region of my groin and flows to the back of my head. Consciously, I would like to go back to sleep again. I would like to forget all. Oh, sweet Jesus, let me die outright. Why should they cure me only to hang me later?

"Mr. Kiunyu, please help raise yourself onto the bedpan," the nurse repeats.

"I don't need the bedpan," I tell her. I feel that I can tell her what I want and what I don't want.

"Are you sure?"

"I will not be using it any more: I am not a baby." I manage to say politely.

"But you can't get out of bed yet." she tells me.

"And why not?"

"Because you are not supposed to get out of your bed." For the first time I look around myself. I am in the same small private ward where Tonia had been housed. What a coincidence. At the botton of the bed and clamped upside-down about three feet above the level of the bed is this ugly plastic transparent pipe dripping into my system through my right foot. My right arm is handcuffed and there is a two foot long chain attaching it to the upper right hand leg of the bed. There is sufficient length of chain for me to be able to move my hand around freely but the fact still remains that I am chained. I am conscious of it.

"Why am I chained," I ask the nurse who is just standing there like an elephant holding the bed-pan.

"The police did it. They have the keys to the lock attaching the chain to the bed."

"Are they allowed to chain patients who are in a state of half coma?"

"I can't tell you that Mr. Kiunyu. I do what the doctor says."

"Which doctor?"

"Dr. Kantai. Any doctor. When the police give orders, every doctor has to obey."

"What about Dr. Kihagi? What became of him? Where is he?"

"You should know that better, Mr. Kiunyu."

"And why should I know better? What do you mean?"

"You were with him, weren't you?"

"With him, of course. I have been with him many times. But what time are you referring to?"

"When he got killed. You should know, shouldn't you?"

"What? Did you say killed?"

"I did".

"What. . . No, no, no! You can't mean that. You've got to be kidding."

"Well, he died in your hotel room, didn't he?"

It doesn't seem to make sense to me. No sense at all. Maybe this nurse is crazy. She could be.

"Did you say he is dead?" I ask emphatically.

"There's nothing to tell. He died on the spot. You should know better since you were responsible." I am all excited. I want her to talk fast but she doesn't. I want to hear it all quickly.

"What about the others. . .the Indian and his thugs?" I am all excited. I am wide awake. I don't even feel the pain in the groin except that my heart is pounding right on top of the wound.

"I don't know. I suppose they were arrested."

"None of them were brought to the hospital?"

"Oh yes. One of them was treated for cuts on the face. He'd six teeth missing. The police took him afterwards. They are putting the blame on you."

"Interesting. Very interesting.. Did somebody visit me?"

"I am not on duty all the time," she shrugs her shoulders and then adds, "Since you are awake and you don't need the bedpan, I will be off to attend to other patients. The doctor may want to come and examine you."

"Oh no. You don't have to leave yet. You have to remove that silly tube dripping into my foot, first."

"I am sorry but I can't do that until the doctor says so."

"Where is he?"

"He said to call him as soon as you are fully awake."

"Why?"

"I don't know. I suppose he wants to determine when you are able to talk to the police."

"Do they want to talk to me?"

"They've been pestering us all morning. I think they want to talk to you very much -- after all, you killed Dr. Kihagi."

"What ! Say that again?"

"That is the story that the others told. You killed him by mistake of course. I am not blaming you. You intended to stab one of your aggressors but stabbed Dr. Kihagi by mistake. Most of us feel sorry for you. He was your friend, wasn't he?"

"Listen Miss, just hold your jaw. Did you say that I am supposed to have stabbed Dr. Kihagi?" I am completely shocked. It's just like Khimji to tell such a fantastic lie. I can see it all. I passed out and Dr. Kihagi died and the only witnesses were the survivors. I shall be alone against four. Nobody else saw the fight. What a damnable skunk Khimji is. What a hateful, filthy, cheating Indian he is. Oh God, how I'd like to strangle him. He might be right though. With the death of Masakalia alone, I am going to hang anyway and I wouldn't hang any harder or more painfully with two murders on my head. I may even collaborate the story just for the heck of it. That would really shock Khimji and his thugs. They wouldn't know what was happening to me. It may even make Khimji love me and remember me with kindness when I am gone, then perhaps he won't pester his sister any more.

"May I go now, please?" the nurse asks. I have forgotten her presence in the room. My mind is wandering.

"Yes, you may go," I tell her. "By the way, what did you say your name was?"

"But I have told you my name before, Mr. Kiunyu," and with that she walks out. I put my left hand through the sheets and feel the bandages all over my body. I don't want to look. I don't like to look at bandages. They frighten me. I am always frightened of what they conceal.

Ha! So I might be accused of having killed Dr. Kihagi? How very absurd: indeed what an invention? What a twist of events. No, I couldn't collaborate with Khimji even for fun. Dr. Kihagi died trying to save my life. He got into the war without knowing what the whole business was all about. I shall always remember him with kindness, may his soul rest in peace. As for Khimji he should go to jail and have a little taste of the African posho. I hope he gets raped by twenty homosexual prisoners so that when he comes out of jail his arse-hole will be so large that he will permanently smear his pants with involuntary shit, the bastard.

I am in the middle of these confused thoughts when the doctor opens the door and walks in. He is rather youngish. He is as straight as a Masai and is extremely good looking. I haven't met him before.

"I am told you are awake and talking, Mr. Kiunyu. By the way, I am Dr. Kantai."

"Glad to meet you Doctor. How are the injuries?"

"You are a very lucky man, Mr. Kiunyu. The stab went through flesh and touched no vital parts so it's just a wound that has to heal. The wound is deep but clean. The knife was sharp but clean. Any risk of internal bleeding has now been eliminated. I expect that the healing will be normal. We simply cleaned the wound and stitched. You are carrying three stitches. I shall get that bottle removed. No reason why you can't eat solids. Your intestines have not been touched. You are a lucky man. How do you feel?"

"Groggy. I feel sort of numb. I can't feel my limbs."

"You've rested them for too long, that's why. We were a little bit baffled. After the blood transfusion, we couldn't understand why you would not recover to full consciousness for so long. We expect to keep you here for not more than two days after which you will of course go to jail or custody or wherever the police shall want to take you. You can come back for change of dressing from time to time if need be, but I do not think that it will be necessary. Your wound will heal easily. But tell me, Mr. Kiunyu, how did Dr. Kihagi get involved in the fight?

What was he doing there? I can't seem to understand that angle."

"You are not likely to understand it from me doctor because I don't know much about it myself," I retort.

"But you called him on the phone, didn't you? That is what our telephone operator says. She listened in on the conversation."

"And I suppose you approve," I retort sarcastically.

"That sounds like a problem in my area and not in yours and doesn't shed any light on my question. Dr. Kihagi was your family friend. My knowledge of him is that he was a straight person who would not normally involve himself in death battles with thugs. The police are puzzled too. Your wife and Julian are even more puzzled. We have all been waiting for you to wake up so that you can shed some light on the matter."

"Oh that matter, I am afraid that I have no light to shed at this moment. Didn't the others explain — I mean the Indian and his group?"

"I am afraid not. All we know is that you and doctor Kihagi were in the room when the Indian and his assistants broke in with the aim of grabbing you and handing you over to the police. The police were all over town looking for you on account of the Masakalia affair. You resisted arrest, so to say, and a fight ensued with you and Dr. Kihagi on one side generally fighting against the others. In the course of the fight, and as a result of good dodging, the knife which you'd aimed at one of the Indian's assistants found its way right into Dr. Kihagi's rear. You stumbled and fell, and on falling on you, Dr. Kihagi got his second wound in the stomach as he fell on the same knife which you were holding upright. The Indian and his assistants had to struggle to disarm you but you armed yourself with a bottle and were going to do a lot of damage with it, but luckily, you were stopped by one of the fellows who admitted stabbing you in self-defence. That is the way it is understood, unless you can shed some more light as I indicated earlier. As you can see for yourself, one does not understand what Dr. Kihagi was doing there."

"You say the story has been published in the papers?"

"It has. The Indian and his assistants are held in custody until you come around and collaborate their story."

"But why hold them in custody? It would appear from what you say that I am the only villain in that scene."

"I don't know. The police may have something up their sleeve. One thing is not clear though. It is not clear why the Indian burst in on you with armed guards and, of course, he had no mandate to arrest you or anybody. You had already fought with him before, so I understand, and the police are looking for a plot. How for instance did he know where you were hiding while hundreds of policemen were combing the whole town with a fine tooth comb and they couldn't find you? Why didn't he tip the police of your whereabouts instead of taking the law into his own hands? If he had not acted as he did, would Dr. Kihagi be dead and would you be in hospital, et cetera? Anyway the police seem to be in possession of some information that warrants keeping the Indian and his guards under lock."

"You must be following the case closely, Dr. Kantai, and I thank you for the information. Incidentally, why are you telling me all this?"

"But you are probably going to be hanged, Mr. Kiunyu. One can't help having some compassion for you — besides, Dr. Kihagi was my friend. I can't help being interested in the case. He was your friend too. In a way, we have a sad common factor."

"You are wrong there. He wasn't my friend. Not the way you think. He was a family friend, if that means anything to you."

"Oh, come, come. You should never speak ill of the dead. But tell me, how come that from the very first day you two met here in the hospital, Dr. Kihagi fabricated a false medical report for you if he was not your personal friend?"

"What are you talking about, Doctor?" I am so suprised at this confession that I have to control all my facial muscles to keep a straight face.

"You know damn well what I am talking about, Mr. Kiunyu, don't you? Your wife hanged herself and you brought her here in a state of unconsciousness and explained her state as resulting from hanging. She had hanged herself as you very well know yourself. The doctor's report talked of something very different. He's explained the circumstances to me. He was doing a favour to a friend. How can you tell me now that he was not your friend? He was. I know that for sure and so do the police. The only thing that nobody seems to understand is why you called him and practically dragged him to his death — so to speak. What I mean is, if you didn't call him, he would be alive today, all other things considered."

I don't know whether it's a trap to get all the dope out of me so that he can pass it on to the police or whether he is simply interested on the grounds that Dr. Kihagi was a sad common factor. I can not imagine that he would go as far as telling me about the false medical report if he really meant harm for me, unless it was a very subtle bait to make me unburden my heart. I have to be careful though. One never knows. I have to use my ears and not my mouth. If Dr. Kantai feels like talking and being friendly, let him. I am however surprised and partly amused at the collusion between the two doctors in changing the Tonia medical report from hanging to epileptic fits or whatever it was. When I remember Tonia denying my accusation vehemently with the put-on innocence and sincerity of a saint and Dr. Kihagi talking about external stimulus and phenomena, et cetera, I can't help but chuckle to myself. So Tonia is such a bloody convincing liar? I would like her to drop in right now and I confront her with the truth.

"Tell me doctor, did my wife actually know that the story about epilepsy was fabricated?"

"Of course she did. You can't make up such a report and not discuss it with the patient otherwise there would be contradictions." He rubs his hands together and continues.

"Fine. Now that you are fully conscious, you may shortly get a visit from the police." He starts moving away. "Perhaps you'll find it easier to talk to them. The nurse will come to remove the bottle."

The door to my cubicle opens and my old nurse friend lets herself in stealthily. It's been quite sometime since Dr. Kantai left me to my thoughts. Must be more than thirty minutes — or fifty. I don't know. I don't have a watch on me. For all that time, I've been holding a meeting with myself where I've been chairman, speaker and the audience, all at the same time. The entry of the nurse is like an intrustion in the Boardroom or like the bell of an alarm clock in the middle of a nightmare. She moves right over to the bed and looks at me without blinking. I am surprised.

"Hey, what's the matter?" I ask her.

"Are you ready for the police?" she asks me in return.

"Does that depend on me? If it does, then I am not ready. I shall not be ready for a year starting next week. Meantime would you please remove that bottle out of my sight," and she does it painfully.

"I don't think that you'll even have a minute, Mr. Kiunyu. They are outside."

"So why did you come to consult me?"

"They wanted to be announced."

"OK. You have announced them. Next time they come around, be sure to get a trumpet. The announcement of such important people should be accompanied by some pomp. Let them in, sister. Cops are nice people to listen to especially when you have made up your mind that. . ."

"Made up your mind about what?" A voice cuts me short as the door is thrown open violently and a bandaged figure walks in defiantly followed by two others in police uniform. Surprised, the nurse almost salutes as she walks out, and after my second look at the bandaged figure standing there right by the bedside staring at me through hard mocking eyes, I have a momentary blackout.

Of all the devils in Rome, I cannot believe my eyes. It must be a nightmare. I don't even know whether I am waking up from a dream or whether I've had a momentary fit out of which I am recovering. I don't know whether the figure has been there for half a minute or twenty minutes all. All I know is that when I focus properly, the bandaged figure in front of me must be the devil's own ghost.

I shut my eyes for a moment and hold my brain. I decide not to think for as long as I can and when my heart, which has been floating in space settles back into its cradle, I open my eyes and focus them unbelievingly on Masakalia. I don't know what to think. I just look at him like a half-wit staring at a crack in the wall.

Yes. It's Masakalia alright. I am not dreaming. He is wearing police uniform and bandages on the head like he should, but I can't figure out why he should be there. He should be dead. He doesn't look soiled or anything, so he did not crawl from any dirty grave. He doesn't look like he has been dug out of any grave at all. He just looks like a bandaged police officer escorted by these two constables who cheated me out of my money and who are standing at attention behind him like idiots. I decide that wonders are many and that surprises and wonders are the same thing and that whatever name you give to a combination of those two phonomena, it could be labelled my constant companion. After all the staring business Masakalia opens his mouth and says enquiringly, "Well?" I reply in the same enquiring tone, "Well?" and we continue the staring act.

After a brief moment, he pulls the enamelled stool used by the nurse and comes to sit by the head of the bed just a few inches from me. He shakes his head as if in disbelief and then says, "Well, what do you have to say, Mr. Kiunyu? Don't you welcome friends when they come to visit you?"

I say nothing. I am still with my friends Wonder and Surprise. Masakalia looks at his watch and then clears his throat.

"Since you won't welcome me, I shall welcome myself. Let me start by telling you, that the first part of this particular visit is meant to be a friendly one so please feel at home. How are you feeling after yesterday's commotion?"

Truth of the matter is, I am taken so much by surprise that I don't even think I can hold a logical conversation with Masakalia. I have seen him in so many dead positions in my mind that I just can't see him sitting there in front of me. I have been imagining that he was buried in a purple coffin — why, I don't know. All I know is that whenever my mind wondered and I saw him being lowered into the grave, the coffin was purple and he was lying on his left side instead of on his back like most dead people do. The funny thing is that I could imagine him in my mind clenching his right fist right there in the coffin and shaking his hand at me.

That was all imagination. Right now the fellow is here right in front of me on what he calls a friendly visit. Well, I must be somebody. To be visited by the dead is no small thing. Anyway, this Masakalia sitting in front of me looks very far from being dead — so what was the blinking nurse talking about when she said he was dead? Isn't that what she said? Something to that effect anyway. She said doctors had lost all hope and that the fellow was dying. She even intimated that by the time I drove from Voi to Mombasa, which is just a few minutes, the fellow would be dead unless I was lucky. Did I misinterpret facts or did I simply draw unconscious conclusions? Why didn't somebody tell me before now that the fellow was not dead? Why did I have to torture myself on his account only to find him sitting in front of me and looking at me with mocking eyes? Was it a coinage of my own mind or did the blinking nurse mislead me? I do not know. I don't even remember whether it was the nurse or the operator. These are useless questions.

Masakalia is here and alive but I can't see why he would need these cheating constables as bodyguards since I am chained and I have no intention of hitting him on the head again.

"Don't you have anything to say, Mr. Kiunyu?" Masakalia enquires after a long pause.

"I'll be dammed if I know what to say. All I can say is that I am glad to see you alive."

"What do you mean? Did you expect to see me dead? So you are the fellow who telephoned from Voi pretending to be my brother. That was very dumb on your part because I have no brother."

I reckon I've just made a grave mistake with my first little speech. Masakalia is not supposed to know that I thought him dead. In fact nobody knows, so I have to debrain-wash myself on that idea otherwise I shall not be able to think straight.

"It's only that I did not expect to see you. Thought you should be in hospital. I didn't make any telephone call on your account.

"Um. I have been in and out of hospital as you can see. I don't have to be in limbo for twenty four hours before I can recover from the effects of a little violence. I am a police officer, you know."

"Yes. I know. For how long were you in hospital?"

"I am surprised that this should be of interest to you, but if you really want to know, I've been on duty since yesterday and I am charged with your case. By the time you were pretending that you were telephoning from Voi, I was being discharged. We told you that little story about my dying condition so that you might do something silly and we catch you."

"Oh, I see."

"That's why I am asking you whether you have something to say on the friendly angle before we get to business."

"I am afraid I find your friendly angle a little bit artificial since between friends, bodyguards should not be necessary. Those two constables robbed me, you know."

"My assistants are not bodyguards, Mr. Kiunyu. I merely want a third party to be present when we get to the real business."

"I see. You want witnesses — that's OK, by me. You may now move onto your business angle. I am ready." I am feeling an utter fool.

"Always the Dodge Kiunyu. Fine. We now get to business. You know the score. I am investigating a police case in which you are implicated in causing grievous bodily harm to a police officer. You are also implicated in the death of a medical doctor. There are other minor charges for which you'll be found guilty by inference if you are found guilty on these two main charges. These two charges are grave, Mr. Kiunyu. You'll most certainly need a lawyer. But tell me, are you in any way sorry for what you have done?"

"Would it help?" I ask him.

"Well, I reckon your question is your answer. Let us not misunderstand each other. Fine. For the first charge, I have no points for which I want clarification from you. I know all the answers. I shall be in the witness stand myself and the police do not deem any investigation necessary. I have made my disposition. It's for the second charge that I want to clear some points with you."

"And how will you explain the motive for my hitting you if you have all the answers for the first charge as you claim?"

"I don't have to answer you. I am putting the questions."

"You'll be surprised, Mr. Masakalia. You'll be surprised that I may have some questions to raise too. It's my health that is at stake and not yours."

"Do you by any chance understand the gravity of these two charges, Mr. Kiunyu?"

"You are charging me, Mr. Masakalia. I've not been officially notified of any charges."

"How can you be so naive, Mr. Kiunyu? I represent the law and I am therefore notifying you officially."

"So what is the charge, murder and assault?"

"I have never taken you for a fool at any one time. You should know the charges. You know your crimes. I can assure you that you will not be framed. You can trust me for that."

"Mr. Masakalia, if the day should dawn when I'll trust you with my life, then I shall know that I have ceased to be me. I shall cut my throat. Anyway, this is all useless talk. Simply ask your questions and go. I want to sleep. I am sick you know. I am in hospital.

"I see. So that is your attitude?"

"Correct."

"And you have given adequate thought to the jam you are in? You understand the implications?"

"That is not a question. I don't have to answer."

"Do you realize that you are talking to the police — that you are talking to the law?"

"No. I am talking to thieves." Masakalia gets off the stool and backs away from me as if I was a poisonous snake. His face is furrowed and his eyes are hard as he spits out words from his tightened lips.

"You have, in the presence of three police officers, made an accusation which I shall certainly add to your charges. You are insulting the law."

"No. I am insulting thieves. The three of you are thieves and being an officer, you are a bigger thief. I am not afraid. I would like this to appear on record. You are a thief, Mr. Charles Masakalia, and I shall denounce you in court. Make it an extra charge and I'll be happier.

"Are you mad by any chance, Mr. Kiunyu?"

"I don't know. I don't think so. What I do know is that I am sick and chained and that the three of you are thieves." The big cop moves over to Masakalia and whispers.

"Leave him alone, Chief. I think you were right about his madness." He whispers in such a way that I hear it all but I don't say anything. What I have decided is that I shall not accept to be bullied. Secondly, I have decided that since Masakalia is not dead, my charges should be nothing compared to what I imagined. If truth were to prevail, the death of my friend the doctor cannot be imputed to me. The only serious charge would be that relating to Masakalia's skull and I would be prepared to tell the whole truth so that he does not escape scot-free to go on bleeding poor folk. Anyway, the very sight of Masakalia puts me into an aggressive mood right now. They should have sent another police officer, but then Masakalia is in charge of the crime branch so he has to do it himself.

The fact of the matter is that I do not know whether my mind is working properly or not. I need time to think. The rising of Masakalia from the dead just about ruined all the beautiful and ugly thoughts I had coined up about death and my neck to the extent that right now I am playing for time to put new ideas together. The only way to gain time is to be aggressive and rude. If I was not in hospital, I know that the blighters would whip the hell out of me, but right now, they can't lay their hands on me. I am protected by my condition and Masakalia knows it.

There are some serious decisions that I have to take. I had resigned myself to jail and death but now things are different. There can only be jail; not death. If there is no fake manslaughter charge on the Kihagi angle — and there wouldn't — then my principal crime will be the bottle on Masakalia's head. I could get as much as five years on that alone, but if the motive is sufficiently diluted by my own accusations in relation to Masakalia's conduct, then I may get two or three years. When you compare this to the rope that has been dangling over my head since that telephone call to the hospital, then you'll agree with me that anything I get will be less than what I expected. That's why I have decided to be forthright with the police 'cause they can't make it worse. It also means that I have to punch holes into the story told by Khimji and his thugs and the only way to do it is by telling white truth. Maybe with a little bit of luck I'll just manage to make it palatable. I have to think it over and I can't do so with Masakalia standing over me.

"Do I take it that you have no more questions, Mr. Masakalia, or am I permitted to call you Charles?"

"Mr. Kiunyu."

"Yes, Charles."

"If you continue in that vein, I shall have you removed from here, sick or not sick, and arrange with hospital authorities that you receive treatment in one of our wards."

"You mean one of your cells, don't you?"

"I said earlier that you are not a fool"

"Go right ahead, dear Charles. Get me removed into a police cell. That sort of thing should improve your case in court."

"Please sir," the big constable pleads, "the fellow is mad. In all my career I have never had to take as much nonsense as you are taking from this man. He's called us thieves. Is this how civilians should respect the police force?"

"Leave it to me Odhiambo. We haven't started on what we came here to talk about." He turns to me and continues in the same breath, "What I want to know from you Mr. Kiunyu is, first, what you were doing and where you were between the time you hit me and the time that Khimji and his assistants found you in room 145 of the Rex hotel having a drink with Dr. Kihagi?"

"I was at the Rex in the same room all the time," I tell him, knowing fully well that he already knows.

"And what were you doing?"

"Mostly sleeping. You may call it taking a vacation. I rested very well."

"Can you please recount the events from the beginning; that is from Wednesday afternoon?"

"Yes. It's simple. If I start with the Railway Club, you called me out and tried to bleed me of..."

"No." he cuts me short, "I am not asking for old history. I am asking you to recount the events from the minute you hit me."

"I am sorry but I thought you wanted to know why I hit you. That should be the beginning. It shows the motive. If it does not interest you, then all I can tell you is that I hit you and walked away to the Rex hotel and got in unannounced right up to room 145 which was still open since I'd quit there a few hours earlier and there I stayed put till you know when."

"Why did you stay put in the hotel? Why didn't you go home?"

'Because your hounds would have been after my skin for knocking you out cold.'

"You accept then, that you were a fugitive from justice for the time you were hiding in the hotel."

"No. I do not accept."

"But you were hiding from the law."

"No. If I was hiding, I was hiding from thieves." Masakalia is livid. I can see his muscles twitching. He didn't like that last bit at all.

"Mr. Kiunyu," he says tersely, "the next time you refer to me or any of my colleagues as a thief, I'll smash your jaw right here in this hospital room and bear the consequences. Just get that right in your thick skull."

"Talking of skulls, yours is not very thin either," I retort. It was a grave mistake. Masakalia moves one step forward and rams his fist so hard on my jaw that I see black Asparagus dancing before my eyes. The bastard, how dare he hit a sick chained man? I feel so bad that all I can do is cry out in anger.

"Continue, you bastard. Continue. Hit me again, you son of a bitch," but he doesn't. He just stares down at me rubbing his knuckles while my left hand is pressing hard on the button for the call-bell for the nurse. He notices my hand and slaps it away from the button and then looks at his constables and then at me.

"That will teach you next time, Mr. Kiunyu. Just get fresh with me next time and I'll smash you whole jaw out of joint."

"You are a thief," I cry out and he comes at me again and slaps me twice in succession just as the door is flung open and Dr. Kantai stands at the threshold staring at the scene with popping eyes.

"What is happening here?" he asks. Masakalia looks at him like an owl, surprised that the doctor witnessed the action, and then puts his hands in his pockets.

"They are torturing me," I blurt out.

"What!" the doctor cries.

"I said they are torturing me. Not the three, only Masakalia here. He wants me to wear bandages on the head like he is wearing." Masakalia's hands shoot out of his pockets and he is coming for me again, but he manages to control himself halfway and with a lot of effort.

"I want an explanation to this," the doctor says calmly addressing himself to Masakalia.

"I am extremely sorry doctor, but your patient aggravated me to no end. I am sorry — but he is responsible. He's extremely abusive."

"So you beat him?"

"I didn't beat him, I hit him."

"What's the difference?"

"OK, I am sorry," Masakalia says with bad grace. "Can I please see you, doctor, outside for a while?"

"Not until I know exactly what is going on. How can you, a senior police officer, come to the hospital to beat up a patient who is chained. Mr. Kiunyu should be discharged by tomorrow and you'll have all the time to question him. How can you start beating him in hospital? That is savage."

"I am investigating a serious case, Doctor, and Mr. Kiunyu is so deeply implicated that we can't simply take insults from him when we are looking for facts."

"So you get your facts with fists? I am afraid, Inspector, that I have no alternative but to lodge a complaint against you. Being a senior offficer you should know better."

"You'll complain to who?"

"To your superiors, of course. To the Assistant Commissioner."

"And what do you think will happen?"

"I don't like your attitude, Mr. Masakalia."

"Nobody asked you to like it. If you really want to know, I don't like yours either. Go ahead and complain if you think it will get you anywhere. This is new Kenya, Doctor. Please look around you. For how long can one look around before seeing daylight?"

"So the new Kenya belongs to the police, does it?"

"Good-bye doctor. I offered my humble apologies and you did not accept. I offer them again. If you do not accept, then go right ahead and do what you deem fit. I shall return in the evening to interrogate Mr. Kiunyu."

"The hospital will have to confirm that he is fit for interrogation, Inspector, so please ring before you come."

"You can't block police work without hurting yourself doctor. I know that Mr. Kiunyu is fit for discussion and I shall return at 8.30 p.m. tonight so you should make sure that he eats his dinner before."

"If your discussion now had to end in patient torture, how do I know that it will not be the same thing this evening?"

"You are not supposed to know, Doctor. This is a police case."

"I am afraid you are wrong. The police case is not in hospital. It is in the police files. What we have here is a patient who is most certainly a hospital case. You can't come here and start torturing patients. You have to wait till they are discharged for them to become a police case."

"I am sorry, Doctor. Really sorry but you are refusing to see my side of the case, so I am afraid I have to ignore yours too."

"You may now go, Inspector. I want to examine my patient." Masakalia and the two constables start trooping out, but at the door, Masakalia turns and points a wagging finger at me.

"Mr. Kiunyu, that was a lot of good time wasted and a lot of bad blood thrown about all for nothing and no good for nobody. If the same thing should repeat itself next time I am around, you'll go back into a coma for a week so wear a civil tongue, my boy. All patience has its limits. For the record, we shall book this first interview as a mere preliminary. Investigation starts tonight."

"And me who thought all along that you were a civilised police officer from Kakamega — how could I have been so dumb," I sneer at him knowing full well that I am protected. He bites his lower lip, shakes his fist at me and then closes the door after him without saying a word. The doctor turns, bends and feels my cheeks.

"Tell me; how did it all start?" he asks me. "I certainly intend to lodge an official complaint." I decide that I can do myself no harm by smearing Masakalia with a little of his own dirt, so I tell the doctor how it all happened leading to my smashing Masakalia on the head and how his nasty behaviour at the hospital was more revenge than anything else, et cetera. I add a bit of salt here and a bit of salt there, and the doctor feels my jaw again. It's swollen where that first punch landed.

"I'll have to make a medical report," he says finally.

"Tell me doctor, can the police budge in on patients anytime they want to?"

"In principle, no. We have to determine whether a patient is fit enough to receive a visit or not."

"So why was Masakalia so sure about his rights vis a vis patients?"

"You heard him yourself. He warned me that this is new Kenya and advised me to look around me."

"So what are you going to do?"

"Leave that to me. The Assistant Commissioner of Police for the Province is Masakalia's own tribesman so I would be wasting my time lodging a complaint in that direction. I'll have to do it different. The way things are going in this country, you can't even get somebody to listen to your complaint unless you have a godfather. It's getting out of hand. If you want something done, you need a godfather and if you do not want something done, you again need a godfather. One has always got to go through somebody else. We have no system. We had a system once but now, the system is vested in those who godfather others. There is of course a lot of give and take but your general welfare depends on whether you are the taker or the giver. Anyway, don't worry. I said I will lodge a complaint and lodge it I will."

All of a sudden, I feel some admiration for this doctor. The fellow is a decent chap in his own quiet way.

"You will not be interviewed again tonight. You are not well. You need a lot of sleep. As the police suggested, you'll have your dinner early — say around 7.45 p.m., after which you'll go to sleep. I shall myself come back around that time to see that everything is OK., but for now I have to go for my own little rest." He walks out and I go to sleep again.

I must have slept for a few hours. When I wake up it is night. The room is in half darkness. I hear an exchange of words outside and then the doctor opens the door, switches on the light and walks in closing the door with a bang as if he was angry with somebody. He walks over to the bed and pulls back the bedding witout a word and examines the bandages over my stomach.

"Not so bad" he says without bothering to look at me.

"Yeah," I grunt. As a matter of fact I am feeling O.K. This last bit of sleep must have done me some good.

"How do you feel?"

"Not bad at all." I tell him.

"Fine." He places his hand about two inches from the wound in my groin and presses. I shriek with pain and he lets go.

"Not too bad," he says. "We'll get the dressing changed in the morning." I say nothing so he continues "Are you expecting your friend Masakalia?"

"He can come and waste his time if he wants to. I am not going to make a formal statement till I've consulted a lawyer."

"If he ever comes at all it will be to break your jaw completely and not to waste his time," he says.

"You mean you can't stop him from beating up your patients?"

"Well, yes and no, but don't worry yourself. I'll fix the bastard. I'll get him."

"What do you mean?"

"Well, you heard him this morning. He asked me to look around me and I sure have been looking around. That's why I am late. Would you expect that I would take lip from an opinionated Kakamegaman and do nothing about it. I don't think that we shall expect much trouble from the fellow from now on."

"What happened?"

"No harm you knowing I suppose. Briefly the fellow has been harassing quite a few people for bribes and not taking their connections into account. He's been very clever about it and always uses blackmail so that the victims can't complain much without exposing themselves. He has hurt one or two who have connections with people close to the top but who have not been able to do anything because the fellow is protected by his tribesman. Just by some stroke of luck, the big tribesman is in big trouble himself over some embezzling case he is involved in with other bigger fish and I reckon that he will be sacrificed in order to save the fish. I have it from a reliable source close to the top who happened, by coincidence, to have been a recipient of the earlier complaints against Masakalia. When I told him of my complaint, he was the happiest man on earth. At least mine was a genuine complaint with no blackmail involved and that seemed to have given him some firm ground for consultation with the top. He made the telephone call to Nairobi in my presence."

"Who is it... I mean your contact who made the call?"

"He's just somebody I know. According to him, instructions may be issued to have the fellow removed. He may even be charged. My contact got the green light to arrange for a short interview with the press. He's already rang a journalist friend of mine to arrange for a short interview tomorrow morning with hospital staff. We'll have the interview right here in this room tomorrow morning at ten." This is too fast for me.

"Do I have to be involved in the interview? Anyway, what would you expect to come out of the interview?"

"Oh nothing much. Simply that police torture at the coast has become so widespread and so commonplace that some irresponsible police officers will not hesitate to torture patients in a government hospital. The journalist will, of course, be briefed by my friend beforehand. What will finally appear in the newspaper will be a double edged dagger aiming not only at Masakalia but also at his senior tribesman who, as I said earlier, is being sacrificed. In a way, I am glad. I'll get a chance of putting the hospital in the news for a change. Maybe we'll get a supplementary budget for some equipment we need badly."

"Who'll be present at the interview?"

"Just the three of us; you, the journalist and myself. Don't worry, I'll do the talking. We shall not need that story of yours showing revenge as the motive for torture. That would damage our story. You will be photographed of course. We have to change that bandage on your stomach and make it wider so as to give the best effect with the camera and then put a compress on your jaw which I see is no longer swollen so that the effects of his actions become more visible. The final version of the story to be published will of course have to be approved by my friend. It's between him and his pressman."

"And will Masakalia be interviewed later?"

"What for? We are the ones lodging a complaint. You can rest assured that whatever will be printed will not hurt your case. It might on the contrary, improve it. Needless to say, the fellow will be withdrawn from dealing with your case."

"Well, I must thank you, Doctor. I am really grateful to you. I swear to God I am."

"I don't know what you are grateful for. It's not for your sake that I went to consult my friend. I went to lodge a genuine complaint like I said I would and like any responsible doctor should. I thought nothing about improving your case and I am not sure that it is improved. The charges against you still remain and before the fellow and his boss are kicked in the ass, they may make it real bad for you just to get even. They'll kick when they can. They are still in office you know. You should expect anything in the way of extra charges but nobody is going to molest my patients leave alone see them without my permission. If you don't want to speak to them just tell me and I wouldn't let them in. I have to exercise my authority here at the hospital. Let the police exercise theirs where they should."

"Did you actually say that the two may be sacked?"

"No. All I know is that instructions will be given from the top for Masakalia to be removed. Maybe transferred from here or he maybe sacked. I don't know."

"And until those instructions are issued, what is to stop him bursting in here and telling you to go to hell?"

"Do you take me for a fool, Mr. Kiunyu? The fellow has already been talked to from other quarters and you can bet your bandages that wherever he is this evening, he's shitting on himself. Anyway, he already knows that he'll be withdrawn from the case so why would he come bursting in here? If anybody comes, it'll probably be another cop."

"Poor fellow. I sympathise with him. What a drop? It's difficult to imagine that fortune is so elusive. I can hardly imagine seeing Masakalia as just another civilian. I can't visualize it. For me, he is the entire police force."

"Don't visualize it, Mr. Kiunyu. What you are going to do now is to eat and go to sleep again and remember before you sleep that what you are calling fortune is not fortune at all. It is ill gotten gains. You must also remember that what will be meted out to him will be just as unfair as what he has meted out to others. Remember also that it will not be out of consideration for a molested patient like you that he'll get the axe but rather because he's hurt the progeny of an elephant. You are just a pawn. Last of all, don't forget that it's mainly through luck on my part that things have taken the turn they have. Don't forget that. I'll drop in to make sure that the nurse has done the bandages right around nine thirty tomorrow morning. Good night."

He goes out and I am left to my thoughts. So Masakalia is getting a squeeze. Who'd have imagined that this young doctor was capable of influencing things the way he has. He is really sure of the outcome, or is he merely gloating? One thing is clear; he is more interested in his own publicity in the press than anything else. Can't blame him for it. If he can get more hospital equipment as a result of the publicity, then that's good for all patients. It's OK for me so long as I don't have to answer questions. I have as yet to start trusting pressmen.

Let's wait and see what tomorrow has in stock for us. I have to expect a call from a different officer of the law, and a press interview. I also have to recruit a lawyer to represent me. I have misgivings though. I feel deep within me that my fate is somehow still tied to this Masakalia fellow. I can't simply dismiss him from the map in my mind. Anyway, we'll see. Fortunes may reverse tomorrow. Who knows. Nothing comes from nothing. I'll not kid myself. After all, I am myself a nobody. A pawn. I have no godfather. I don't even have a father without the god prefix. My father was a nobody. Nobody but a long-term jailbird. I am son of nobody. Nothing more than a simple Son of Woman.

SEVEN

Saturday Morning

Well folks I think I've to start saying good-bye to you all 'cause I don't think that you'll be hearing from me for sometime from now. I am tired. I've had a hectic week and I reckon that as weeks go, that was a week that was. The reason why I am pulling the curtains shut is because I am sick of this mucky, humid, heat-ridden and corrupt air that hangs around Mombasa. I need fresh air in my lungs. I shall be going up-country maybe tomorrow or day after tomorrow or any day thereafter when I shall feel myself safe and fit for a drive up to Nairobi. If what Dr. Kantai hinted to me was true then you wouldn't be seeing me around here no more. I'll leave Mombasa behind me and forget it the way a cow forgets its droppings. That's what I would like to do; move away from here and stay moved.

You are probably wondering whether I am out of my mind but I can assure you that I am wide awake and sane. If you are surprised, I am not. In a corrupt atmosphere, everything is possible. You must be ready for anything or everything or both.

What happened was, the press interview took place as planned, and Dr. Kantai did all the talking as I knew he would. I really don't know why the interview had to take place in my hospital room 'cause I practically had nothing to do with it except that I was photographed. Dr. Kantai answered all the questions including those directed at me. When the interview was over, Dr. Kantai escorted the pressman out and then came back after five minutes.

"What did you think of the interview?" he asked.

"Well, it was your interview. I think your presentation was fine, but I couldn't see why you had to add so much salt."

"The reason why I had to add what you call salt is that Masakalia has actually been fired. He was officially fired this morning. From here, the pressman is going to have a short interview with the police boss who will confirm the firing officially. The article in the paper will end up with something to the effect that the Assistant Commissioner of police for the Coast Province is deeply dismayed at the inhuman behaviour of the officer who inflicted actual bodily harm to a hospital patient, and has therefore dismissed him on the spot. Since they are fellow tribesmen, the powers that be will not be blamed. Nobody will be blamed but the fellow tribesman. Everybody else will be protected. The actual truth will not be known. He may, of course, blame you for it, but I doubt that. He is not foolish. He knows that the decision has been taken from the top and that the hospital affair is just a red herring."

"But I thought that his boss was in trouble too?"

"He was in trouble, but he is no longer in trouble. There's always some trading in these underground dealings, and Masakalia has been traded. He was the cheapest commodity on the market, and he's been sold first. He's no longer in the market. He's been sold and taken. What happened is that his boss was involved in clove smuggling in conjuction with some other big fish close to the top who has pleaded to the top for clemency, and since it would have been difficult for the smuggling case to advance without revealing the identity of the fish, investigations by the Special Branch have been stopped by order from the Attorney General's Offfice. There will be something in the newspaper tomorrow advising the public that the Attorney General has determined that the allegations about the smuggling of cloves from Zanzibar were utterly baseless, and that the story had emanated from some undesirable characters in Zanzibar who have now confessed to have fabricated the story for personal profit. You'll never hear of that case again. In exchange for immunity, the fellow was asked to do something about the troublesome Masakalia. In a way, they'll kill two birds with one stone. They'll show that the police force is not involved in any dirty game, and make that falsehood more convincingly true by showing that bad elements in the force are being removed mercilessly. Very clever, don't you think?"

"Very clever indeed, I must say. But tell me, who is immune from the effects of corruption in this country?"

"Nobody, my dear fellow, except beggars and the general masses who can shout and nobody hears. Don't think about it. Just do your thing and keep out of trouble. By the way, our type of corruption is not as bad as some people are likely to make us believe. We are doing better than all the countries around us right now because we pretend less. Money changes hands pretty fast here but with some of our neighbours, there's just not the money to change hands. When they boast that their system is better because now they have no beggars hanging around in the towns, they simply forget that they have no beggars because there's nobody to beg from. Beggars can't beg from beggars."

"You sound like a politician, Dr. Kantai."

"No. I am not and I'll never be. Anyway, forget it. I should be doing my rounds. I don't expect to be seeing you again unless you do something silly to your wound. For the time being, you are discharged. You can come back for out-patient treatment but further hospitalisation is no longer necessary. As I told you when we were arranging the bandages for the camera, your wound is OK, or will be, if you don't forget the antibiotic dose I prescribed earlier. You can leave the hospital as soon as the police come round to unlock your chain. They have been informed that you'll be discharged."

"Really, Doctor do you think it is fair to discharge me when you know damn well that those blasted cops will simply escort me from here to a cell in my present position. Is it very fair?"

"I am not very sure about that. I can't tell for sure but I think that you may be in for a big surprise. Don't quote me but I think you may be let loose to recuperate at home."

"But, doctor. . ."

"I said don't quote me," he cuts me short. "Why don't you sit or lie tight and wait. If what I heard was right, then you will change your views about corruption. Sorry I must get going," and he left.

I have only one half minute of reflection when the door is opened and in comes the bandaged head of Masakalia followed by his whole body.

His entry caught me in mid-thought and I resented it. I was expecting a different police officer. I resented his presence although I was sorry he'd been given the axe.

"Who let you in?" I demand furiously.

"Nobody stopped me," he answers cheerfully.

"Do you have the keys to this goddam chain?"

"Hey, hey, slowly man. I was wondering. . ."

"Well, if you don't have the keys, you may go," I cut him short. "I want the fellow with the keys."

"Why the bad temper? Why get mad at me before you know what I have to say. I have not come here as a police officer. Oh, no. I am sacked with effect from today. It's my last day in the Force. My last day as a civil servant. I am coming as a friend."

"OK, but do you have the keys to this goddam chain? I am discharged you know."

"My god! What an impatient fellow. Where do you think you'd go when you left here? Please listen. I shall be brief. I have to talk to you this morning. Tomorrow, I shall not be able to do anything. I can't set my foot in the office tomorrow. What I have in mind has got to be agreed on today and executed today. Please listen. I have lots of problems too, and so have you. Let's do something this morning. It's my last morning as a cop."

"Go ahead," I tell him. He is speaking in an agitated manner, but there is none of the usual police tone in his words. It was just plain Masakalia as a poor individual begging me to listen to him. Anyway, I am neutral.

"I have a proposition which may sound mad to you, but which I consider sound. I am sacked and my name shall be ruined, so I can't get a job immediately. I have to bide my time. I shall go back to Kakamega, but I don't want to go back there and just sit. I have to do something for which I shall need help. You know we are near the Uganda border. It's just a few miles if you don't follow the roads. Now there is a lot of lucrative business going on that very few people know about. I'd like us to get into it before a whole mob gets wise and starts cutting each others throats."

"What business?" I ask, getting interested.

"Coffee. Uganda coffee. For one hundred Kenya shillings, you get as much as one thousand Uganda shillings. With the Uganda shillings, you buy coffee from ordinary people at twice or thrice or four times the usual price, bring it across the border and sell it in Kenya. Alternatively, you may have to buy it using Kenya shillings bearing in mind the black market conversion rate, and it comes to the same thing. There is the other possibility of exchanging Kenya goods for coffee 'cause they have nothing in the shops in Uganda. That bastard, Idi

Amin has ruined that country, and keeps the foreign exchange in his own house from where he dishes it out in cash the way he wants. Morally, we shall therefore not be robbing Uganda. Farmers get more for their coffee and old Idi will have less money with which to buy guns to shoot the farmers. That way, you do some good for Uganda while also doing some good for Kenya and yourself."

"That's what I want to talk to you about. I need somebody to work with me. I need a Kikuyu. Most of the few people in that business are your tribesmen. I need somebody who knows the ropes to take care of the selling angle. For the beginning, we shall not attempt to transport and sell our buy to the coffee authorities in Nairobi. We shall simply buy and sell right there by the border. Profits would be much higher if we could sell direct to the Coffee Authority, but then the risks are high. The distance is too long and the capital investment required would be too high. Anyway, the big buyers require police escort, otherwise their trucks would be stopped en route, and we are not likely to get such favours from the police. We are small. Anyway, would you be prepared to come along with me if I, in turn, arrange to destroy the files with your charges?"

"Can you do that with impunity?" I am very surprised.

'Just leave that to me. I am being sacrificed because I've demanded gifts from thieves who happen to be under the shadow of some mighty elephant. It has nothing to do with hitting you in hospital and I hope you are broadminded enough to dismiss that as an insignificant happening. You are being used as a pawn to knock down another pawn. That other pawn is me. We are both pawns. Seriously, I want to set you free while I can. That is today. Not merely because I want you to help me out with this border business, but also to get even with the bastards. How I hate them."

"How can you do that? The Kihagi case is a murder case. How can you extricate me completely without getting the law to come after you?"

"OK. You might as well know. It's all done. I didn't sleep last night. That's why I couldn't come to see you as I said I would. I told you that I am ready to set you free even if you decide to come along with me or not. It's true. You are free of all charges. You can go home the minute they discharge you from the hospital. The police have no case against you."

"Please explain." Instead of explaining, he took a key from his pocket and opened the lock to the cuff chaining me to the bed.

"It may sound paradoxical, but I have done the opposite of what everybody would expect me to do. Everybody would expect that I would smear your case so that it looks worse than it actually is and I don't mind if they go on thinking so. In a way, my fate is somehow interwoven with yours. I can't get you out of my mind. You do not behave to me like other people behave to me. When I make my demands from other people, they behave like sheep, as thieves should, but you fight. You are the only person on earth to hit me when you couldn't take it anymore. I thought about it for a long time. I realized that there were limits. It was a good lesson, but of course you need not have hit me so hard. Anyway, I've thought about it for long hours and finally put all the blame on myself. Morally, I think you are innocent of that incident, so not only have I withdrawn the case in my heart, but last night I destroyed the file. You are free of that charge. There is no living trace except these bandages on my head and the scar, which will soon be covered by my hair."

He pauses for a long while and I get the urge to light a cigarette. I have not smoked since I got booked into the hospital, and I am determined to kick the habit. Why I got the urge, I don't know.

"On the Kihagi case, the thugs have confessed. They are still in the cell. From the very beginning, I knew that Khimji was lying. You were not very helpful to me yesterday morning, but I had a chance to talk to your friend, Dr. Kantai, who is incidentally very happy that I am getting the axe, but who told me a few things you'd told him, and with that, I got working on the thugs. They are in different cells, so I tricked them. First of all, I took two false signed statements to the thug whose teeth you knocked out, knowing fully well that he passed out quite early during the fight. The statements were supposed to have been signed by his friends accusing him of having stabbed Dr. Kihagi. I told him that he'd be charged with murder and that his friends were going to be state witnesses. You should have seen the poor devil Anyway, to cut a long story short, he signed a statement showing how they were hired by Khimji, how the entry of Dr. Kihagi into the room surprised everybody, and how the fight started and continued till the moment you clobbered him and put him out. I repeated the same trick with the others till the whole truth came out. I have a signed statement from the thug who stabbed you and then stabbed your doctor friend to death. The poor fellow is pleading like mad and blaming it on Khimji, but he has been charged with murder. He may escape with manslaughter, if it can be shown beyond any reasonable doubt that there was no premeditation. Anyway, all that will be required of you is to be a witness for the prosecution. I am afraid you can't run away from that. You will be the chief witness, but since the fellow has confessed willingly, all that will be necessary is for you to corroborate. As a matter of fact, you may not be called at all unless the judge deems it necessary. Not unless the three of them claim that the statements they have signed were obtained under duress and are therefore unacceptable. There was no duress, so I don't see that situation arising."

"What about Khimji? Did he sign a different statement?"

"The fellow is a tough egg to crack. I didn't have a chance to work on him last night, so I paid him a visit this morning. He had to read all the other statements, word for word, before he'd consent to change his story."

"So he did?"

"No, he didn't."

"What happened?"

"He offered me twenty thousand shillings to extricate him completely from the case and to have his name cleared."

"How can you do that?"

"My friend, this is my last working day. I can't possibly leave twenty thousand shillings when I am being sacrificed for hounding thieves. Khimji is free. I set him free. Not for twenty thousand, though. I thought forty thousand was more appropriate for the trouble, and after a lot of opposition, he accepted. I have already been paid, and as I say, Khimji is out of the cell."

"I still don't understand. The statements of his thugs will incriminate him."

"But who cares? Who cares how the case will proceed? You can count me out. I'll be in Kakamega then. I merely destroyed his original statement and convinced him that I'd have the statements of the thugs changed, but I couldn't be bothered. I am handing over the files to John who will temporarily act in my position, and it will be for him to start looking for any documents he finds missing. I'll give him five thousand shillings and ask him to go get a fresh statement from Khimji. Maybe Khimji will pay him something. Who knows? The bastard stinks with money and most of it is illegal money, so why should I miss my sleep?"

"Is this John in the whole picture? I mean, is he likely to. . .?"

"Don't worry yourself. Even my boss is in the picture. He's my friend you know. He knows everything, so don't bother your head. The only thing he doesn't know about is the forty thousand. He only knows about twenty which we have already shared equally, ten thousand a piece. That leaves twenty five after I give John five. Not too bad and not too good. Anyway, you can't buy coffee even when its cheap with newspaper cuttings. One needs pink Kenyattas in liquid form. So that's that. You haven't told me what you think."

"I can't tell you what I think before you spell out what the *modus operandi* will be. What is there in it for me? You say you want assistance, but what are the pecuniary benefits attached to that assistance? What are the costs and the benefits?"

"That is simple. First of all you accept that we go into it as friends. Secondly, we accept that it is illegal and therefore risky. It's risky business and that is why I am roping you in. You've taken big risks before. The worst thing would be to be shot by Amin's soldiers, but they are human beings. They also need money and Kenyan goods, so we have to be prepared for that sort of thing right from the start. Given that there is this inherent risk, we go into the business as partners, and not on the basis of employer-employee. We share out the profits on a pro-rata basis depending on how much each of us puts in. Since, however we shall plough the profits back into the business, I am prepared to lend you some of my money to be repaid from future profits until we are equal partners having equal shares and sharing the risks and the proceeds of the business fifty/fifty."

"That sounds very generous of you. What do you have in mind as a starting figure?"

"I reckon we shall have to start small. I've been thinking that sixty thousand would be OK, as a starting point until we get a clear picture of the lay of the land. We are not going to have a registered business as such. We shall have to operate on trust. It's the only way in such a business. Ideally, of course, I should contribute thirty thousand and you do the same."

"My dear man, I don't have anything near half that amount; at least I couldn't spare that much and I'll be damned if I'd put the lot into such a risky business if I had it. Anyway, I am, in principle, willing to come along. We can discuss the details later. I want to think. But tell me, why all the generosity? Why me?"

"Because you nearly killed me, you bum," and he laughed. "But seriously, and this may sound funny, we have a lot in common. As a policeman, you do not know your friends till you are sacked. Now that I've been sacked, I should expect to count my friends on a hand with amputated fingers, and if I linger around here, I could very easily find myself in jail for the same reasons that I am being sacked. The big fish that I have touched for a few coins are still around. I really have no real friends. I am being honest to myself. I hate this system, but I have to be like everybody else. If I can't get a job, then I have to trade and I have to do so with somebody who understands me. I think we understand each other. We are both bad, not because we are bad at all, but because we are small and not afraid. On the question of generosity, I really don't think I am being generous. I am just being practical. We have to sell the coffee to some big fish who are mainly your tribesmen and who are only willing to buy from somebody they can trust. I have been in the police. They wouldn't trust me. So selling to your tribesmen becomes your department and of course you'll be handling the process. If we are not equal partners, I wouldn't be able to sleep for fear that you'll take off with the whole collection. We have to to be equal. Equality breeds trust."

"But what about the initial investment?"

"OK. Let's say you have around fifteen thousand. That's fine. Keep five and I'll lend you twenty. That way, you'll have thirty and I my thirty so that we start with sixty. We share profits equally and you reimburse my twenty from your share of profits in due course. I see no reason why we should not start as soon as this Kihagi case is heard and I got the court registry clerk to fix it for Tuesday for mention. I don't have to give evidence in the goddam case, because I am no longer a cop, so I am lucky. I was with John all along, so he'll be able to testify for the police. What I'll do is leave Mombasa tomorrow.

I am no fool. I wouldn't stay here one day longer than is necessary. I'll go to Nairobi and stay with a friend while I give myself a short holiday and will keep in touch with you till you are able to join me and we travel to Kakamega together. I have built myself a small house there and you'll be my guest until you make your own accomodation arrangements. My telephone number while in Nairobi will be. . . now, where is that piece of paper?"

He searches all his pockets and finally finds the piece of paper he is looking for in his hind pocket, mixed up with a lot of currency bills.

"Here, you keep this. The fellow I'll be staying with is called Luseno. This is his house phone. If he should pick up the phone, don't let him get an inkling of what we are on about, but you can always leave innocent messages with him. And how shall I be able to get in touch with you?"

"From here I intend to go home and as soon as I can drive, I'll get the hell out of Mombasa. As a matter of fact, I am feeling OK, so I don't see why I can't drive. There's of course the question of being called to court as a witness but again I don't just have to hang around for them old friends of yours so that all they have to do is pick up the phone and summon me to court. It's for the prosecutor to look around for his witnesses. All things being equal then, I'll drive up to Nairobi tomorrow and book myself in some cheap hotel. From there, I'll contact you myself. I think that it's better that way."

"Fine. I think it's a damn good idea to get them looking for their key witness and please make sure that they fly you first class from Nairobi and pay a handsome per diem for the time they require your services. I got to be on my way now, so see you sometimes next week."

We shake friendly hands and he leaves. I really have no comments on the whole affair. I don't know whether it's funny or crazy or simply unreal. Is life just a vicious circle? Was Sheila then right about starting from mud and ending up in mud? Can the circle be broken? I'll be damned if I know. Anyway we'll see.

Masakalia has gone one minute when my navy friends Jim, Claude and Harry troop into the ward room. They are looking healthy and wild.

"It is not yet the visiting hour old chap, but here we are," Jim says. "Man you are good at the disappearing act. You disappeared easier than the shifta. Anyway, how are you and how is the knife hole in your what-do-you-call-it?"

We shake hands and exchange pleasantries and I explain briefly the lay of the land after which I tell them that they can give me a ride home 'cause I am discharged. I ring for the nurse and ask her to bring in my clothes and she does. I strip off the hospital garments and get dressed while my friends are watching.

"I thought it was a small knife hole," Claude exclaims. "How come you have your whole stomach area covered with bandages?"

"I am just carrying some extra dressing for a rainy day. Had to wear it wide for camera effect. The wound is only half an inch wide and has three stitches which are expected to disolve in due time. I am OK, but I have to take it easy for a while."

We drive home but Tonia is not at home. You may not believe it but I am happier not to find her at home. I'd telephoned earlier from the hosptial before the interview with the press, asking her to come over later in the morning 'cause I'd be discharged, but she hung up on me without as much as saying a single word. Just the first hello and no more. I have a score to settle with her.

What we do is, we decide that since I am off booze and smoke for the time being, them navy fellows are going to fetch some beers and drink while I organise my things at home. I get into the kitchen and put fifteen half litre-bottles into a carton and then get this curry can I hid behind the fridge and shove the contents into my hind pocket. I decide that this might be the last drink with these chaps so I might as well do the buying. I get my car keys from upstairs and then ask them chaps to pass by Marshalls garage and get the windscreen fixed. I count out what I think would be required in terms of Kenyattas plus twenty percent for cotningencies and give it to Jim. He and Harry get into my car while Claude drives his own car.

"See you in thirty minutes folks."

"More like an hour, I would say," Claude says. "We are going to fetch the booze from our Mess where it is cheaper and it might take sometime to fix your windscreen. Anyway we'll be here as soon as we can but by the way, what about a roast chicken — a whole chicken. You will be needing some lunch you know."

"O.K. I have no objection to the chicken." And they drive off. I get back into the house and dial late Dr. Kihagi number. Julian must be a very sad lovely woman. I would like to express my condolences. After three rings she picks up the phone and I say;

"Hi ! Julian, this is Dodge. I am at home and was wondering whether Tonia is with you. My main reason for calling is however to express my . . ."

"You ! ! !" she banged down the phone so hard that I imagine I hear it break. I replace the receiver back slowly and ease out of the bedroom into the lounge. I think all women are against me. I am in for more trouble than I perhaps imagine. But why? Why? Why wouldn't my own wife want to see me when I am hospitalised and why wouldn't she even want to say a simple hello? Why should her friend adopt the same attitude. Hey, hey. This is nonsense. I have to do something about it. I have to bring about some face to face confrontation. We have to talk things over or shout things over. They say that silence is golden but I don't see what is golden about this type of silence. I am angry.

"I march right back and dial Dr. Kihagi's number again when Julian picks up the phone, I start talking straight.

"Would you please tell Tonia that I want to see her straightaway and to make it snappy!" and I bang down the phone hard. I feel better. Trouble is I don't even know whether Tonia is with Julian but I feel better all the same. I'll sit and wait.

Saturday Afternoon

If any of you folks imagine that I am going along with the Masakalia plan, then you haven't been with me the whole week. You have been elsewhere. If you'd been with me all along, you'd know that I'd decided to quit them dark alleys of life otherwise I wouldn't have wasted my half-full bottle of beer on Masakalia's hard head. There are no two ways about it. Black stuff is out and out in as far as I am concerned. No more of it will be mixed up with my person.

There comes a time when one has to come to terms with oneself.

There comes a time when one has to hold a serious meeting with oneself on questions like, "Who am I, where am I going, where did I come from and where do I want to go? What is life all about and what do I want to do with mine and why?" That is the crucial question "Why am I here? I am here yes, but to do what, when, how, and why? What can I do and what should I do, and if I know, why should I do it at all? For what purpose? For who?" If the answer to all these questions is reduced to an amorphous nebulous mass that takes no shape in your head; if the answer is nothing but a humble void in your think-tank, do you then give up the ghost and float aimlessly in space or do you, like an honest explorer, determine that there must be a way to the other side of the hill? There must be a way through all the natural but hostile obstacles in the desert of life to some friendly human shore. There must be a place where man is man and woman is proud of it. That is the place I am looking for. It's where I must go. As an explorer, I have to find the way. That place is right here. Right up in your coconut head, so all you have to do is think properly. That's all you have to do. Think properly. It's what I haven't been doing the whole week and since you have been with me all along, maybe you haven't been thinking properly either.

What would I want to do with my life? The answer is simple. Nothing for myself. I can see nothing that I would do for myself that would make me really happy. The alternative is only one; do something for others. And what can I do for others? Anything I can think of wouldn't be original and is likely to be doomed to failure because I don't have the right answer to, "How?" Them goddam politicians and fat cats wouldn't let you do a thing; so how? Simple. Become a politician and a big fish and then in the long, long run become the "Head of State. That is the only way you get doing something meaningful for other folks on this African continent. I can't be wrong. The politician has the last word. He determines what is democracy. Even the cracked-up boors down in South Africa talk of democracy; so may they all go to hell. I've got it. I got the answer. The politician, be he a traditionally elected politician or a self-appointed politician from the Armed Forces imposing his rule by the gun, the difference is the same. They are both politicians except that often the latter doesn't know the difference or the absence of a difference. Anyway, whatever the difference, that is the place to be. Right at the top or near the top. It's all that counts; power. How you get it is absolutely immaterial. Just get there and when you are there, do your thing. That's it; just get there by fair or foul. The means don't count.

The thing I'd like to do is put all these corrupt bastards in jail. I'd like to rid the country of corruption and give more power to the people. There's no way I could start doing this sort of thing unless I was some Attorney General or the Minister of Home Affairs. Being no goddam lawyer, I stand no chance for the first option so I have no choice but aim for the second — but how?

Well you may think I am nuts but I aint. You can almost always do anything you put your mind to so long as you keep at it till death says hello and that's what I am going to do. No kidding. What I'll do is, I am going to leave Mombasa as I told you earlier but I wouldn't be going to Nairobi as you might be thinking. Oh no. I am going right back to Kaheti.

Kaheti is the place where my mother was born so it is my legal home. I went there first time when I was around eleven years old only to find my old grandmother one month dead. She had this small plot of land of around four acres and since I am the only living descendant from her loins then this piece of land is mine by right. Maybe some punk is farming it illegaly but that is no matter so long as he is willing to transport himself elsewhere when I show up. That's where I will go. I will build myself a small timber house and then I'll start participating in what some folks call civic activities around the area and then when the time for elections comes, I am going to propose myself as a party candidate within the community. The incumbent member of Parliament for the area is very unpopular mainly because he is extremely fat and sleeps in parliament, but also because he is known to have appropriated, for his own personal use, public funds contributed by the poor for *harambee* projects aimed at expanding schools and churches in the area. He is not likely to be re-elected and the only viable contender is another fat fellow who is also likely to sleep in parliament. Current talk back around Kaheti is that both of these fellows are so fat that even if either of them used all the pages of the week-end newspaper to wipe off the shit from the folds of his ass after a diarrhoea session there'd still be some grains of maize left lingering in the ass hole region. It's all exaggerated stuff and nonsense but it gives you an idea of the amount of love that folks have for these two well-fed gentlemen. That's how much they are loved. It's all crazy stuff but our poor voters will always be voters. They can vote you in or out for the same reason.

Anyway I am going back to Kaheti and I am going to stand for parliamentary elections which are some four months away unless the old man changes his mind. I am not very much known in the area but who knows? The people are looking for a new face. They are looking for some son of the land who will not sleep in Parliament and I don't look like the sleeping type. I'll give it a try just for the heck of it if nothing else. I must explore. I am an explorer by nature. Them educated young folks from the area are not interested in politics. They are just happy working their civil servant lives away in Nairobi. Maybe I'll use them to campaign for me. They are the ones most dissatisfied with the incumbent and the pretender to the throne.

Hey! I am thinking too fast. I'll have to plan my campaign. I have no money for the campaign. It's an expensive affair. I'll have to figure out a successful campaign that will cost the least. For a buccaneer of my experience, I should be able to work out some strategy based on simple human nature and feelings, but constructed upon sound practical statistics.

Here's the plan developing in my mind. The people must be taken by surprise. Surprise always works if you catch everybody with their pants down. It's risky too, but an explorer has no surprises. He is always moving into the unknown at any moment. He is ready for everything. That's what I'll be. An explorer.

What I'll do is, I'll first obtain the names and addresses — village by village, of all registered voters in the constituency from the register. At the same time, I will make a thorough investigation into the allegation that Mr. Kariuki, the incumbent, used for his personal purposes, poor people's harambee money. This is going to be hard but the information doesn't have to be the sort of stuff you can use in a court of law. It must be such that he can't go to law against me because of fear of the whole truth coming out. Then I am going to prepare this long letter which I shall address to every registered voter linking Mr. Kariuki's big belly and buttocks to the diverted public funds. I must accuse him of at least ten counts of dishonesty in the letter, including blowing dust at innocent folk as he drives away in his Mercedes which is also probably procured from public funds. I shall lament in the letter that the character who is proposing himself as an opposer to the incumbent might be requiring a little bit of the same stuff just to maintain his belly at its present size. I have to say all those things in a very circumspect way so that the letter can't be used as evidence of slander in a court of law. It would just be a serialised stencilled letter with each voters name written at the top in ink and which I will make sound rather personal thus giving the impression that I know these folks. I'll make it sound intimate and the question thereafter will be,"Who is this fellow?" "Who is this savior?"

I will distribute the letters to the different villages myself just to save on postage stamps. Two days later I'll get into the most popular bar in Kaheti, which is where Kariuki drinks, and after two drinks, deliver this little speech practically accusing Kariuki of being a thief. I'll make my speech whether Kariuki is there or not. If he is not there, his henchmen will be there anyway. I'll have with me one or two fellows who wouldn't be wise to anything but who will make good witnesses. In less than two minutes after the beginning of my speech I am sure to be attacked especially because the barman is Kariuki's cousin. That would be the real beginning of my campaign. I must have some commotion. Somebody to blame for the violence. People like violence generally so long as they are not involved personally or they hate it. They can't be indifferent. They will talk about it. I will make sure that I lose the fight but of course I shall not allow them to break my bones. Then I shall lodge a complaint. I'll make it so big that the press will be drawn in. The press will spread the case over the newspapers because anything about parliamentary candidates is juicy news during the campaigning period. My beating will be tied to my brave and public accusation of Mr. Kariuki and will be sufficient publicity for me for the campaign. It wouldn't really matter who the newspaper favoured. Kariuki would be the loser. There's nothing that the innocent voter appreciates as much as a personal letter and if this is backed up by some brave personal attack on the incumbent, the campaign is just about over. The pretender will be lost in the process for playing no tangible role. Anyway that's what I'll explore.

The only other strategy I would explore if I didn't feel so sure is the use of the Nyakinyua women. These are the old ladies in the villages who enjoy good talk and good game and who are around forty five to sixty years old and participate fully in local politics. It so happens that there are usually more women voters than men around the villages. I could identify the most influential Nyakinyua in each village and kid her along about this nice time I am going to give her one of these fine days because she's still young, attractive and desirable as soon as I am through with this election formality. None of them would believe such stuff, but they'll still get a hell of kick out of it. You never can tell; some will even believe it. Anyway, they wouldn't be talking about some fat fellow at all. They'll be talking about the old Son of Woman and that's me. I may even screw a few of them Nyakinyuas just to let them know that I mean business. Anyway I am going to explore all these possibilities. Why not?

The other thing I am going to do is explore means of getting close to the old man, the President. There's no point my getting elected to parliament if he wouldn't give me some influential post. How I'll go about that, I don't know yet. Can't figure it out right now. One thing is true though; if I have to lick his sandals, I jolly well will lick them. I'll lick them real clean. I'll go further. I shall lick the gout off the bottom of his swollen feet and I jolly well don't care whether you despise me for it or not. Why should I care? What I want is the Ministry of Home Affairs and you don't get that sort of thing unless the old man can trust your tongue.

What I will do when I am Minister of Home Affairs is that I'll put half of the country into jail. No kidding. Any of you corrupt bastards and shady characters are going to end up right in the can. The common man will breathe for a while because there wouldn't be any of you goddam godfathered grabbers and goofers around. You will be in prison grabbing dust. I'll straighten you out real upright so please vote for me.

So there you are; Mr. Dodge Kiunyu, M.P. for Kaheti and Minister of Home Affairs. You are welcome right now to join me in the crusade. I wish my dead mother could come back to life for one short day and see her son sitting in this ministerial office. What a thought. Anyway, I don't think that I would put prostitutes in jail. Mother wouldn't forgive me for that.

I am in the middle of these thoughts when I notice Tonia and Julian standing right there in front of me. I didn't hear them come in and right now they look like ghostly apparitions. They don't seem to tie up with this voting system I just worked out.

"You've been talking to yourself for the past two minutes or so about jail and women. I thought you came from hospital and not jail, my dear Dodge. What is it all about?" It is Tonia talking and I am so much taken aback that I have no words. She pats a seat for Julian and sits herself opposite me. It looks like the shattering of a wonderful dream. The two women look unreal to me. You wouldn't believe it but they just look like people I knew many years past. Very funny. Me, I am in Home Affairs. It is too real and vivid for me to switch.

"Did you hear me?" Tonia repeats and I just stare at her like a goon. I am no longer here. I am far away. I am a Minister.

"I told you he wasn't normal," Julian tells her as she crosses her legs. "Just look at him".

I don't know what I look like and I couldn't care. I hear and I don't hear. Gosh! I have to get out of my timber house at Kaheti and get back to Cliff Avenue. That's where I am, isn't it? Right here in Mombasa and I am not even drunk. I shake myself up to the present and instead of saying good afternoon or sorry or anything, I simply get up and proceed to the toilet. No sooner do I close the door behind me than I start sneezing. Where the sneezing comes from, I don't know. All I know is that I sneeze. Haachio! My groin is also sneezing with pain.

I was going to have to settle it out with Tonia so it might as well be now. I know I am going to have trouble with her but nothing like the big thing I have ahead of me. I get out of the toilet as Dodge Kiunyu and not as Minister of Home Affairs and say hello as if I am seeing the women for the first time. Nobody replies so I sit down right where I was sitting down before and face Tonia.

"You wanted to see me, so here I am," she says. "Since you have found your tongue, give it mouth".

"Well, I am out of hospital," I tell her.

"I can see that for myself", she tells me in turn. "What did you want to see me about? I would have imagined that from the hospital you'd be getting into remand, how come you are here?"

"I wouldn't be getting into any remand because I have committed no crime and I am not charged with any crime. I am free". I tell her.

"Good to hear that. What did you want to see me about?" I can see that she does not intend to be friendly. She is antagonistic. Both of them are looking at me with disgust but are hiding it behind a cloak of forced tolerance.

"Can I please talk to you alone Tonia. I have one or two things I want to talk to you about".

"You know the answer to that, don't you?" She says tersely. Well I am beat. If I was going to go through life like this, nobody would give me a vote even for the village council so I decide to come to the point, Julian or no Julian.

"I'll be going up-country so I thought you should know".

"You could have said that on the phone or did you expect that I would help pack up your stuff?" I say nothing. I have no energy for this sort of thing.

"OK," she says, "so you are going up-country. Would you mind telling us how the whole thing happened? How and why did Dr. Kihagi die and what were you doing with him in that brothel hotel? Since you are going up-country we are entitled to some truth."

I tell them the whole story right from my entry to the Railways Club to the bottle on Masakalia's head, Khimji and his thugs and my new post as Minister of Home Affairs. When I finish, there is only one small comment from Julian.

"I told you he was mad."

Tonia stares at me with incredulous eyes and asks, "So in effect you called Dr. Kihagi to his death?" I decide not to answer. I would be better off very far away from here. The way these two women are looking at me leaves nothing for the imagination. I am the devil. It's no use. I've told them practically everything that there is to be told on the matter the way I think they should understand it but I reckon I failed in my mission. I knew I would fail but I had to clear some part of my conscience. I made no impact. I reckon I made matters worse. I would have been better-off keeping my mouth shut and simply walking away with my few belongings and disappearing from the foul and filthy air hanging around this Mombasa island. I should be miles away but deep inside me, I don't want to leave Tonia unhappy. I want her to understand my point of view; at least for the future. That is why I said the most stupid thing in the circumstances. I don't know why but I simply said, "I shall not contest the divorce. I don't want to cause you any more problems."

It was really dumb of me to say such a thing. Tonia reacted in the most unfriendly way possible especially in the presence of Julian.

"I believe you expect me to thank you for that; well, you have my thanks whatever they are worth. However, let me tell you one thing; you are the last man I'll ever want to meet again in my present and future lives if I should be born again. I wish you luck wherever you are going but in case some of your madness should luckily evaporate from your head, you'd better know that your crazy dream about getting along in politics will never come true. How do you expect to transform yourself from a small-time, small-minded, town-gutter, black marketeer to the position of a respectable politician. Just go. Get the hell out of here. Let there be no further explanations. It's better that way. Let your madness guide you through the dark alleys to hell, Mr. Minister, but go! I shall not hold you back. God be with you."

I have no force to say anything. I believe I am completely spent. Strange. What she says seems to come from very far. It goes in through one ear and out through the other. It's as if I am a witness and not a participant. I feel compassion for Tonia. Somehow I love her for hating me. It is a strange feeling. I have absolutely nothing against her. I wish her all the joy in the world. As for me I am far. I am very far. I can see the timber house on my grandmother's village plot. I can smell the village. I can smell the dust. It is better than anything around here. It is the dust of life. The dust from which all life springs. Reddish-brown fertile dust that has its origin from the same volcanic eruption that gave birth to mount Kenya. I am far away. I can see snow-covered volcanoes. Tonia's words are now very far away. I hear them because I am here, although I am four hundred miles away. God! I think I am sick, but she doesn't stop.

"Do you by any chance stop and think about all the harm you have done not to me and Julian alone but to yourself and all those people who have had some contact with you. Do you? Do you by any chance understand that you are a carrier of a contagious disease that has no name? Is it not possible that you can see inside yourself and see for yourself what you truly are? God bless you. It is your life. I don't want to sound unkind. I am not trying to be unkind. I did not come to see you in hospital because as far as I am concerned, you are dead. You are dead to me but just in case you do not understand, I am dead. I am dead to you. I do not exist. It is not me that you are seeing. No. I am not the Tonia you know. I am a different person to you. When you become Minister of Home Affairs in hell, you will understand."

It is a far away speech. I forgive her for everything and forgive her for nothing. I am mentally too far away to care. Her words take me even further. They take me to Sabuyo Settlement Scheme near Nakuru when Tonia pulled wool over my eyes and weaved this weird story about my having illusions and not having met her at all, when she was stealing my money and just after I'd given her the first and very brief screw on the couch. I didn't get to know the truth till I came out of prison and I in turn waited for her to get out of prison to recover my money which all ended up in my being hooked up to her and bringing her down here to Mombasa where we were not known as jailbirds. I married her after three months of honeymooning.

She's trying to pull the same type of wool over my eyes and this finally brings me back to the present circumstances. I can see myself sitting down facing Tonia and Julian. It doesn't change anything though. My mind is too far made. I am going to Kaheti and I'll fight for parliamentary elections and lick the old man's gout for the Ministry of Home Affairs. Tonia's words sound like corruption. They sound like corruption that must be stopped. They sound like part of the selfishness inherent in the life style of the "haves" vis a vis the "have nots". The oppressor crushing the oppressed. I feel pure. Crazy. I identify the two women with the evil that is going on around us. I identify them with the borrowed, but ill adapted, western way of thinking while I see myself as a simple native son mixing and mingling with the native dust on which the future of the nation will be built. All of a sudden I feel near and far away from them. I even start wondering whether Tonia is really my wife. I am crazy. I must be or maybe I am simply sick. Perhaps I should go back to hospital. I am sick.

What I do is, I just get up and say "You are very nice people therefore what you say must be correct. God bless you", and I proceed to the bedroom. I have only one idea on my mind; I have to pack and go. I am almost walking in a daze and I start packing in a daze. I don't really care what I am doing. All I am doing is picking things and throwing them into my brown leather suitcase. Somehow I get some pleasure simply picking things from the wardrobe and throwing them into the suitcase without order.

Within a short while I've filled up the suitcase and a large sisal market bag. I am all packed. I am in the process of locking up the suitcase when I hear some commotion outside. I dash our carrying my two loads.

What is happening is that my navy friends just got back with this crate of beer and a roast chicken and they meet Tonia and Julian as these two are just getting into the car to drive off I don't know to where. I can't believe that Tonia is just going to drive off the last minute of my departure and not at least watch me as I disappear from her life. Anyway that is not important. What is important is that she is asking these friends of mine what they have come to do around here, et cetera and would they mind transporting their food and drink and any other stuff elsewhere, et cetera, et cetera.

I look at the scene and decide that it will be my last embarrassing moment because I am not going to be embarrassed anymore. It all looks childish, Tonia throwing her feminine weight all around the place. Instead of getting angry I start feeling genuine pity for her. Real pity. God! I wish I could take her along with me but that is a wish that can never become a horse so there's no point imagining beggars riding.

It is all right gentlemen, I say behind Tonia's back. She whirls round to face me. "My wife is right. You have to take your food and drink elsewhere but since you have taken possession of my car please wait for me. I am coming along with you." They all look at me with their mouths agape and bulging eyes. "Somebody please help me get this stuff into the boot."

"What is happening, old chap?" Jim asks, but I don't reply. I move round and get the boot of the car open as everybody looks on. Nobody offers to help me. I carry my suitcase and my sisal bag, shove them into the boot and then bang it shut.

"Let's get moving," I say but they don't move. Nobody is moving. I am the only one moving. I get into the back seat of the car among the crate of beer and the chicken and repeat; "Hey! Let's go," and this time Jim and Claude seem to awake to the situation and hop into the car.

"Where are we going?" Claude asks. I don't answer him because right now I myself don't know where we are going, so instead I look at Tonia who still looks surprised and say. "I am sorry, but good-bye," and then I tap Claude by the shoulder. "Drive man!" And he drives.

As we approach Nyerere Avenue Claude finds his voice and asks, "Where are we going?"

"Anywhere you like," I tell him. He pulls alongside the road and kills the engine.

"What is going on, Master Dodge?"

"OK." I tell him. "Drive to the Railway Club. I'll explain," and he gets the car moving.

There are very few people at the Railway Club and I pick the quietest corner which we normally call the Colonial corner on account that the remnants of the old colonials who are still members of the Club prefer that corner in order to keep away from nigger noise.

The barman comes over and I point out at the crate of beer and tell him he can have it. He looks at me and then at everybody and asks "Why?"

"For nothing," I tell him. "Keep it in your bar till we need it next year."

"I am sorry, Sir, but I do not understand. I cannot possibly keep .."

"And on how many occasions have I told you not to call me Sir?" I cut him short. "Take the crate and go and then come right back for orders." He picks the crate and goes. My friends are looking at me as if I've become a little god. Truth of the matter is I am still feeling far and near and I still have Tonia on my mind.

What we do is we ask for drinks from our stock and I proceed to tell my friends of my future plans and my intention to get the hell out of town and be in Nairobi for dinner tonight. I tell them about my whole campaign for election into parliament and even lament that unfortunately I had no pretentions for the Ministry of Defence which would have probably enabled me to do them navy chaps a little favour like building more civilised barracks for singles.

They don't say anything much but I can see that they think I am crazy only they are not prepared to tell me the bitter truth the Tonia way. Some ice is developing. We eat the chicken almost in silence. I feel uncomfortable. Why can't they see that it is a logical thought. Who is born a politician? Who has no right? Why should it appear strange that I, Dodge Kiunyu, could be Minister of Home Affairs? What is strange about it? It looks very simple to me. There are only two things to be done. Get myself into Parliament and that should be easy so long as nobody else but the incumbent and the pretender are my rivals and then and even before then do proper boot-licking which shouldn't be a difficult thing given that the old man wears sandals on account of his gout. How can my good old friends fail to see the simplicity of the whole thing? Anyway, maybe I am crazy.

More people have started coming to the Club. I can see that they are all wondering what the hell I am doing here instead of being in jail 'cause everybody knows that I cracked Masakalia's skull. We get a "hi there" and again a "hi there" and a wave of the hand but no more. I reckon I have become the fellow you know but you don't want to know. Maybe I am wrong but I don't feel any warmth although this place is generally and normally hot and humid.

I make up my mind in the spur of the present minute and I get up. I have to leave. "I have to make a phone call", I say and I move to the call box. I insert a coin and dial Dr. Kihagi's number. There's no answer and bang down the phone. I just have this urge to say something nice to Tonia before I leave. I don't know why. Maybe I have some guilt conscience. I simply want to tell her that later on if everything worked okay for me she shouldn't feel too arrogant to join me. That's what I want to tell her. I re-insert the same coin and dial my house. No answer. Oh, hell! Why should I bother? So what I do is I re-insert the same coin and dial Khimji's number. I am hoping he is away. All I want is to say goodbye to Sheila. She deserves a cordial parting.

"Hello, who is it?" It is Khimji. I decide that if he as much as hears my voice he will give Sheila hell for nothing so I just hung up. I feel sorry for my coin which is now swallowed by the machine and decide that I have enough of them silly telephones. There are no telephones in the village. You go to look for people and have to talk to them face to face. It was more human. My original intention was to call Zick in Nairobi and tell him I'd be coming over but I have ended up not calling him. I could always get in touch with him when I get to Nairobi. I'd know where to get him.

I get back to the table and I don't even sit down. If I am going to drive to Nairobi with this bandage around my groin, then I can't afford to take any more liquor. What I do is I rub my hands together and say, "Any of you folks want to spend a week-end up country?"

"Nairobi or Kaheti?" Claude asks.

"Nairobi of course." They look at one another before Jim speaks.

"You know old chap, I reckon you are acting as if you are born again but right in my dome I know you'll always be the Son of Woman you've always been. I don't think we'll miss you for long. You'll be right back here when you are tired of village dust and you'll be trully welcome. But say, why don't you try to make it up with your woman? You know women, one minute hot and cold the next minute. She could soften if you tried. What do you think you'll be doing in the goddam village where they never even heard of birth control pills. Man, you'll end up a father of twenty bastards. Sit down and relax. You have a wound to heal. There would be no point going up-country unless you changed your mind to go along with Masakalia in his lucrative exploits so long as you'll be man enough to rob him. That is the only thing that looks logical to me."

I don't say anything and I don't sit down. My hour has come. When Jim was talking, I was far away.

"I mean it really. I'll pay for your hotel in Nairobi and you can come down by the six o'clock train to be here six a.m. on Monday. No kidding. Let's go."

They just looked at one another as if they are also very far away.

"You really mean it, Dodge?" Claude asks.

"That's what I've been trying to tell you the whole afternoon."

"I'll be damned!" he says, and I ask him for my car keys.

"Good bye and wish me luck," I say as I walk towards the car? I wave at them as I turn on the ignition but they do not wave back. They are just staring. They do not believe it. It doesn't look real. Even for me, it doesn't look real. As the car moves forward and I am heading towards the exit from the club, I imagine I am going to wake up and find myself in my bed. I am dazed and my car smells of village dust.

By the time I get to Voi I am extremely conscious of what is happening to me. What is happening is that because of the bumps on the road my groin is hurting like Jesus on the cross and I can't possibly drive one more mile. As I turn into town, there are these two hitch-hikers; a man and a woman with a large white paper poster on which there is only one word written in large letters — NAIROBI. I stop alongside and simply ask, "You folks going to Nairobi?" and they reply in one voice "Yes." They sound like Americans.

"Any of you drive?" And again "Yes!"

"Hop in." I said.

I drove to the gas station and asked the weird looking attendant to fill up the tank. While he was filling up I handed over the key to the male hitch-hiker who was husband of the other and wh   epeated

207

his name three times and three times it passed through one ear and out through the other. I asked him if he knew Nairobi well and he told me that he knew the Norfolk hotel very well and that they were already booked there for two nights. I told him that I was also going to the Norfolk so could he drive 'cause I was a wee bit tired and he thanked me ten times.

They took the front seats while I stretched myself on the rear seat and we took off. There was a one-sided conversation for around fifteen minutes before I popped off and got lost into sweet slumber. I only remember getting myself half angry before I popped off on account that them Americans were rich and therefore had no business hitch-hiking like they were poor folks. It was mockery to poor folks who hitch-hiked because they couldn't afford to pay for their transportation. The other thing I remember is a tap on the buttocks and an American voice saying to me.

"Hey sleeper, we are there. We are at the Norfolk."

I rub my eyes and focus. I sit up. The air is fresh and cool. It feels good to the nose. I get out of the car and say good-bye to my friends who make straight for the reception desk while I get into the driver's seat and head off. All of a sudden I feel that I don't want to stay one minute in Nairobi. Not one minute. I am nice and rested. I drive to Vic Preston's petrol station fill up the tank and get them to clean my windscreen of all the dead insects. I take the museum road and step on the gas till I get to Karatina.

It was a one and half hour drive that left me hungry and tired. It is eight thirty five in the evening when I stop the car in front of this little hotel some fellow has just put up in town and which is called the "Elephant Castle". There is nothing elephanty about it except that it is all round and nice so I reckon that the fellow was thinking about the elephant's foot but not an elephant house. The place wouldn't contain many elephants. Anyway it is a nice joint and I don't get very disappointed when they show me into my room. I am in New York — I mean that is the name of my room. Instead of numbering the rooms, this fellow, I mean the owner of the joint, gave each room the name of some famous town and that's how I am in New York. Quite an original fellow.

Anyway this is where I'll spend the night. The place is not expensive. Kaheti is only some twelve kilometers away so I reckon I'll use this joint as my operational base till I have put up my timber house at Kaheti. There's a lot of timber around Karatina and that will make things easier.

So what I'll do is, I'll take my shower and then go down and have some country-side dinner. Then I am going to sleep like Jesus and tomorrow I'll start my new life.

I'll start by giving Zick a telephone call in Nairobi first thing in the morning to arrange with him a trip to Kiambu for an early introduction to the old man. That has to be fixed first. It has to come before the elections and I know that Zick will be able to arrange it. He has been arranging all sorts of things for the old man's farms so he is a frequent and welcome guest at the palace. All I have to do is start talking about cows and creamy milk and such stuff as artificial insemination to the old man and I shall be in business. Anyway that is the first thing I'll do: call Zick.

The next thing I'll do is call this number that Masakalia gave me and hope that he wouldn't be around 'cause all I want to do is leave a message saying, "Regret but Mr. Dodge Kiunyu has resigned his post. Acknowledgement unnecessary. Work shall go on without him. Best seasonal wishes". Masakalia will understand. Poor devil.

I feel sad about letting him down but then there comes a time when a man has to make up his mind and make it hard. Sorry, poor devil. I hope you make enough money out of illegal Uganda coffee deals before I am Minister. After that, you won't get a chance of touching any black stuff except in jail. Anyway good luck old friend. I have to try my luck in a different direction and maybe if I succeed, I shall hire you to capture crooks. Anyway, good-bye.

The third thing I am going to do will be three things. I'll ring Mombasa just for the heck of it and let Tonia and my navy chaps know that I am nice and arrived and ready to start my dusty life and reiterate my invitation to Tonia to join me when I am nice and seated in the Home Affairs chair. She will of course bang down the phone in my ear, but so what? If it makes her feel better by so doing, then the better my conscience. Anyway, I shall expect her to bang the phone and when she has done so, I shall curse "bitch!" knowing full well that I am cursing into a dead phone. As for divorce, she has it without asking. As far as I am concerned, I am single whether that is good or bad for me as Minister of Home Affairs.

The last Mombasa call will be for Sheila. I'll just say good-bye and let her know that I am in this up-country place where I intend to get permanently localised. Simple information for my conscience. By nine o'clock in the morning I must be through with all those calls 'cause from then on, I won't be having the time to make calls around. I shall be waking up early in the morning to be at the timber house construction site by eight o'clock everyday except Sundays and that for around a month after which I have to move from this joint into my timber joint.

My campaign for Parliamentary elections will start thereafter as I told you earlier so all I have to hope, for the moment, is that my small groin wound heals as Dr. Kantai said and I think he was right. All the way from Nairobi to Karatina, the wound didn't talk so the doctor was right or it is simply that the road was smoother or both or neither. All that I take to heart is that the wound was silent. Anyway, we shall see.

Meantime, my friend, I am afraid but I have to take leave of you till after the elections. For the time being, please wish me luck. I need it. I shall need the presence of your kind thoughts all along through the campaign. I cannot win in isolation.

I can win nothing for myself. It is not for myself that I'll go through this trying election exercise with all the unforeseeable dangers and pitfalls that will probably break my back. No. It is not for me. It is for what I want to do to you crooks in the first instance and also for doing something small for the honest. But. . . but. . . am I honest?

What type of man is an honest man? Maybe he is nothing but the opposite of a dishonest fellow. Jesus should know. Me I don't. So why worry? Columbus was a great explorer who thought that America was Asia, but that did not stop him being a great explorer, so again stay with me and give me your vote. This is not the last time we shall be meeting. It's only mountains that don't meet. Take note however that the next time we meet you wouldn't be meeting my lowly me — oh, no. You will be meeting the Honourable Mr. Dodge Kiunyu, Minister of Home Affairs at your service.

So there you are my friend. You know all about me now and in the future, and that's all I am going to tell you for now. Not because I am tired and hungry but simply because you know as much as I do. After all you have been with me for a whole week and you haven't told me one little thing about yourself. Maybe you'll want to tell me something about yourself the next time we meet and I'll probably tell you a few more things about Government business from the point of view of the Ministry of Home Affairs.

Till then my friend, please accept my very humble, reluctant and sleepy farewell. I really want to stay with you but I am tired. Really tired. I'll have to skip my dinner and just turn in. I am dozy. All I want to do is shut them silly eyes and dream away. You'll be welcome in my dreams. Visit me in my sleep and let's float together in the realms of the everlasting. Come and float with me. I want to float with you. Let's enjoy heavenly sleep together. Let's rest them bones. So goodnight, good-night to you of the earth. Me, I am gone. Yes, come sweet slumber, come. If I should dream, let it be about votes. Yes, votes. Votes for the son of woman; I shall need them vote...

The End